THE TEN
THOUSAND

portal wars II

Allan

system 7
publishing

Crimson Worlds Series

Marines (Crimson Worlds I)
The Cost of Victory (Crimson Worlds II)
A Little Rebellion (Crimson Worlds III)
The First Imperium (Crimson Worlds IV)
The Line Must Hold (Crimson Worlds V)
To Hell's Heart (Crimson Worlds VI)
The Shadow Legions(Crimson Worlds VII)
Even Legends Die (Crimson Worlds VIII)

The Fall (Crimson Worlds IX)
(November 2014)

War Stories (Crimson World Prequels)

Also By Jay Allan

The Dragon's Banner

Gehenna Dawn (Portal Worlds I)

www.jayallanbooks.com

THE TEN THOUSAND

The Ten Thousand is a work of fiction. All names, characters, incidents, and locations are fictitious. Any resemblance to actual persons, living or dead, events or places is entirely coincidental.

ISBN: 978-0692296134

Whoever fights monsters should see to it that in the process he does not become a monster. And if you gaze long enough into an abyss, the abyss will gaze back into you.

- Friedrich Nietzsche

Part One
Anabasis

Chapter 1

From the Journal of Jake Taylor:

Trust. It is the hardest thing to embrace, especially when you have seen what I have, been through the hell to which I was consigned. Yet it is also one of the greatest things man can experience, to rely without doubt on others, to know they are there for you, that if your vigilance fails they will step in and lend you their own strength.

It is something people don't understand well. They place their trust carelessly, recklessly, seeking to feel better, to convince themselves they can rely on those who have not earned such confidence. Organizations cannot be trusted, nor governments. By their very nature, they are changeable and soulless, subject to the caprices of those in positions of power.

It is a great fallacy that groups and institutions are trustworthy, a foolish misconception that continually causes mankind to make poor choices, to tread down dark roads that lead to slavery. Vigilance is the cost of freedom, questioning everything and demanding proof of all you are told. Yet that is a heavy burden, one most people cast aside for the drug of false trust.

My life has been one of sorrow and pain, inflicted on me by an evil regime bent on maintaining its power at all costs. All I once believed in was a lie; those I called my leaders were soulless monsters. I was a fool, believing in things because I was told to, because it was easier, because I did not think for myself. I am as guilt-stained as anyone, for once I willingly followed the powers I am now sworn to destroy.

My men, and those we must now fight as well, are all victims of this nightmare. Many innocents, led by lies into an unjust cause, will die before the stain is washed away. There is nothing I can do to prevent this. I must do what I must, regardless of the cost.

But there is good, even in the pit of hell, for it was in the middle of my ordeal that I rediscovered trust. In my battles there were men in the lines next to me, fellow-soldiers who fought with me, bled with me - who risked their own lives to save mine. I have served 14 years with these men at my side, protecting my back through the horrors of Gehenna. Through the years of deadly warfare those men became closer than friends, closer than brothers. I trust each of them with my life - a trust that has been forged through long years of bitter service together in hell. I know every one of them will do what I ask, no matter what the cost. I can never achieve the victory I pursue without the aid of those close to me, my comrades in arms.

But there is a weakness there too, for I know too well the difficulty of the task ahead of us, and I fear my friends, many of them at least, will die before it is over. They will die because of where I send them, the orders I alone give them. And I will see their cold, dead faces staring back at me for as long as I live.

"Keep moving. I want you in position and ready to fire in ten minutes." Major Karl Young stood on the small rock outcropping, waving his arms to urge his troops forward. It was almost time.

Young was a true veteran, a ten-year man. He'd survived more than a decade in the burning hell of Erastus, and that was as true a mark of toughness as any warrior could bear. He was as close to fearless as a man could be, the survivor of a hundred bloody combats. But he was excitable too, prone to loud outbursts and over-the-top enthusiasm - so much so that his friends and comrades called him Frantic.

The troops were moving forward. He had a full battalion, all enhanced Supersoldiers. They were jogging faster than any normal human could sprint, carrying their full load of exos as they did. Young's troops were moving to flank the enemy, part of General Taylor's plan to cut off and surround the advancing UN forces. Young could feel the victory within their grasp, and it showed in his shouts and gestures. He was earning his nickname with every yell and wave of his arms.

His people were moving forward through a narrow defile, with high rock walls on either side. They were well in advance of Taylor and the main force. When the general launched his frontal attack, Young's battalion would emerge from their hidden position and take the enemy in enfilade, just as Bear Samuels' troops would hit the opposite flank. The Alantrian forces were marching through a tight valley. They'd have a hard time repositioning to face the threats coming in from all sides. Trapped between converging fields of fire, they would be slaughtered. At least that was the plan.

Young was aware that most of the soldiers they were facing were involuntary conscripts, just like him - and the rest of his men. He didn't have any hostility toward the Atlantrian troops. Indeed, he sympathized with them. But the battle was almost underway and his blood was up. Once the fighting started, he knew it was either his people or the enemy. There was no room for hesitation in combat. Sparing an adversary was likely to cost the lives of one of his own – and that was unthinkable. There was an unbreakable bond connecting the men who'd shared the hell of Erastus, stronger even than that between soldiers elsewhere. General Taylor had tried to show the Alantrian troops the truth; he'd beseeched them to desert UNGov and join the Crusade. If they wouldn't listen, Young thought grimly, there was only one option. They would die.

"We're in position, sir." Lieutenant Hemmer's voice came through Young's implanted comlink. "The head of the column has reached the designated deployment area."

Young nodded, a pointless gesture since Hemmer was almost a klick forward of his position and there was no visual link active on the com. "Very well, Lieutenant." Young tried to hold back the excitement he always experienced in battle. His face was flushed, and he felt the heat around his neck and ears. He was a gifted officer and one of Taylor's most trusted compatriots, but he always had to struggle to keep himself calm. Frantic had earned his nickname more than once. "You may begin deployment."

Almost time, Young thought, feeling his hands shake as they usually did before battle. Almost time. He closed his eyes for a few seconds and took a half a dozen deep breaths. Just like always, he thought…the same as every battle you've fought before. But he knew that wasn't true. This would be their first combat off Erastus, and they were facing a group of troopers just like them, men who'd been lied to and pressganged into fighting an unjust war. Before, when they'd killed, the soldiers from Erastus had been facing the Machines – and then an army of UN career enforcers. Now they were about to engage soldiers who had been taken from their homes and shipped to a strange world to fight, men who should be their allies, but weren't.

He took one last breath and flipped on the unitwide com. "OK, 5th Battalion…prepare for battle."

*   *   *   *   *

Jake Taylor stood inside the HQ tent, staring at the monitor. The plan was complex, a series of maneuvers so intricate he wouldn't have even attempted them with any but his own veteran officers and men. There were no less than six columns on the move, and when they completed their respective marches, all of UN Force Alantris would be enveloped – and subsequently destroyed in detail.

"It looks like everything's going according to plan, Blackie." There was a touch of sadness in Taylor's voice. He would do whatever was necessary to destroy UNGov, but annihilating these soldiers, conscripts ripped from their lives just as he and his own men had been, was something he abhorred. He would do it because there was no alternative, but the thought of it made him sick. For an instant he wanted to leave HQ and run away – to hide in the wilderness and let someone else bear the burden. He inhaled deeply and clamped down on those thoughts. His men were all sworn to see this through, and Taylor had promised to lead them if they would follow. He'd never break that pledge, not while he still drew breath.

"We're spot on, Jake." Tony Black was Taylor's second-in-command, his most trusted friend and confidante. "The men are maneuvering like they're on the parade ground." Black had been a little concerned about the complexity of Taylor's plan, but the troops were coordinating flawlessly, and the hapless enemy forces had no idea what was about to hit them.

The UN forces on Alantris had been dispersed when Taylor and his people arrived, conducting the types of search and destroy missions common to the middle stages of a pacification campaign. The Machines had been forced onto the defensive on Alantris, but they still held large areas of the planet. Had held, at least. As soon as Taylor's people came through the Portal the Machines broke off and withdrew from the planet, leaving the two human forces to face each other alone.

The Alantrian army hesitated for a few days, uncertain what was happening. Then word came through the Portal from the high command on Earth. The human invaders were rebels, murderers who had slaughtered their comrades. The orders were straightforward – attack and destroy them.

Taylor broadcast his entreaty for the Alantrian troops to join him. He told them of UNGov's perfidy and the great fraud that caused the war. A few scouts and outposts deserted to join his force, but his story was just too far-fetched for most to believe. The propagandists from Earth had gotten to them first. They told them Taylor would lie to them, tell them crazy stories to try and subvert them. The Alantrians were confused, but most of them remained in the ranks and prepared to meet Taylor's army. They'd been following orders for a long time, and most of them couldn't imagine another course of action.

On Erastus, Taylor had been well-known, one of the senior officers, the first Supersoldier and a celebrated Ten Year Man. His words carried credibility, and the troops there had flocked to his banner. But no one on Alantris knew anything about Jake Taylor – except what UNGov was telling them.

Taylor's army was concentrated, drawn up in formation all around their entry Portal, so the Alantrian forces formed up as well, and marched on their positions. Jake let them concentrate and advance, keeping his troops in place while they did. His apparent lack of aggressiveness lured his adversary in, and the enemy's confidence soared. There were over 22,000 combat troops on Alantris, including a healthy core of veterans. Taylor's forces numbered less than 14,000, and that included a large contingent of support personnel. The Alantrians expected to overwhelm and destroy the invaders, but they didn't know that 10,000 of Taylor's troops were surgically-enhanced Supersoldiers and hardcore veterans of the most hellish world where men have ever fought.

"Majors Young, Samuels, and Daniels all report their troops are in position." Black stared at Taylor, realizing the general wasn't listening. His friend had drifted into one of his periods of introspection.

Black couldn't imagine the burdens Taylor was forced to bear, and how difficult it was for his friend to order the attack on an army of fellow-conscripts. Tony Black had grown up on the streets of the Philadelphia Metrozone, one of the most dangerous urban enclaves in the world. He'd known brutality since he was a child, and he'd learned to fight, for a scrap of bread or a dry place to sleep, at an early age.

Taylor, on the other hand, had grown up on a farm. He'd known hard work and poverty, but not the constant violence and filth of the ghetto. Black knew Taylor was a veteran now, one of the toughest who'd ever lived. But he'd also experienced love and family. Taylor acted like he'd forgotten about all of that, but Black knew it was still there, the flickering remembrance of a better time and place. He wasn't sure if it did his friend any good, but he knew it made it that much more difficult for him to issue the orders.

"Jake?" Black raised his voice a little.

Taylor shook out of his daydream. "Yeah, Blackie…understood." Even when Taylor wasn't paying attention, the NIS implanted in his brain recorded everything he was told – along with every bit of sensory input.

Black looked over at his friend, but Taylor didn't say anything else. "Jake…do you want to commence the attack?"

Taylor hesitated for a few seconds. Then: "No, Blackie. Not yet." He stared back at his friend, and Black could see an instant of weakness in his eyes. "I want to address the enemy one more time first."

Black let out a deep breath. He understood Taylor's hesitation. But he also knew they had to win the battle. They were about to hit the enemy with a surprise attack from all sides. Warning them didn't make any sense, at least not militarily. But he knew better than to argue with Taylor. "OK, Jake, but try to keep it short. Every minute we give them to react is going to cost more of our men before the battle is over."

"Maybe there won't be a battle." Taylor's voice was soft, with an odd tone. "Maybe they will understand." He took a breath, knowing in his heart he was fooling himself. "Maybe they will understand…and we won't have to kill them all."

Black nodded slightly. "Sure, Jake. Maybe." But he didn't believe it – and he knew Taylor didn't either.

                    *   *   *   *   *

"Attention all soldiers of UN Force Alantris." Taylor stood next to the HQ tent, looking out in the direction of his deployed army. He couldn't see the troops from where he stood, except for the reserve formations lined up waiting for the orders to advance. But he knew where they were, every squad, every man.

"This is General Jake Taylor, the commander of the Army of Erastus. I am addressing you one final time before battle is joined. My people and I are just like you, soldiers conscripted into the ranks for life, sent to a distant world to battle an alien enemy." He paused for a few seconds, his mind racing for what he could say to convince them. To save them. "Like you, we once believed in that cause. Whatever suffering we endured, we knew we were protecting our homes, our families." Another pause, shorter than the first. Taylor could feel Black's tension as the seconds ticked off. It was time to launch the attack. "But that was a lie, a foul deceit conjured by those who used it to seize power."

He held the Tegeri amulet in his hand as he spoke. The device was allowing him to communicate with every soldier in the opposing force, to slice through any jamming or other attempts to block his signal. "Watch your com units…witness what truly happened on the first colony worlds so many years ago." He turned a dial and pressed a small button.

He remained silent for a few seconds. He knew the amulet was projecting the image of the colonial massacres on every com unit in UN Force Alantris. He couldn't imagine the power that transmission required, the sophistication of the alien device he held in his hand.

He hadn't thought much about it at first but, as he began to discover the capabilities of the amulet, he came to realize that Tegeri technology was far in advance of Earth's. The Machines, he realized, should have been evidence enough of that fact. The manufactured biomechanical soldiers were extremely sophisticated, and Earth science couldn't begin to replicate whatever process created them. But their weapons and equipment were more or less the equivalents of those possessed by the Earth armies and, in 45 years of constant war, the Tegeri never employed anything more advanced. War on the Portal worlds had been largely a contest between equals, at least in terms of armament.

Now Taylor was beginning to realize the Tegeri could have utilized far more powerful weapons. Indeed, he wondered if they couldn't have easily crushed the human armies, even destroyed Earth itself. Almost certainly, he thought in answer. The fact that they didn't was just more evidence to support the honesty of T'arza's claims…and the basis for Taylor's crusade.

"What you have just seen is the truth. The images you have been shown before are fabrications, lies designed to get you to fight. Earth's government is the true evil, one that must be destroyed so our friends and families – all those we left behind forever – can at last know the taste of freedom." There was strength in Taylor's voice, and conviction. But there was a hint of desperation too. Not because he couldn't destroy those who ignored his entreaties. Just the opposite. He knew he could annihilate the soldiers of Alantris – and if they refused to yield he would do just that. More innocent blood on his hands.

"Now, soldiers of Alantris. You have a choice. Drop your weapons and join us. You will not be harmed if you do. You have my word." He paused, and when he continued his voice was dark and foreboding. "If you remain in your lines…if you stand with the evil of UNGov, we will destroy you utterly. For this battle is for the future of mankind, and there is no place for mercy or weakness with those who fight to keep mankind in chains."

He cut the transmission and turned slowly to face Black. "OK, Blackie. Maybe that will reach a few."

Black nodded. "I'm sure it will, Jake. You're becoming quite eloquent."

Taylor suppressed a laugh. Words like 'eloquent' never sounded quite right in the thick urban accent Black had never been able to shake.

Black knew Taylor better than anyone. He understood his friend's need to try again, to do all he could to save some of those men. But he knew just as well that Jake Taylor would never allow pity or guilt to stand in the way of the crusade. He would see every conscript on Alantris dead on the bloodsoaked field if that is what victory required.

Taylor turned and walked back toward his tent. "Give them 20 minutes, Blackie." His voice was thick with sadness and fatigue. "Then launch the attack."

$$*\qquad*\qquad*\qquad*\qquad*$$

The field in front of the line was covered with bodies, but Samuels' troops kept firing, raking the formations caught out on the flat, open ground. "Pour it into 'em, boys." He knew what he was supposed to say. His voice was calm, just what his men expected from their commander. But inside, he wanted to drop to his knees and wretch his guts up.

Bear Samuels had been a gentle giant from Alabama when he first arrived on Erastus, and he'd somehow managed to retain a remnant of that good-natured innocence, even after all the years of brutal combat. He'd become a good fighter and a strong leader, at least in battle against the Machines. UNGov's propaganda had turned the Tegeri's manufactured soldiers into pure manifestations of evil, and for years Samuels and his comrades had believed it all. It was easy to slaughter an enemy you thought of as soulless murderers, but killing other human beings didn't sit well with him. The men he'd fought in the last battle on Erastus were government thugs, bullies and institutionalized killers, at least. He imagined all the people they'd executed or dragged away to the reeducation centers as he led his men into battle against them. It helped him get through the fight, to deal with the guilt of gunning them down.

The soldiers his people were massacring now were different. They were ordinary men, just like he had been, like all his fellow soldiers on Erastus. The fighters out in that plain, dying in bunches under the withering enfilade fire, were conscripts, ripped from their homes and families just as he had been. They'd been kids, barely adults, when they were taken from all they'd known and sent far from home to fight a brutal war, never to return. Nothing he could tell himself made him feel better about what he knew he had to do. Nothing but his faith in Jake Taylor.

Taylor had taken him aside one night after the battle against the UN forces on Erastus. The two of them killed a bottle of Bourbon and talked all night. Samuels never knew where Taylor found the whiskey, but the things his commander and friend told him that night would stay with him as long as he lived.

He would draw his strength from that conversation, and he would do whatever had to be done, no matter how upsetting he found it to be. Because if he didn't, what had happened to him, to Taylor and all their comrades – even to the men his troopers were slaughtering now – would never end. Unless UNGov was destroyed, generation after generation of young conscripts would be fed into the machine. The war wasn't about holding back a bloodthirsty enemy; it wasn't even about conquering the Tegeri. It existed for one purpose, as a source of propaganda to preserve UNGov's dominance over a humanity too frightened to stand up for its own rights.

Taylor was right, Samuels thought as he watched the murderous fire from his autocannons tear apart the hapless enemy formations, now little more than terrified mobs, as they tried to flee. There was no choice, no other way. He had to do this; his men had to do it. No matter how they felt about it.

No more than a third of the enemy had made it past the flanking forces, and their formations were shattered. They were heading back the way they'd advanced, a tumultuous, panicked mob, fleeing wildly.

Samuels watched them sadly. Yes, he thought, head back toward your bases. Right into Hank Daniels' waiting line. Daniels, Samuel knew, had no pity at all for them.

*   *   *   *   *

"Get those guns set up and ready to fire." Hank Daniels stood a few meters behind his firing line, barking out orders to his sweating troops. "Now!" His force had gone the farthest, and they were spread out in a long formation along the enemy's rear, completing Taylor's envelopment.

The battle was already underway. Colonel Black had hit the enemy frontally, driving into them with such ferocity they broke and ran almost immediately – right past the two flanking forces Taylor had positioned along their route. He tried to imagine the horrendous losses Bear and Frantic were inflicting on the panicked soldiers as they fled past their prepared flanking positions.

The Alantrian army was experienced from over a decade's continuous combat, but they'd never encountered anything like Taylor and his veterans before. Supersoldiers, stone cold killers forged in the furnace of Gehenna, no warriors who existed could stand against them, not without staggering numerical superiority.

Daniels knew what was happening, even though he couldn't see it. The Alantrian lines, what was left of them, were buckling. Their formations were melting away under the sustained fire of Taylor's perfectly placed flanking forces. By the time they reached his position, they would be a routing, panic-stricken mob seeking only to escape. That's were Daniels' people came in. His troops were stretched out all along the enemy's rear — now the direction in which they were running – waiting. Taylor's orders were brutally clear. Allow no one to escape. He was to accept any surrenders he could without endangering his command, but not a single enemy soldier was to get off the field. Not one.

Daniels treated Taylor's orders like they were commandments from heaven. Spider Daniels had served under Jake Taylor for all the years he'd spent fighting on the brutal battlefields of Erastus. His devotion to his friend was total, verging on fanatical. Daniels was a true believer, his mind and soul given without reservation to Taylor's crusade.

Daniels was the angriest and most resentful of Taylor's top officers, the one most determined to destroy UNGov. Taylor, even, had mixed feelings, his convictions still tempered by doubts, despite the steel-hard image he portrayed to those around him. He hated UNGov, and he wanted to free mankind from a totalitarian nightmare. But he was uncomfortable with the cost his men – and the people of Earth - might be called upon to pay.

Daniels was driven by pure rage. He wanted to tear down UNGov brick by brick, to strangle the life out of every member of the Secretariat personally. He didn't share Taylor's sympathy for the people of Earth, at least not completely. He hated the government, but he blamed the people too, for their gullibility, for their willingness to wear the shackles they'd forged for themselves. Daniels blamed the government for sending him and his comrades to Erastus, but he held the civilians accountable as well, for it was they who allowed UNGov to control them.

"Enemy forces approaching, sir." Captain Hollis was Daniel's aide and the battalion's second-in-command. Hollis was a desert rat from the old American southwest. West Texas, Daniels' NIS reminded him. The neural intelligence systems were enormously useful devices, and they'd saved the lives of many of his comrades – but Daniels sometimes missed being able to forget trivial facts.

"Battalion…" - Daniels' voice was firm, commanding - "… prepare to fire." He looked out over the open plain, a stretch of ground utterly devoid of cover that Taylor had chosen carefully. There wasn't a rock outcropping or small dip in the ground anywhere. Just one long ridge in the distance, a rise the enemy would crest before fleeing into the vast open space in front of Daniels' position. It was the most perfect killing zone he'd ever seen. And it was almost time.

He saw motion in the distance, along the top of the ridge – then, a few seconds later, a mob of panicked, fleeing soldiers rushing up and over the hilltop and into the wide open grasslands. They were running right for his position, fleeing directly into his carefully targeted fields of fire.

He stared at them for an instant, watched as they approached, a wild disorganized mob. With his enhanced eyes, he saw them in the open long before they would spot his own dug in troopers. He felt a moment of pity, but it was fleeting. Taylor had offered them not one, but two chances to yield. Most of them had spurned both. Now they would pay the price. He spoke calmly, almost coldly into the com.

"Fire."

*   *   *   *   *

Taylor stood next to a makeshift table, really just a piece of scrap metal sitting on two saw horses. He had been listening to the reports on the com, but he'd stopped hearing them after a while. They were all the same from every corner of the battlefield. A few of the enemy were able to surrender and were taken prisoner. The rest were dead.

Taylor had planned the envelopment as a battle of annihilation. He knew what he had to do to win this war, the level of ruthlessness it would take to give his people even a small chance of fighting their way to Earth and overthrowing UNGov. But knowing something and living with it are two different things. Taylor the general – the crusader - had planned the battle he needed to serve his purpose. But the man had to deal with the consequences of what he'd done. UNGov had ripped these men from their homes and families and sent them to Alantria – and Taylor had killed them. He had killed them all.

He imagined the troops of the army he'd just destroyed, most of whom lay dead across 25 square klicks of ravaged ground. There were veterans out there, soldiers like himself who had adapted and learned by hard experience, surviving battle after battle. He knew there were recruits too, the FNGs who'd stepped through the portal in the days and weeks prior to the battle. They were young kids, mostly, with no idea what was coming for them. They'd have been the first to die; they would have stumbled cluelessly into his soldiers' fields of fire or crowded together in terrified masses, presenting unmissable targets to his gunners. The veterans would have held out longer, at least a little. But it didn't matter. They were all helpless newbs against Taylor's hell-hardened cyborgs.

"How many?" He was still looking out across the field, an odd expression on his face.

Black stood behind him. He paused for a few seconds, considering playing dumb. But that would serve no one. He knew what Taylor wanted to know – and Jake was well aware that he did. Game playing would serve no purpose. "About 1,100 successfully surrendered, Jake."

Taylor was silent for half a minute, still staring out at the clouds of smoke drifting over the field. "So we killed 20,000 men today." His voice was deadpan, without emotion. Successfully surrendered – the words stuck in his mind. How many, he wondered, tried to give up toward the end? How many did his soldiers shoot down in the confusion as they were trying to yield? Perhaps, he thought, he was better off not knowing. It served no purpose to dwell on such things.

He stood motionless, watching the orange sun setting slowly over the field. And this is just the beginning, he thought…we have so far to go. He sighed softly. So many more to kill.

Chapter 2

The Final Report of General Zacharias Fox:

We have been defeated on all fronts, and our inner defensive line is crumbling. This enemy is like nothing we have faced before. Our forces have been unable to stop them in any engagement. They move with great speed, and their endurance is astonishing. My forces have been unable to meet them effectively on equal terms, or even with a numerical advantage of two or three to one.

I estimate that approximately 20% of my effectives have deserted or surrendered, and the units remaining under my command are at or below half strength. The enemy is rapidly approaching, and I don't know how long we can hold out without immediate assistance. I am urgently requesting reinforcements before it is too late to save...

Transmission terminated.

"The news from the Portal worlds continues to be uniformly disastrous. It would seem that we can now add Pacifica to the list of fallen planets."

Raul Esteban leaned back in his plush leather chair, laying the glowing tablet and its disturbing report on the table as he stared thoughtfully at the snowy peak of Mt. Blanc in the distance. The top half of the mountain was shrouded with dark clouds. There was a storm heading toward Geneva, and Weather Division was predicting a bad one. Days of snow and sub-freezing temperatures. Esteban felt a touch of irony. There was another storm also, one currently lightyears away, but it too was approaching. And it was looking like a bad one as well. Far worse than anything he'd seen coming when Jake Taylor and his troops first rebelled on Erastus.

"I daresay we are witnessing the effectiveness of Secretary Keita's Supersoldier program, though in a manner we did not anticipate." Esteban's voice was hard to read, but that didn't stop everyone in the room from trying. They were edgy, nervous. The Secretary General was not a patient man, nor was he tolerant of failure. The other members of the Secretariat plotted and schemed, making their plans for the day when Esteban was gone...but there wasn't one of them with the strength or courage to go up against UNGov's unquestioned leader. "Taylor has managed to turn a considerable number of the soldiers on Alantris, Mariana...and now Pacifica, boosting his strength considerably." He paused, still staring out across the Swiss countryside a kilometer below. "But it is the altered troops, the Supersoldiers, who are in every way the heart of his force." Another pause, shorter than the last. "Ten thousand men. And they are beginning to threaten everything."

Esteban was the most powerful man on Earth and the closest thing mankind had to an absolute ruler. He'd been one of the prime movers in the great fraud that induced Earth's nations to surrender their sovereignty, to give up their freedoms and independence in exchange for protection from a bloodthirsty alien enemy...a danger, it turned out, didn't actually exist. Esteban and his co-conspirators sent their thugs to murder colonists, and they framed the Tegeri for the crime. In the process, they instigated four decades of interstellar war, all in a ruthless bid for power. A very successful one. They had gained complete control over all mankind and imposed their own world order, almost bloodlessly – except for several generations of soldiers who died in the sands of distant worlds, fighting an unjust and unnecessary war. Esteban had always believed the greatest weapon for controlling people was exploiting their fears, and he and his cohorts had proven it decisively.

But political power had its limits, and mortality was the

greatest. When the cancer that was steadily destroying his brain finally killed him, the last of the men responsible for the greatest lie in history would be dead of natural causes, having reworked human society and reigned for 40 years as a ruling elite. Esteban and his cohorts had tasted more power than anyone since man had first gathered together to build crude villages and begin civilization's ascent. But in a few months, half a year at most, the last of them would be dead.

Earth had known many dictators and absolute rulers, but not a lot of them had managed to die peacefully in bed. Esteban drew satisfaction that not one of the members of the original cabal had been assassinated or deposed. They had seized control of mankind, and the miserable sheep inhabiting the world's former nations largely obeyed their masters with almost no serious instances of rebellion. Until now.

He inhaled deeply, turning his eyes back toward the men seated around the table. The Secretariat of the United Nations, the supreme governing body of a united Earth. The first Secretariat had consisted entirely of his co-conspirators, but now Esteban was the last of the old guard. Soon, he knew, he would be gone as well, and the grand plan for world government would finally pass entirely to the next generation of chosen elites. He and his peers had made their bid for power and succeeded. He wondered if there was anyone else at the table with the same drive and ability as the men who'd forged UNGov's supremacy. He and his original comrades had chosen all these men, promoted them through the bureaucracy, and carefully selected those few who would ascend to the ultimate height of power... the Secretariat itself. Some had been favorites, sycophants of the most powerful of his peers, but others had clawed their way to the top on the basis of ability and ruthlessness.

He had once thought a few of them might be worthy, but now he was questioning that assessment. They'd proven unable to deal with Taylor's Rebellion, as it had come to be called in the closed confines of the Secretariat. And they still seemed far more interested in their internal power struggles than addressing the matter forcefully. He understood. Anyone who took the lead on solving a problem also risked taking much of the blame for failure. Esteban saw it throughout the layers of the bureaucracy he and his cohorts had built. They had been men of action, unafraid to stake their claim to power and do whatever was necessary to make it reality. But those who had come after were ruled more by caution than courage. They had been given power; they hadn't seized it. And they lacked the dynamism of their predecessors.

"It is essential that we destroy this upstart and his band of fugitives before they are allowed to progress any closer to Earth." Jake Taylor had led his ten thousand warriors from the hellish inferno of Erastus through Portals that had been held by the Tegeri, routes unknown to anyone on Earth. There was no way to predict where Taylor's army would appear, no rational method for planning a defense. And Taylor's force, led by the Ten Thousand, the surgically altered Supersoldiers, was slicing through the standard UN forces like a knife through butter.

"Gen…Taylor…" - Samovich thought better of according Taylor his self-proclaimed rank – "…is a significant threat, but not one we cannot handle." Anton Samovich was one of the top members of the Secretariat, with a strong chance to succeed to the Secretary-General's chair when Esteban finally died. He'd been damaged politically by the insurrection, but he was a survivor. He had sponsored Anan Keita's appointment to the Secretariat, and Keita had been responsible for the Supersoldier program. A lot of the stink of the current crisis had splashed on Samovich, but the wily operative had managed to limit the damage. Samovich's portfolio was internal security…and he'd used his resources not only to hold down the masses, but also to build up considerable dossiers on his associates on the Secretariat. Corruption was endemic throughout UNGov, but that didn't prevent the dogpile when someone was exposed. Blackmail was a highly effective form of political power…and no one on the Secretariat doubted Samovich's willingness to follow through on a threat.

Chang Li sat on the opposite side of the table, staring skeptically at Samovich. Li was another senior member of the Secretariat, and Samovich's primary rival for the Secretary-General's chair. The rivalry – and seething hatred - between the two was well known, and the Secretariat was divided into three camps. Samovich had four solid supporters, as did Chang. The neutrals, the other three votes that would decide who became the next Secretary-General, would go to whomever could offer the highest price. Even in a thoroughly corrupt system, there were those who had mastered the art better than others, and Li and Samovich were two of the best.

Li was about to speak, but Esteban beat him to it. "What action would you propose to contain this problem, Secretary Samovich?" Esteban turned back from the window, his eyes focusing on the Russian's like two lasers. "Because your efforts to date have not exactly inspired confidence."

Samovich sat firm, unmoving under the Secretary-General's withering gaze. "I propose we match like with like...that we confront Taylor's Supersoldiers with our own."

A murmur rippled across the massive table. The enhancement program had been suspended immediately after the army on Erastus rebelled. UNGov was accustomed to whipped supplicants, not dangerous and defiant rebels, and the Supersoldier program had taken most of the blame for the disaster on Erastus.

Esteban continued his stare. "Do you think that is wise?" His tone was sincere.

"Yes, Secretary-General, I do." Samovich returned the hard gaze. "Taylor's men have been far more dangerous and troublesome because they have had the modifications..." – he glanced around the table, settling his gaze on Li – "...but blaming the rebellion itself on the mods, as if stronger muscles and greater endurance drove these men to insurrection, is a foolish political game, beneath the dignity of this august body." His eyes did not waver from Li. "One we no longer have the luxury to pursue. It is time for us to put aside petty political squabbles and take decisive action to end this costly and destruction revolution before it spreads further. And to do so, we must be able to match our adversary in every way."

Li stared back, his face flushed with anger. Samovich had boxed him into a corner. He'd used the Supersoldier program against Samovich every way he could, but now he remained silent. It was played out, and he knew it. Things were getting serious…Taylor and his people were beginning to look unstoppable, and UNGov had to do more than just sit and hope one of the planetary armies pulled off a miraculous victory. If Li argued against Samovich's proposal, he'd be expected to offer an alternative. Inaction was no longer a luxury they could afford, and simply reinforcing every colony world, waiting to see where Taylor's people might emerge, was untenable. And Li didn't have anything else. He struggled to remain calm on the outside as he nodded to Samovich.

"Very well, Secretary Samovich." Esteban leaned back in his chair. "What do you specifically propose?"

Samovich let out a quiet breath. He'd won this round. If his plan worked, if he was able to stop Taylor's Rebellion in its tracks, he'd be halfway to the Secretary-General's Seat. If it failed…well, that would be a problem, not only for him, but for UNGov as well.

"Taylor has approximately 9,600-9,800 modified soldiers remaining per out latest estimates. He had almost exactly 10,000 when he left Erastus, and he has fought three planetary campaigns since. His losses have been disturbingly light, and mostly among his non-modified troops." Samovich paused, thinking for a second how much speculation he cared to offer. "I would estimate, based on desertion reports and strength levels on the planets involved, that approximately 6,000 soldiers have deserted and rallied to him, adding to the 3,500-4,000 unmodified personnel he had on Erastus." A wild guess, he realized, but he was sure his numbers were close. "Of those, perhaps 1,500 of the non-modified personnel have been killed or permanently incapacitated by wounds."

There were scowls around the table, mostly on the faces of Li and his allies. "These numbers are wild supposition," he interrupted. "There is no factual basis to back these estimates."

Samovich was going to argue, but Esteban beat him to it.

"Secretary Li, we are attempting to craft a viable response to the current crisis. I agree that Secretary Samovich's numbers represent his best guesses, but I question if there is better data available to us." He stared at Li. "Do you have a methodology to suggest that offers greater accuracy?"

Li sank back into his chair, a sullen look on his face. "No." He sighed softly. "I do not."

"Then I suggest we put political infighting aside and allow Secretary Samovich to continue." He looked back at Samovich, motioning almost imperceptibly for him to go on.

Samovich looked at Li then back at Esteban. "Thank you, Secretary-General." He shot another lightning-fast glance at Li before he continued. "I propose that we produce our own force of 20,000 enhanced soldiers and keep them ready to intervene when Taylor's people hit a world we are able to quickly reinforce from Earth." He ignored the stunned looks around the table. "It will be an expensive project, I realize, but a necessary one. I do not see another reliable way to defeat Taylor and his forces."

"The cost will be astronomical." The voice was a different one, deeper, with a heavy Spanish accent. Enrique Cruz was one of Li's cronies, a man who hadn't had a thought of his own in years. "On a program that has failed utterly?" He paused, glancing back at Li before he continued. "You do recall that Taylor's soldiers on Erastus were the field test for the program. Look how that worked out."

"Yes," Samovich snapped back. "Look how that worked out. They have obliterated every force they have engaged, with a ratio of casualties inflicted to those sustained of 20-1. I submit that the program itself is a profound success and, further, that we stand little chance of defeating Taylor's people within an acceptable time frame unless we can match their abilities."

"I believe Secretary Samovich is correct." Esteban's voice was firm, confident. He had made a decision, and he wasn't inviting further debate. "I do not believe it will be overly difficult to add a course of mental conditioning to the program to prevent a repeat of Taylor's unfortunate treachery, do you Secretary Samovich?"

The Russian nodded gently. "No, sir." A short pause. "Not at all. Indeed, I believe there are a number of options to ensure obedience among the modified troops."

"That should address the concern over another Taylor incident." Esteban panned his eyes across the table. "Indeed, perhaps we should introduce a program of conditioning to our normal training regimen." UNGov had never bothered to indoctrinate or brainwash its draftees. They were all sent off-world, to planets they would never leave. They had no options but to fight. There was no retreat, no mustering out. Defeat meant death for them all.

That was before the Tegeri intervened and turned a UNGov planetary army into a dangerous rebel force. The game had become more complex, and there was no room for carelessness. "Yes," he continued after a few seconds' thought. "I believe we should institute an immediate program of mental conditioning for all inductees." He looked down the table. "Does everyone agree?" It was a perfunctory question. No one was going to argue with the Secretary-General.

Samovich nodded and joined the chorus of "Yes, sirs."

"Very well." Esteban looked back at Samovich and returned the Russian's nod. "You may begin preparations for the selection process. I presume you will need veterans for the program." A small frown crossed his lips as Samovich nodded his assent. Pulling 20,000 men from the planetary field forces wasn't going to be easy. Most of those armies were still fighting the Machines and the Tegeri. UNGov couldn't just withdraw all the veterans from those formations, not without the fronts collapsing on a dozen worlds. "We must be careful where we draw down the required forces." He stared over at Anan Keita. "Your thoughts, Secretary Keita?"

Keita had remained silent during the meeting. His portfolio was interplanetary military, and the present crisis fell directly within his purview. But he was also dead center for taking the blame for the debacle on Erastus. He'd survived and maintained his Seat only because Samovich decided it would be more costly politically to sack his newest ally. Keita was grateful to dodge a bullet, but he didn't fool himself. His position was still tenuous at best, and he'd made sure to tread cautiously.

"My thoughts, Secretary-General?" Keita was caught by surprise. Samovich's influence and power had saved him from an ignominious impeachment – or worse - but he wasn't expecting to be consulted on anything of import.

"Yes, Secretary Keita," Esteban said, his tone impatient. "What are your thoughts on finding the 20,000 subjects for the reboot of the Supersoldier program?"

Keita cleared his throat. "Well, sir…I suggest we withdraw 25% of the two to five year men from each disputed colony world to form the required cadre. Then…"

"Some of those campaigns are still in the early stages of pacification," Li interrupted. He spoke calmly, but his body language showed his tension. If Samovich's plan was successful in destroying Taylor and his people, he would be a hair's breadth away from Esteban's Seat. Li had no illusions about long surviving Samovich's ascension to the Secretary-Generalship, no more than the detested Russian would if Li won their power struggle. "Indeed, a withdrawal of that many veterans would severely endanger many of the campaigns."

"Which is why I was going to propose doubling the numbers of new recruits sent to each world." Keita glanced at Samovich, noting a slight nod of approval from his mentor. "I would expect casualties to spike sharply, especially among the new troops, but I believe that is an acceptable price to pay."

"It's not simply casualties among the recruits. It is logistics, supply, transport." Li's voice was marginally louder than before, and his hands were pressed flat against the table. "More troops require more equipment. They will overburden the training facilities." He stared at Keita. "Have you considered all of this, Secretary Keita?"

Keita took a deep breath. He'd been silent for a long time, but the nod from Samovich and the attention from the Secretary-General encouraged him. It would take bold action to rehabilitate his political position, and now was as good a time as any to begin. "I have considered all of that, Secretary Li.

However, despite such concerns, we are faced with a problem that must be addressed. Whatever the cost, whatever the inconvenience of our solution…it is almost certainly less destructive than doing nothing and allowing these rebels to continue their rampage." He stared right at Li, mustering all his courage to do it. "Wouldn't you agree, Secretary Li?"

Li looked like he'd tasted something sour, but he just returned Keita's gaze and said, "Yes." A short pause. "Indeed you are correct, Secretary Keita. Doing nothing is not an option." Li suppressed his anger. He knew when to fold a losing hand.

"Very well…" Esteban rose as he spoke. "…then Secretaries Samovich and Keita are authorized to develop a comprehensive plan for the implementation of Project Supersoldier to create a force of 20,000 modified soldiers to face Taylor and his rebels." He glanced briefly at Keita then settled his gaze on Samovich. "They will report to this body for final approval once the plan is ready for implementation." He moved his head to the side, looking around the table and settling his focus on Li. "Are we all in agreement?" It was a rhetorical question. No one had disagreed with Raul Esteban in decades, at least not openly.

"Then it is decided." He turned back toward Samovich. "Anton, we are all depending on you. I trust this plan will be carefully designed and flawlessly implemented." There was menace hiding in the pleasant, businesslike tone. Esteban was giving Samovich another chance, but he was signaling he wouldn't tolerate a repeat of the previous failure. "I want Taylor and his forces completely exterminated." He paused. "Do you understand me?"

"Yes, Secretary-General." Samovich felt a vice clamp down on his guts, but he fought to remain calm. "I understand perfectly."

Chapter 3

From the Journal of Jake Taylor:

There is a man...a boy, really. I see him in my dreams. He is me, I know...a young man who no longer exists, except to haunt my sleep. He beckons to me, beseeches me to pull back from the course I have undertaken, to think as I once did, with kindness and mercy and laughter. He begs me to stay away from the abyss, to pull back from the edge, but I ignore him and plunge forth anyway. He is a foolish child, an innocent who knows nothing of the universe, nor the darkness that infests it. He has not stared into the eyes of true evil, and he knows nothing of the things I must do to destroy the serpent that has swallowed mankind. My actions, brutal though they may be, are not my choice, they are my sacred duty. I have allowed myself to become a monster so that I may have the strength to slay a creature far worse and much darker.

The boy comes every night, offering me the humanity I have lost. But I send him away each time, banishing him to the forgotten past where he belongs. For he is a shadow, gone for-ever, and humanity would be nothing but a burden to me now. Where I must go, he cannot come. He is weak, and I will need all the strength and resolution I can muster.

Taylor looked out over the blasted plain, watching his troops advancing into the withering fire. They were going down in clumps, five or ten at a time, but they kept pressing forward, barely hesitating as they climbed over the fallen bodies of their comrades.

The sky was deep red over the field, and the soldiers fought in an eerie, crimson twilight. There were large pits all across the plain, deep fissures billowing great plumes of sulfurous smoke, like huge shadowy towers rising into the darkening sky.

He watched his men moving across the hellish landscape, grimly advancing into the deadly fire. At least half of them were down already, but they pressed on, following his orders with all the strength and determination they could muster.

He saw Blackie leading a column toward the main enemy strongpoint. His force was melting away behind him, like an ice cube on a hot day, but they kept going, returning fire as they slogged toward the enemy. Taylor's eyes were fixed, watching his closest friend lead the shattered remnants forward, ever forward. Until a shell landed right next to him, and he simply vanished.

"Blackie!" Taylor screamed, his hands balled into clenched fists.

He woke suddenly. He was covered in cold, clammy sweat, the light sheet on the cot almost soaked through. The dreams had been getting worse, and more frequent too. He hadn't told anyone, but he was down to 2 or 3 hours of sleep a night. At best. He could feel the cumulative effects, the exhaustion building inside him, but it still took him hours to get to sleep at night and, when he did, the nightmares came.

He looked down at his palms, now covered with purplish mottles where his enhanced muscles had turned his fists into vices. He stared as the bruises began to fade as his equally-improved healing abilities kicked in. My God, he wondered, what the hell did they make me into?

He shivered. The cool air from the half-open tent flap felt frigid to him. He pulled the sweat-soaked sheet off the cot and tossed it on the floor, reaching out for the heavy blanket folded up on the table next to him. He shuddered again as he spread it out over the camp bed and pulled it up to his neck. Juno was a temperate planet, with cool breezy summers and mild winters.

Its moderate temperatures and gentle breezes made it a virtual paradise, one of the most pleasant worlds men had ever found. But 14 years fighting in the burning hell of Erastus had left Taylor sensitive to the cold. It had been a year since he'd left the burning sands of the world his people called Gehenna, but he still hadn't gotten used to it, at least not completely.

It had taken months just for his body to adapt to the absence of chronic dehydration. It was impossible to drink enough fluids on Gehenna, and the planet's relentless, searing heat made you sweat out every drop of your ration. Acclimating to Erastus was an unpleasant process, but eventually the body adapted, even to that hell planet's seemingly unbearable conditions. All of Taylor's veterans had been lean and taught, their skin paper-thin and tightly stretched across their muscular frames.

When they left Erastus for Vincennes, they found an environment they couldn't have imagined, a cool, rainy planet with water everywhere. A soldier could just drop a few decon tablets and drink a lake dry – and a few of them tried. Their bodies, fully-acclimated to a moisture-deprived state, reacted harshly. Crippling headaches, vomiting, diarrhea. Practically the entire force was down for the first few days. Fortunately, Taylor, concerned at first with putting distance between his army and whatever forces UNGov might push through the Earth-Erastus portal, had chosen an uninhabited planet for the first transit. He'd wanted them to have some breathing space while they organized themselves and planned their campaign. Their crusade.

Taylor's body had been no less shocked by the change of environment than anyone's. He recovered from the worst of it in a few days, just like everyone else, but some of the effects lingered. His fully-hydrated body felt bloated and sluggish for months until he finally adapted. He felt normal now, accustomed to carrying an extra five kilos of water weight. But the cold still sliced through him like a knife.

He tossed and turned, trying without success to get back to sleep. He was tired, and he knew he needed the rest, but part of him was glad for the restlessness. There was a price to pay for sleep. The nightmares waited for him when he drifted off.

Finally, he gave up, rising with a grunt and wrapping the blanket around him. He walked over to the campaign desk in the corner of the tent, sitting in the small folding chair and poking the workstation's screen to bring it out of sleep mode.

The glow of the screen cast a ghostly pale light on the walls of the otherwise dark tent. There were rows of figures on the screen, unit strengths mostly. He nodded absent-mindedly as he scanned them. Losses had been light in their first few planetary campaigns, far lower than he'd feared. The human armies his people had faced seemed even less able to counter the abilities of his enhanced warriors than the Machines on Erastus had been. The battles had been routs, debacles. The poor conscripts in the planetary armies never had a chance.

Well, he thought, a caustic grin on his face, you made us into what we are, and now you will reap what you have sown. Of course, those doing most of the dying so far were innocent. It had been the politicians who'd sent his people to Erastus and devised the programs that stripped them of their humanity…made killing machines of them. The men dying under his army's guns were other victims, coerced or tricked into fighting an unjust and unnecessary war. But there was no other way. Those who would not join his crusade had to be destroyed. The politicians, the puppetmasters behind the great evil, they would also pay. Taylor would make sure of it. But he had to get to them first. And that meant destroying those who fought for them, even if they were poor, brainwashed cogs in the machine.

He imagined the growing fear in the halls of power on Earth, the top politicians and their cronies listening in stunned silence to the dispatches coming in, reports of armies destroyed, worlds lost. Taylor's mind pictured the endless debates and political infighting. He wondered, how would they react? What would they do to counter him?

He punched a key, bringing up another group of figures. Deserters. That's what UNGov will call them, he thought. The soldiers of the planetary armies were men just like Taylor and his people. They were conscripted or compelled to enlist, press-ganged the way Taylor himself had been. They were victims just like the soldiers from Erastus. Family, friends, home - all had been stripped from them. If most of them had been assigned someplace less hellish than Erastus, that was a meager blessing compared to all they had lost.

Taylor hated killing those men, and he was thankful for those who'd joined his crusade, the meager few he hadn't had to kill. Every one of the others sliced into him like a knife.

It had been different in the final battle on Erastus. Those men had been UNGov thugs, career enforcers who'd spent their lives bullying a cowed civilian population. For them, there had been no pity in Taylor's soul, and he hadn't hesitated an instant before ordering the last 12,000 of them summarily executed. He and his men were fighting a great evil, and there was no room for doubt of half-measures. UNGov was a cancer, and it had to be destroyed completely, every cell of it torn from the body of humanity.

The planetary armies were different, and he did everything possible to spare as many as possible. He broadcast his appeals to them over their own com lines, beseeching them to join his crusade. He told them the truth of the war, how UNGov and not the Tegeri had murdered the early colonists. He appealed to them all, as one of them, as a man who'd lost all everything, just as they had. And they came, some of them. Singly and in small groups, they abandoned their lines and crossed over. In the last campaign, Taylor managed to persuade 30% of the soldiers his army had faced to switch sides and join the crusade. But that left 70% unconvinced - or too closely guarded by their officers and afraid to flee. And Taylor had no choice but to kill that 70%. Nothing could be allowed to stand in the way of his crusade, not hesitation, not pity…nothing.

He sighed as he glanced at the preliminary scouting reports for Juno. It looked like the UN army there was 21,000 strong, the largest force they had yet faced. More innocent victims, more hapless conscripts to massacre. He nodded and stared at the screen, his resolve building as grogginess faded away. Yes, he would kill them, all who didn't join the crusade. There was no choice, and remorse was only another weakness. And there was no room for weakness. None. Taylor needed strength, and the cold-blooded resolve to see this war through to victory.

He punched at the workstation's keys, pulling up maps and troop dispositions. The intel was sketchy and incomplete. Taylor had imposed rigid limits on the use of drones and other ordnance, and he'd rejected every request to relax the stringent rules. If they ran out of ammunition and other vital supplies, the crusade would be over. They'd won their battles quickly so far, and they'd more than replaced their logistical expenditures with captured stores. But they had a long way to go, and they couldn't count on an uninterrupted streak of rapid victories.

Taylor sat quietly, reviewing the newest intel. Thanks to the Neural Information System implanted in his brain, he would remember everything he read. The NIS wasn't a computer or artificial intelligence, but it did organize and expand his brain's capacity to store and retrieve information. It was a constructed eidetic memory, one he'd found to be extremely useful in the field.

He typed a few digits on the keypad, and the columns of numbers on the screen were replaced by a diagram, a series of dots connected by a spiderweb of thin lines. The Tegeri had shared all their knowledge of the Portal network, and it was far more extensive than UNGov knew. There were Portals everywhere, on Earth, on other worlds, far more than the UN forces knew about.

One of the dots was flashing blue. Juno. There were ten lines reaching out from the small blue circle – all Portal routes connecting the planet with other worlds. Taylor focused on one of them, leading to Oceania. That was the route the UNGov forces had taken. Earth to Arleon to Oceania to Juno. Taylor's people could advance that way toward Earth, but that wasn't his plan. Arleon was completely pacified, the Tegeri and Machines driven off the world entirely, and it was still occupied by its victorious planetary army. Oceania was 70% occupied by UN forces, the war there starting to wind down as the enemy forces pulled back from a defensive line they had held for a decade. There was still fighting to be done, and years of final search and destroy missions would follow before the Machines were completely expelled, but UN Force Oceania was definitely ascendant. It was a difficult invasion route to move that way toward Earth, one cutting through two of the strongest-held worlds under UN control. And if he advanced overtly and directly toward Earth, he knew his people would face every bit of force UNGov could throw in their way, anything they could pour through the Portals to reinforce the planetary armies.

No, Taylor wasn't going to lead his people down that bloody road. There was another route, one the UN forces knew nothing about. The Tegeri had been on Juno for centuries, and they'd mapped out all of its Portals. One of them led to a planet unknown to the Earth authorities, a world the Tegeri called Lorus. And that world led to another, and another – until finally the route ended at an undiscovered portal on Earth itself, one hidden in a cave in the northern wastes of Siberia. A remote, unguarded backdoor to the home world.

It was exactly what Taylor wanted, a way to get back to Earth without charging into the teeth of UNGov's heaviest defenses. Some of his officers had wanted to march right through the Erastus-Earth portal, but he knew that was folly. No 10,000 men ever made could openly storm the combined defenses of Earth's sole government.

Taylor had known from the start he had to find a way to get to Earth without running right into UNGov's massed defenses – and the undiscovered portal offered just that opportunity. His ten thousand modified Supersoldiers could never defeat the combined might of Earth's oppressive government. Taylor knew that, though he exuded nothing but confidence in public. The army had 9,000 additional troops on its rosters, unmodified soldiers from Erastus supplement by men who'd deserted the UN ranks to join the crusade. They were normal soldiers, if mostly veterans, and far too few to alter the overall calculus.

The war to free Earth would be fought by millions, not thousands. His men would have to disperse, form the nuclei of a hundred centers of resistance, raise up the population to fight for their freedom. Taylor couldn't even imagine the final cost of the war. Governments never yield power willingly. They will consume their citizens, massacre them in unimaginable numbers, poison the world, even destroy themselves with bitter infighting, but they never give up their power voluntarily.

The crusade would have to obliterate UNGov root and branch, defeat all their soldiers and security forces, hunt down and execute every member of their leadership. There could be no half measures, no mercy; the rot had to be cut out, down to the bone. Millions would die, Taylor knew. Cities would burn, disease and pestilence would ravage the world. Man had meekly surrendered to those who would rule over them as their masters. Taylor was resolved that crime would be washed away, in blood if necessary. He had no illusions of the cost mankind would have to pay to regain its lost freedom. The price of liberty was a lesson mankind would have to learn again.

He sat at the small campaign desk, staring at the fabric walls of the tent. How, he wondered, did I end up here? Taylor had been born in the New Hampshire countryside, far from the centers of power. His family had been poor; virtually everyone outside the government was. But they were fortunate in ways too. They were farmers, and that accorded them some meager privileges. The production of the farms was always in great demand, and UNGov coddled the farmers, at least compared to the way it treated other citizens.

Earth's teeming masses were adequately fed, more or less, but they subsisted on chemically manufactured foods and algae derivatives. Most of the world's farmland was blighted and polluted, incapable of yielding more than a fraction of the output of decades past. But those in positions of power and privilege wanted real food - fresh fruit and vegetables and meat, not the manufactured gruel the population consumed. So, as long as the food kept flowing to the restricted markets, the government mostly left the farmers alone.

They weren't wealthy, despite the demand for their production. UNGov buried them under fees and taxes to recoup most of their income. But they did have access to real food, and that was a fringe benefit the millions living in the cities could only dream about. Taylor still remembered his mother's apple pie fondly, and he realized what an unattainable luxury that was to most of the people of the world.

Taylor sighed, and his expression morphed into one of sadness, melancholy. The thoughts of home were gloomy ones to him, images of what he'd lost, what he could never have again. It was a place to which he knew he couldn't ever return, not really. Taylor had allowed himself to be conscripted and sent to Gehenna to save his family's farm. That had been his sacrifice, to leave all he knew and go to fight in hell to save his loved ones from ruin. But that Jake Taylor was gone, turned into a cold-blooded killer, half machine and soul-scarred from 15 years of war. His family and friends wouldn't even recognize him; he would be a stranger, one they would fear.

He was half machine now, the perfect warrior, but no longer quite as human as he once had been. He imagined seeing his family again, wondered how they would react to how changed he was, both inside and out. What would his mother think, looking into his eyes? Would she be repulsed at the metallic constructions implanted where his natural gray ones had been? Could he endure his mother staring at him, trying without success to hide her revulsion at what she saw?

Taylor knew he was a monster; his enemies had made him into that. It was more than the implants, more than the robotic eyes and ears. He knew he had become something dark inside too, an inhuman force, intent on destroying his adversaries no matter what the cost. He was no fool, nor did he allow himself any fantasies about what lay ahead.

Jake Taylor would do anything at all to destroy UNGov. He would kill without mercy, and he would see his loyal followers, victims all, just like him, wiped out to a man. But he would not be diverted from his purpose. He was obsessed, driven, determined at all costs to rid mankind of what he saw as an unholy evil.

Deep in thought, he lost track of time and didn't notice the shaft of hazy morning light pushing through the partially open tent flap. The sounds of the camp stirring to life were commonplace and routine, and he ignored it all by habit. But he swung around when he heard Colonel Black poke his head through the tent, his hardened battle reflexes reacting on their own in response to the new presence.

"It's just me, Jake." There was a combination of amusement and tension in Black's voice. Taylor had been so tightly wound since the last battles on Erastus, Black half expected to get his head blown off one morning. He pushed through the flaps and into the tent.

"Hey, Blackie." Taylor's tension faded, and he sank back into the chair. "It's almost time to address the enem...local forces." Taylor had to keep reminding himself that these planetary armies were conscripts just like him. Just like the rest of his men. UNGov usually had some pretext to offer a recruit the chance to "volunteer," but that was just a veneer to hide the fact that they were drafting soldiers and sending them away, never to return. It was typical government style, he thought, and they made it seem like they were doing the recruit a favor by allowing him to enlist. But it was bullshit, just one more damned lie perpetrated by a totalitarian regime intent on controlling every aspect of human society.

"What about some breakfast, first? You've got to eat, Jake." Black was Taylor's oldest companion, and the two were closer than brothers. Or had been. Taylor had become larger than life since the last battles on Erastus, his mind and spirit dedicated to destroying UNGov and ending the pointless and wasteful war against the Tegeri. Black's loyalty was without question; he would follow Jake anywhere, to the ends of the universe if need be. But he could feel his friend slipping away, along with the rest of the man Taylor had been.

"Oh...yeah, I guess." Taylor looked up at Black. "Can you just send an orderly in with one of those nutrition bars?" A short pause. "And some water." There was still an odd tone in Taylor's voice when he spoke of water. No one who had fought on Erastus for 14 years would ever get completely used to being able to drink his fill.

"Sure, Jake. I'll take care of it right away." There was a touch of sadness in his voice, though Taylor didn't notice. His attention had already turned back to the workstation. Black knew Taylor was only doing what he had to do, and he supported him completely. But he missed his friend too, the brother Taylor had been to him through the years of hell on Erastus. He knew he'd never have made it through without that companionship, and he mourned the loss. He realized there wasn't much left of Jake Taylor, the man. He'd been consumed by the leader, the crusader.

"Blackie?"

Black turned to face Taylor. "Yeah, Jake?"

"Can you get that comlink set up for an hour from now?" He glanced at the small chronometer on the workstation. "Say, 0700?" Juno's day was almost a copy of Earth's, just fifteen minutes shorter.

"Of course, Jake. It's done." Black turned again and slipped through the door of the tent, leaving Taylor to his work, his endless work.

Chapter 4

From the Tegeri Chronicles:

Know all who read this Tome, the tale of those who came before us, wise and powerful, and of the great evil that came for them. For our history is long, and our Chronicles tell of the Ancients, those we once called gods, benevolent and fatherly, who mastered the secrets of the universe millennia ago.

They tell also of the Darkness, the Destroyers, who came and swept away the Ancients, vanquishing all in their path, ignoring only our ancestors, primitive and beneath their notice.

The Ancients built the Portals, and for uncounted millennia they danced among the heavens, the great black gulfs between the stars no barriers to their wisdom and knowledge. They shepherded our race, leading us slowly toward civilization, forward to the day we might join them, and explore the universe at their sides.

Alas, such was not to be. The Ancients were gone to their doom before our race matured, and the heavens grew silent. But they left us the Portals...and all they had taught us.

Somewhere, it is said, the Ancients also left us all of their knowledge, hidden, a key to the secrets of the universe. We have searched for it for centuries, and we must never cease in our efforts. For it is also said that one day the Darkness will return...and we must be ready.

The Great Cavern of the Tegeri was massive, a single chamber lying deep beneath the Sacred Mountain. It had been the birthplace of Tegeri civilization, the gathering spot of the first of the young race to come together and build a society. It was the holiest of locations on Homeworld, and the Great Council still held its meetings there, as it had, uninterrupted, for long millennia.

"T'arza appears to have chosen well, for the human Taylor has proven to be a highly effective leader." The First of the Council stood at the head of the great table, his robe reflecting the rainbow of colors emanating from the luminescent crystals on the ceiling 100 meters above. The First was old, ancient even by the standards of the long-lived Tegeri. He spread his hands in the symbol for appreciation and recognition of achievement.

T'arza stood at his place around the table, as befitted the leader of a great house. He bowed his head in response to the First's words and gestures. "My thanks to you, Honored First. I am pleased that Taylor has achieved success to date." He paused, a troubled look on his face.

"Please, T'arza, share your thoughts in full with the Council." The First spread his hands as he spoke. A gesture of security, an invitation to speak at will without fear of condemnation. "You may share freely."

"I am concerned, Honorable First." He glanced around the table, locking eyes briefly with the members of the other ruling houses in turn. "We have placed an immeasurable burden on one individual and assigned to him a seemingly hopeless task."

Tegeri society was loosely constructed, as befitted a race that valued personal freedom above all things. The old families constituted the Council, as they had since the dawn of civilization, but they met rarely, and usually only in times of crisis. Indeed, before the war with the humans began, there had been over a hundred revolutions of the sun without a gathering. The Tegeri had few laws and little tolerance for burdensome government. Freedom was sacred to the Tegeri, and it was restricted only when absolutely necessary to maintain a functioning society. As a race, they lacked the drive to impose their will on others, and they shared a common work ethic. The leadership of a house was considered a burden one was obligated to bear, not an opportunity to accrue personal power.

The First bowed his head slowly, an acknowledgement that he recognized the merit of T'arza's concerns. "Indeed, we have placed a great burden on Taylor. We did not, as you know, do so without considerable thought. Yet for all this body's long deliberations, we were unable to divine an alternate plan."

T'arza bowed his own head, a recognition of the truth in the First's words, but his expression was still unsettled. "It is truth, Honorable First. Yet I wonder if perhaps we should assist him more directly. There are New Ones on many of the worlds along Taylor's path." The New Ones were the manufactured entities the humans called Machines. They'd been created by the Tegeri, first to replace their slowly dying race, but then to face the human armies invading the Portal worlds. "Perhaps they should aid Taylor's forces instead of withdrawing and allowing the human armies to fight each other." T'arza's voice was slow, halting. He knew his words were unwise, spoken without the requisite forethought. But he felt responsible for Taylor, and he couldn't think of another way to aid the human.

"Indeed, T'arza, we have discussed this at great length in prior sessions." The First's voice was filled with compassion. "You are deeply honorable, and it is no surprise you feel the Kzarn'ta, the blood debt, to the human, Taylor. Yet it is not by lack of willingness that you do not aid him further, but simply because there is naught that you can do."

T'arza had enticed Taylor to pursue his current quest. For a Tegeri, such an act created a reciprocal responsibility. Kzarn'ta was a Tegeri concept, a combination of guilt and familial duty. It dishonored T'arza to convince Taylor to fight a war and then to withhold aid in that conflict.

"Your feelings are pure and do honor to your house, T'arza," the First continued, "but you bear this responsibility in error. We withhold support not from a lack of will, but because such aid would hinder rather than aid Taylor's efforts." His ancient eyes met T'arza's. "All of the humans on Earth believe we murdered their colonists, that we massacred even the young as they tried to flee. They have been at war with us for 70 revolutions of the sun." Tegeri years were shorter than those on Earth, and the 45 Earth years of conflict had been almost three-quarters of a century on the Tegeri calendar. "Taylor's success will require him to persuade many of his fellow humans to join his cause. Were he seen as our ally, that task would become immeasurably more difficult." He paused, a look of distaste on his face. "We are all aware of the propaganda the human government has employed against us. Most of the population of Earth views us as monsters, murderers who slaughtered helpless colonists." There was revulsion in the First's voice, but wisdom as well.

T'arza crossed his arms, placing his open hands upon his chest, the Tegeri symbol for agreement. "You speak truth, Honorable First." He paused for a moment then added, "Nevertheless, I wish there was more we could do to aid Taylor."

"He has the amulet," the First replied, "and he begins to understand its true power. Do not underestimate the value of that you have already given him."

T'arza crossed his arms again. "Yes, Honorable First. You are wise. Indeed, he has quickly discovered many of the amulet's capabilities." Taylor had used the device to project the true images of the massacres on the early human colonies. It had been UN forces and not the Machines who destroyed the settlements, an act that profoundly confused the Tegeri at first. The very idea of killing innocents to assist in a power struggle was an alien concept to them. No Tegeri would ever formulate such a plan and, if one did, he would be driven by shame to take his own life in atonement. The two races were genetically similar, but human psychology was vastly different than Tegeri.

"Taylor has discovered the communications capability of the device, and he has used it to great effect." The First nodded slowly. "Indeed, he has achieved considerable success to this point, and the knowledge we provided him of the Portal network will be invaluable as well."

"You speak truth, Honorable First." T'arza bowed his head.

"Yet you are still troubled, T'arza. Are you not?"

T'arza hesitated, looking back at the First but saying nothing. "I bid you to speak your mind at full." The First fixed T'arza in his gaze. "For your word carries great weight on this Council."

"Yes, Honorable First. I concur with the logic of what you have said, yet I find myself conflicted." T'arza paused, the discomfort obvious on his face. "Taylor is indeed a highly capable human but, even if he fights his way back to Earth, how can he possibly defeat the combined resources of an entire world?"

"He cannot." The First spoke slowly, deliberately. "We do not trust in his victory solely by force of arms." He gazed at T'arza with ancient, watery eyes. "Indeed, we place our trust not only in Taylor, but in all the humans. For it is in their race as a whole that our only hope lies. Taylor's crusade can succeed only if the people of Earth rise up and support him – and overthrow their sadistic and repressive government." The First paused, and T'arza could see the uncertainty in his eyes.

"Taylor must succeed, and we must have faith that he will. For most of a century we have fought the humans. We have long realized their dysfunctional leadership was to blame for the war and not some inherent evil in their souls. I cannot understand the methods by which the humans select their leaders or the lack of wisdom they appear to employ in the process. I have often wondered if we do not share the blame for this tendency, for we visited them centuries ago and, while we sought only to aid them in developing their civilization, we allowed them to view us as gods. We did no more than the Ancients did with us, yet perhaps the humans were more susceptible to blind obedience and unquestioning worship. I fear we may have contributed to infantilizing their understanding of leadership."

The First turned to look around the table, gazing for an instant at each of the assembled Elders. Finally his eyes returned to T'arza, and he spoke softly, a deep sadness in his voice. "We have fought this pointless and wasteful conflict for decades, meeting the human armies with weaponry similar to their own. We have held back from deploying our greater technology and allowed the New Ones to suffer thousands dead in battles against an enemy we could have long ago destroyed."

The First's voice changed, his grief for those lost in the war obvious in his tone. "Such is the path we have chosen. Eradicating the humans, destroying their race would be a moral crime unequalled in our history...and it would doom us to destruction as well, for we need our brother race to face what is coming." The First spoke slowly and with great emotion, even foreboding.

"For the Darkness is returning. The Seers have felt its approach, and there is no doubt. We have little hope to defeat this evil, that which destroyed the Ancients, alone. We must have the humans as allies. For if we do not stand together to face what is coming, our races will surely die...and naught but the unburied dead shall remain on our silent, windswept worlds.

Chapter 5

Classified Secretariat Directive:
To: Chief Surgeon, Supersoldier Program
From: Anton Samovich, Secretary of Internal Security

You are hereby authorized and instructed to implement the proposed frontal lobe interdiction procedures set forth on the attached schedules on all Black Corps trainees prior to deployment. As we have suffered considerable control problems with the previous group of modified soldiers on Erastus, it has been deemed necessary to supplement standard conditioning with these surgical procedures. We consider it of crucial importance to eliminate the capacity of the enhanced soldiers to exercise free will and to ensure their unquestioned obedience to orders. The potential long term effects to the candidates have been reviewed and determined to be insufficient cause to cancel the procedures, particularly as current plans call for the survivors of the strike force to be euthanized upon completion of the mission. The Secretariat has voted unanimously to approve this resolution.

Samovich stood atop the raised platform, watching the recruits moving swiftly across the training field. No, he thought, not recruits, certainly not anymore, if that label had ever been accurate. The Black Corps began mostly with veterans, and now they were surgically modified and fully trained to fight with their implants and exos. The soldiers marching before him were the ultimate warriors, ready in every way to face Taylor's forces.

The Supersoldier reboot had gone well, better even than he'd expected. He'd been observing all morning, watching the Black Corps troopers put through their paces for his benefit. The modified warriors could run 40kph, at least for short bursts, and their artificial eyes could see three times as far as a normal human's. They had better stamina than an unmodified soldier, and twice the strength. Each of them was superior to a normal man in every aspect.

There was more to the soldiers of the Black Corps, Samovich knew, than their enhanced physical capabilities. Their neural implants would allow them to remember everything they saw with complete recall, and that knowledge would always be there, pushed into their conscious mind, even when they were scared or tired or overwhelmed. They would never forget any aspect of a battle plan; they would remember every centimeter of terrain they saw, recall every bit of cover wherever they passed.

Samovich had managed to pull over 15,000 veterans from the various planetary armies, replacing them with a flood of new recruits. Overall, the whole thing had worked fairly well. There'd been some minor setbacks, but mostly the lines were holding everywhere. Casualties were off the charts, especially for the newbs being pushed through the system in larger numbers, but Samovich considered that a perfectly acceptable cost. If producing his veteran cadre cost an extra 50,000 casualties among the recruits, so be it.

The other 5,000 candidates for the program were the pick of the conscripts. Samovich would have preferred to have all veterans, but he'd bled the line commands as much as he dared, and he still had a shortfall. The only other option was delaying the deployment of the Supersoldiers, and that was out of the question. Taylor was rampaging from planet to planet, his army an unstoppable force, utterly destroying every UN contingent they met. Wherever Taylor and his people marched, the Tegeri and their Machine soldiers pulled back, allowing them to pass freely. Any place humans were battling each other, the aliens stepped aside and let the two Earth forces fight it out.

Samovich was counting on his new Supersoldiers to wipe out Taylor's army. They were equals, products of the same set of enhancement procedures. But Samovich had twice as many of them. He'd have had three times as many, or even four, if it had been remotely feasible. But producing even 20,000 enhanced warriors in such a short time had almost stripped the planetary forces of veteran cadre and bankrupted UNGov. Twice as many would have to do.

A victory would restore the situation on the frontier, allowing the UN planetary armies to continue their respective conquest and pacification campaigns. But there was more to consider than just the tactical situation. For Samovich, everything hung on the outcome of the battle against Taylor. Victory would provide him almost irresistible momentum toward the Secretary-General's Seat when Esteban finally died. Failure would, even more definitively, result in his complete political destruction, and probably his death at the hands of an ascendant Chang Li. No, there was nothing more important than destroying Taylor.

Samovich had taken on considerable additional responsibility, handling every aspect of the Supersoldier program himself. It was a step out of bounds for him. The off-world military was Anan Keita's portfolio, not his. But the wily Russian wasn't about to trust his fate to Keita's handling of things. He'd micromanaged every aspect of the training program himself, turning his fellow-Secretary and ally into a rubber stamp.

A man in a black combat uniform, a modified soldier with exos fully deployed, came running toward the platform, interrupting Samovich's thoughts. He looked up and said, "Would you like me to parade the troops again, Mr. Secretary?" He looked like a grizzled veteran who could blast the skin off a recruit with just his voice, but when he spoke to Samovich, his tone was downright obsequious.

"No, Colonel. I have seen enough." He stepped up to the rail and looked down at the officer. "When will they be ready to ship out?"

"Anytime you are want, sir. They are fully operational."

Samovich smiled. "Very well, Colonel. You will have your

orders shortly." Very shortly indeed, he thought. Just as soon as we know where Taylor and his rebels are planning to hit next.

*   *   *   *   *

Samovich leaned back in his chair, twisting his neck, trying without success to get comfortable. He felt the fatigue in his entire body, and he struggled with the effort to stay focused while his mind and body screamed for sleep. Supervising the Supersoldier program was a full time job, even more than that. But he also had his own portfolio, internal security. Keeping an entire world pacified and under constant surveillance was not easy, and it was proving more difficult than usual in recent months, requiring a greater amount of his attention than it ever had before.

UNGov had clamped down hard on all information regarding the rebellion on Erastus, but it was almost impossible to keep something completely secret. UNGov had sent 50,000 security troops through the Portal with orders to destroy Taylor and his rebels. Not one returned. The troops who were lost weren't lifetime conscripts, they were professional UNGov security forces. They had friends and families and, despite the best efforts of the propaganda machine, their disappearances had gone largely unexplained. It was easy enough to crack down on a few overzealous family members who became too aggressive in their quest for answers, but that did little to change the fact that there was a lot of simmering anger out there.

The increased conscriptions were also causing discontent. The normal program of disguising the draft by recruiting petty criminals and tax delinquents was entirely incapable of raising the numbers of troops Samovich needed to replace the veterans he was pulling out of the line units. Rookies had ten times the casualty rates of veterans on some worlds, and Samovich found himself replacing the replacements at an alarming rate. It had taken well over 100,000 raw trainees to take the place of his 15,000 veterans, and raising those numbers so quickly had forced UNGov to drop its amnesty pretenses and simply conscript openly – and forcibly - from the lower classes.

He tried to get ahead of any problems, determined to stamp out unrest before it could spread. He'd ramped up the issuance of warrants for reeducation, hoping to instill more fear in the population and discourage any unhealthy interest in what was going on. Reeducation was promoted as a government service, an effort to treat dangerously psychopathic citizens before they could damage the greater good. Samovich knew the truth, of course. The facilities returned a few heavily conditioned inmates back to their former lives to maintain the official image but, for the most part, they were death camps, designed to quietly elimi-nate the most problematic citizens before they had a chance to cause any real trouble.

His efforts had so far prevented any major civil disobedi-ence, but he knew there was a pressure building, and that por-tended future trouble. Brutality could crush imminent rebel-lion, but it was a tool that demanded selective use. In the long run, too much of it upset the delicate balance that had ensured UNGov's power for so long. Samovich's department worked to instill fear, without inflicting too much pain. A man, even a craven one, backed against a wall facing his own imminent death will fight to survive.

The secret to effective sustainable oppression was leaving the citizens just enough that they feared losing it. Push them too hard, and they will feel they have nothing to lose. A pop-ulation that reaches that point becomes very dangerous. The oppression becomes counter-productive, as each brutal crack-down only causes the rebellion to spread. The mob becomes an animal, fearless, violent, deadly.

Earth's population was disarmed, at least as much as UNGov had been able to enforce, but hundreds of millions of people were hard to control, even when they were throwing bottles and your forces had automatic weapons. Samovich knew his enforc-ers could crush scattered riots, even localized rebellions, but he also realized there was a tipping point when the security forces would be too few to deal with the situation. He was determined to make sure that never came to pass.

The war, he knew, was a major part of UNGov's program for suppressing dissent. Whatever discontent rippled through the population, it was quickly overcome by fear of the Tegeri. The thought of murderous alien monsters bursting through the portals and rampaging across the Earth was enough to keep most of the population in line. Without that overall fear, old nationalistic feelings would surface and threaten the world unity UNGov provided.

The people accepted things like rationing and the lack of freedom because they believed UNGov protected them. But the whole thing was a lie, one created by the governments itself. If Taylor and his people got back to Earth they would attempt to spread the truth and strip away UNGov's veneer of propaganda. It was a risk too terrible to contemplate. Taylor and his army had to be destroyed before they could find a way to return to Earth. No matter what the cost.

The com unit buzzed. "What is it?" he snapped. It had been a long day, and he had a headache. He wasn't in the mood to be disturbed by some petty problem or another.

"It's Colonel Larrison at the communications center, Mr. Secretary. I have priority one orders to contact you at once with any news of the Erastus forces."

Samovich felt a surge of adrenalin. "And?"

"We just got word, sir. They are emerging from a previously unknown Portal on Juno."

"Thank you, Colonel." A smile crept on Samovich's lips as he cut the line and punched in another connect code. Juno was just two transits from Earth. The Black Corps could be there in a matter of days. "Colonel Patel, it is time. You are to assemble the Black Corps at dawn and prepare for immediate transit. Taylor's army has just emerged on Juno."

Chapter 6

From the Journal of Jake Taylor:

When I was a kid, I used to get a strange feeling whenever a blizzard was coming. My mother used to tease me about it, and my brother and sister used to tell me I was crazy. But I knew it was real. Whatever the weather report said, my instinct was always right. I could never explain it, or even describe the feeling very well. But it was always there in my gut, right before the storm.

I almost forgot what snow was in my years on Erastus, the idea of a blizzard slipping away like some distant memory that no longer seems real. I may have grown up in the chilly hills of New Hampshire, but I truly came of age in the sunbaked hell of Gehenna, and my childhood memories of winter storms and snowball fights slowly faded away to shadows.

I hadn't thought of that feeling in years, not until the other night. I had it again. I almost didn't recognize it after all these years, but then I realized what it was. I talked to the weather team, but they told me there was no chance of a storm. None at all.

But I am still troubled. My feeling was never wrong before, and I don't expect this to be the first time. There is some kind of storm coming, a big one. I can feel it. I don't know what it is, but it will be here soon.

"Attention all personnel serving in the formation currently known as UN Force Juno. This is General Jake Taylor, commander of the Army of Liberation." They'd changed the name, part of an overall attempt to recruit more personnel from the planetary armies. Every man who came over to their side wasn't just a soldier added to the cause – it was one fewer they had to kill, one less weight on their consciences. Taylor hated anything that seemed like propaganda, but he couldn't argue that recruitments were up sharply since the first encounter on Alantris. I will use the tools of my enemy, he thought, to destroy him.

Taylor stood on the smooth ground in front of the main headquarters tent. He clutched the amulet T'arza had given him in his left hand as he spoke. The alien device had turned out to be much more than just a short-ranged projection system. Indeed, its reach was at least planetwide, and its power was enormous. It was the mechanism Taylor used to communicate with the planetary armies, and the signal it generated burned right through any jamming attempts.

Taylor finished his speech, the same one he'd used on the other worlds. He'd refined it a bit here and there as he'd become a better propagandist, but the essence remained the same. He was telling them all the truth, sharing with them the bitter realizations that had come to him when he was a captive in T'arza's underground complex on Erastus. It all made sense once you understood, but it was a lot to accept so abruptly. He was stripping the soldiers of Juno of the one thing that made sense in their lives, tearing away the solace they drew from the belief that their sacrifices were protecting Earth from a terrifying enemy. It was a harsh reality he was delivering, but one he knew every soldier on the Portal worlds needed to know.

He was hopeful as he finished speaking and signed off. The drone reports suggested the army on Juno was large, over 25,000. Perhaps 5,000 of them, or even 10,000 would come over. Taylor felt a rare flush of optimism.

"You're getting good at that, Jake." Black smiled and nodded to his friend. "I almost believed you this time." He winked at Taylor and let a short chuckle escape his lips.

Taylor nodded. "Let's hope. Every one of them that comes over is one less we have to fight." One less we have to put in a grave, he thought, but didn't say.

"Yep." Black glanced back toward the spot where Taylor had made his speech. "We should know soon enough. I'll launch a flight of drones in an hour. We may be able to get some idea of movements from their bases."

Taylor nodded. He knew it was more than just convincing a few troopers he was telling the truth – he had to reach a critical mass of sorts. It took enormous courage for a soldier to walk out of a base alone, abandoning his post because he realized the cause for which he fought was a bad one. If only a few scattered troopers tried to leave, they might be detained by the other men, prevented from simply walking away from their positions. Many of those who believed Taylor's words would still refuse to leave their comrades behind, and they would be hesitant to argue out loud for their fellow-troopers to join them in deserting.

However, if he convinced enough of the soldiers in a given post, the momentum swung the other way. Men would go along, follow their fellow-troopers, even if they were unsure it was the right thing to do. Taylor was telling them the truth, so he was sure he could convince any doubters who came along with their comrades. All he could do was hope he'd reached enough of them to make a difference, to save some lives.

"Alright, Blackie, you're in charge." Taylor started walking back to his tent. "Come get me when the drone reports are in." In the meantime, he had work to do. He knew the Juno forces weren't all going to come over…and he had to finish the plan to kill the ones who didn't.

*   *   *   *   *

Lucius Vanderberg stood bolt upright as he addressed the assembly, his scarred face twisted into a vicious scowl. His uniform was jet black, from head to toe, the two small platinum fists on his collar identifying him to all as a UN Inquisitor.

Few of the soldiers on Juno had ever seen one of UNGov's

top enforcers in person. Most of them had been pressed into offworld service for unpaid taxes or other petty offenses, hardly the kind of thing that got the attention of the likes of Vanderberg. Inquisitors dealt with crimes like sedition and treason, transgressions UNGov took very seriously indeed. Empowered as judge, jury, and executioner, an Inquisitor was a grim figure, one who inspired fear wherever he went. Merciless, pitiless, and relentless, they were the iron fist of UNGov's control over mankind.

Vanderberg had arrived a few weeks before Taylor and his people came through the Portal. Anton Samovich had deployed his elite security forces to the various planetary armies, seeking to curb the growing desertions. With Taylor using Portals unknown to the UN forces, there was no way to predict where his people would emerge. So Samovich pulled enough Inquisitors from their normal stations to cover every world currently occupied by UN armies. Vanderberg and his team had drawn Juno.

The black clad figure stared at the lines of troops standing at rigid attention before him. There was an angry restlessness in the formation, but fear kept any open defiance in check. He turned, looking back at the blood-spattered wall…and the several dozen bodies piled up a few meters away, next to a freshly dug pit.

"I repeat, no disloyalty will be tolerated in this army. You are UN soldiers, engaged in a virtuous battle against the alien enemy, and you are expected to behave as such." His voice was cold, emotionless. "All traitors will be dealt with in precisely this manner." He moved his arm, motioning toward the mass of bodies, as his deputies shoved another ten soldiers toward the wall. The prisoners' eyes were downcast as they shuffled forward, the shackles on their legs restricting them to tiny steps. They were wearing the brown uniforms of UN Force Juno, but all insignia of rank or unit affiliation had been torn off. They had cuts and bruises all over their arms and faces, the marks of brutal interrogation and harsh captivity.

They had abandoned their posts, attempted to flee to the

enemy after Taylor's address. A few of their comrades had made
it, but most of the escapees were apprehended by Vanderberg's
patrols. Many of them were slaughtered in the field, gunned
down where they stood, but the Inquisitor's orders had been
clear. He wanted live prisoners. He wanted to show the rest of
the army how he intended to handle disloyalty.

The deputies pushed the prisoners against the wall, hooking
their arms into the shackles protruding from the bloodstained
concrete. A squad of ten of Vanderberg's men stood silently,
watching as the last of the prisoners was chained in place. The
squad commander looked back at the Inquisitor, waiting for the
order to proceed.

"Pay close attention, all of you…or you will end up chained
to this wall." He turned to face the squad. "You may proceed,
Lieutenant." His voice was utterly without pity.

"Detachment, attention!" The lieutenant's voice was sharp
and crisp, like the crack of a whip.

Vanderberg panned his eyes out over the assembled soldiers.
They were restless and angry. The men against the wall were
their comrades, whether they had attempted to flee or not. But
Vanderberg had kill squads positioned behind the formation,
and the soldiers were drawn up without their weapons. Any
resistance would be futile. It could only serve to line up more
men against that wall.

"Detachment, ready!" The lieutenant's eyes were fixed
straight forward, staring at the wall, and the ten men chained
there, about to die.

A couple of the condemned men were sobbing softly, but
most of them were silent. They stood almost motionless, in a
state of shock, confused looks on their faces. They'd been badly
beaten in captivity, and many of them were barely aware of what
was happening.

"Aim!" The lieutenant glanced briefly back toward Vanderberg, acknowledging the Inquisitor's brief nod with one of his
own.

"No! Please, no!" One of the men against the wall broke
down and begged for mercy. He lunged forward, but the chains

held fast and he fell back, losing his footing. "Please…"

"Fire!" The lieutenant's command drowned out the prisoner's pleas, and the squad opened fire at full auto, the hypervelocity rounds ripped into the writhing bodies, almost tearing them to shreds. It was over in a few seconds, the ten prisoners dead, their riddled corpses hanging grotesquely by their shackled wrists.

Vanderberg glared at the lines of troops as a detachment unshackled the bodies and hauled them away. His gaze was a taunt, a dare for them to try something, but they just stood in place. Some were silent, others gently sobbing, but none broke their ranks. Their will to resist was broken.

"Next group." Vanderberg's voice was grim but matter-of-fact. He was ordering the death of ten more men with no more emotion than he might show reading a stack of reports. He was fairly certain he'd made his point, but he was going to be damned sure before he was done. There were another 200 prisoners to go.

*   *   *   *   *

"How many?" Taylor's voice was shrill, stunned. He was usually unflappable, but he couldn't believe what Black was telling him. He stood motionless in the center of the camp, his mind racing to grasp the data his number two had given him.

"About 300, Jake." Black was looking down at his feet as he spoke, his own surprise and disappointment obvious in his tone. He forced himself to look up and make eye contact with Taylor. "That's it. There's no other activity, no sign of any other troops moving in our direction."

Taylor felt as if he'd been punched in the gut. What had he done? How had he screwed up? They'd gotten thousands of converts on the last two worlds, small percentages of the total forces involved, but considerable numbers nevertheless. Now almost nothing. Something was wrong.

"We're still studying the drone data, Jake, but it looks like they've pulled back into their primary base areas and abandoned their peripheral positions. With the Machines gone, they've buttoned up in the forts near the Portal, and there's almost no external activity." Black stood next to Taylor as he spoke. He knew his friend was blaming himself, wondering why so few had responded to his appeal this last time.

"Jake...it's nothing you did. We don't know what's going on. Maybe they've got a strong commander here, and they wouldn't abandon him. Or a martinet who clamped down hard and prevented most of them from getting away. UNGov might have gotten the word out to the planetary armies, warned them about us." He paused. "We just don't know yet. Maybe we'll have a better idea after we review the rest of the drone footage."

Taylor nodded but didn't say anything. I'm going to have to kill them all, he thought grimly. It had been no different on the last world, not really. About 3,500 troops had surrendered on Tannenberg, but that wasn't even 20% of the overall forces present. Still, Taylor had drawn solace from 3,500 lives saved, even as he'd massacred the 15,000 who'd remained in the ranks against him. But 300? That was so few there was no comfort to be gained, no way to even lie to himself. He was going to have to destroy the entire army on Juno, all of them.

"Maybe we'll get a surge later." Black's voice cut through Taylor's dark thoughts. "It's still early, Jake." He managed to sound almost convincing, but Taylor knew his friend didn't really believe it. Almost all the troops who'd come over on the other worlds had done so almost immediately. Time only gave the commanders on the scene more time to regain control over their soldiers.

"No." Taylor's voice was like ice. "No, Blackie. They had their chance." He was staring off across the empty plain. "They had their chance...and we have a job to do." Taylor could feel the change inside him. The conflict was falling away, at least for the moment. Jake Taylor, the man, didn't matter. His petty guilt and grief were of no account. He was the leader of the Crusade, and the cause was more important than any man...than any 10,000 or 100,000. The future of all Earth's people hung in the balance. Victory was all that mattered, whatever the cost.

Black just stood in the middle of the camp, looking back at Taylor but saying nothing. He knew the pressure his friend was under, and he'd seen the conflict inside Taylor, eating him alive. The mood swings, the long periods of introspection. Black knew there were two Jake Taylors fighting for control. The man, the loyal friend and comrade who had served so many years at his side. And the leader, the crusader…the dark psyche forged in the instant Taylor learned the terrible truth about UNGov and the war, a creature of pure duty and vengeance. He wasn't sure which of them would win the battle for his friend's soul. The crusader probably had a better chance of winning the war, but Black knew that would be the end of the man who had been his friend. Taylor would be consumed. There would be nothing left of the human being.

"Let's get the army moving, Blackie." Taylor's voice was cold, precise, completely without doubt or hesitation. The crusader was firmly in control now. "I want Hank Daniel's people on the move in half an hour." He was still staring off across the plain. "It's time to destroy UN Force Juno."

*   *   *   *   *

"Report, General." Vanderberg's voice was gruff. He stood under the harsh white light, reading a dispatch on a small tablet as he barked out the command.

"The enemy force is advancing on our primary base locations." General Samuelson stood in center of the command bunker, staring at a large display as he made his report. There was fatigue in his voice, and depression. Samuelson wasn't a conscript; he was a UN appointee like all the planetary commanders. But he had led UN Force Juno for more than ten years, and his loyalty to his men was strong. Watching this UN thug execute over 400 of them had sickened him – and his failure to do anything to prevent it was weighing on his conscience.

Samuelson took a deep breath as he stared at the main tactical display. "I am going to send ten battalions to set up a defensive line in the White Sand Valley…"

"Negative," the Inquisitor interrupted. "You will prepare to defend the inner perimeter…" – Vanderberg paused as he glanced up at the main display and its map of Juno's close-in firebases – "…along a line from Base Echo-3 to Base Tango-4."

Samuelson stared at Vanderberg silently for a few seconds. The Inquisitor's presence made him nervous and interfered with his concentration. Finally, he cleared his throat and said, "Do you think it is wise to allow them so close to our innermost positions?" The line Vanderberg had specified was very close in, less than 100 kilometers from the Portal. Setting the first defensive line there yielded an enormous amount of highly defensible terrain to the enemy.

Vanderberg sighed, clearly annoyed at the need to explain himself further. "Yes, General, I do believe it is wise, or I wouldn't have ordered you to do it." Vanderberg stressed the word 'ordered,' emphasizing the fact that UNGov had placed him in command of Samuelson and all his people. "Please allow for the possibility that there are other factors at play, details to which you are not yet privy."

The Inquisitor's arrogance was almost intolerable. Samuelson could feel the surge of anger, his hand twitching. He fought the urge to let it drop to his holster, to pull out his pistol and splatter the brains of the man who had murdered his soldiers all over the control room. Nothing would have pleased him more than putting a bullet between Vanderberg's smug eyes. But that would be a moment's satisfaction, followed inevitably by his own death. And UNGov would just send someone else to replace Vanderberg, probably an even harder-nosed SOB.

"Very well, Inquisitor." Samuelson felt futility push the rush of anger away, leaving only a deeper fatigue. "Then that is where we will stop them."

Vanderberg glanced up again. "Stop them?" There was a trace of amusement in his voice, a mocking tone he made little effort to hide. "You think your men will stop them?" His eyes locked on Samuelson's. "No, General. Your men will delay them. Briefly. Then they will smash through your lines and advance on the Portal." Vanderberg looked back down at the tablet, his eyes panning over the dispatch it displayed. "Which is exactly what I want them to do."

Chapter 7

UN Directorate of Internal Security
Field Report Summary – Secretary's Eyes Only

This is a Priority Two Communique. I have compiled a report
on the increasing levels of civil disobedience and dissent noted
in our last monthly assessment. I have identified two individual
problem areas responsible for 94% of the net increase in sedi-
tious and unlawful activity.

There has been a significant increase in unrest among families of the security forces lost on Erastus. I recommend that the
Information Directorate be instructed to create and disseminate
a more comprehensive and convincing explanation for the loss
of these personnel. Concurrent with this activity, I propose a
200% increase in deportations to the reeducation facilities to
facilitate acceptance.

The other major cause of unrest is the increased conscription. The problems have been sporadic in most areas, but
open rioting has occurred in both the Philadelphia and Warsaw
Metrozones. I suggest the immediate dispatch of Public Watch
teams to clear the streets and restore order. – Rashad, Omar
(Deputy Director, Internal Security)

"The Black Corps is ready to transit. They require only the
authorization of the Secretariat to proceed." Samovich stood
before his colleagues, his eyes focused on Raul Esteban. The
Secretary-General looked noticeably different than he had the

last time the supreme body sat in session. He was pale, and his skin hung loosely over his bones. His once thick hair was gone, and he wore a small cap that covered his almost-bald head.

He's lost at least fifteen kilos, Samovich thought, trying not to react, as his gaze panned over the most powerful man in the world. He felt a sudden sense of urgency. Esteban had been undergoing treatment in an undisclosed location, and none of the other members of the Secretariat had seen him for several months. Samovich realized with alarm that Esteban was declining significantly faster than he'd expected. He didn't have as much time as he'd hoped. Soon it would be the moment to make his bid for power. He wanted Jake Taylor's scalp in his belt before that day came.

"Reports indicate that Taylor's forces have invaded Juno." Esteban spoke, slowly, softly, his once commanding voice reduced to a scratchy, forced whisper. "That would seem to be an ideal location to intercept him. The local army is quite large, and it is only three Portal transits from Earth." He coughed, a deep throaty attempt to clear the congestion from his chest. "What logistical preparations have you made?"

Samovich nodded slightly, still trying to hide his shock at Esteban's condition. "We are prepared to launch the operation within hours of this body issuing its final approval. I have, on my own authority, already dispatched the Black Corps to central Africa to prepare for transit." The Portal to Arleon was located deep in the Congo Basin.

"You have overstepped your sole authority, Secretary Samovich." It was Chang Li. The wily Chinese politician rarely challenged his rival openly in session, usually opting to have one of his allies do it. But Li, too, was unnerved by the decline in Esteban's health. If the Secretary-General was close to death, Li knew he had to stall the operation against Taylor's army, at least until Esteban was dead or had stepped down. If Samovich pulled off a quick victory, Li knew he'd have big problems – and with 20,000 enhanced soldiers, supported by the 25,000 men of UN Force Juno, even Li expected him to win. Taylor and his people were as good as dead. And Li would be too, if he didn't figure a way to delay the operation.

Samovich was about to respond, but Esteban beat him to it. "I disagree, Secretary Li." He paused, catching his breath before he continued. "I believe Secretary Samovich showed admirable initiative in positioning the enhanced troops at the Portal in anticipation of an operation this body is almost certain to approve. I do not see that he exceeded his mandate in any way." He paused, coughing a few times before continuing.

"Indeed, Secretary Samovich's suggestion to deploy Inquisitor teams to the planetary armies appears to have produced immediate benefits." He glanced down at the tablet on the table in front of him. "Not only did the Inquisitor on Juno notify us immediately when Taylor's army transited to the planet, but he also appears to have reduced desertions by a factor of ten." He paused again and glanced briefly at Samovich. "Whatever his responsibility for the unfortunate lapses that initially allowed this rebellion to occur, I completely approve of Secretary Samovich's subsequent handling of the matter."

Li stood stone still, finally just nodding and saying, "Yes." It took everything he had to hide the frustration…and the fear. If Samovich pulled this off, Li knew he was in big trouble. "Of course you are correct, Secretary-General."

"Very well." Esteban looked around the table. "May I assume there are no further objections then?"

The room was silent. A few of Li's allies glanced over at him, but he shook his head. This wasn't the time, not with the Secretary-General taking such a clear stance. Li knew he had to prevent Samovich from winning a fast victory, but he'd have to do it covertly. He knew he didn't have the support to act officially through the Secretariat, and making a futile effort would only damage him further.

"It is decided then." Esteban turned toward Samovich. "Secretary Samovich is authorized to immediately commence transport and subsequent combat operations against the rebel Taylor and all forces under his command." Esteban paused, struggling to take a deep, raspy breath before continuing. "It is time to end this rebellion before it is allowed to spread further."

He glanced around the table one more time. "Secretary Samo-vich, you are to instruct the Black Corps that all rebel forces and their supporting elements are to be exterminated." There was a grim finality to his strained tone. "This rebellion is to be utterly and completely destroyed…with no trace of its existence remaining."

"Yes, Secretary-General." Samovich was suppressing a smile. The meeting had gone better than he'd dared to hope. "I will see it done."

"Very well." Esteban was clearly exhausted. His breathing was ragged and he was pale as a ghost. "Then we shall adjourn for now, though we will remain in extended session until this crisis is resolved." He rose slowly, painfully to his feet. "We will reconvene in three days, at which time I trust Secretary Samovich will be prepared to update us on the transit of the Black Corps and its supporting elements." He nodded once and walked slowly toward the door. He had a motorized chair for getting around in private, but he refused to use it in front of his associates on the Secretariat. He didn't believe in showing weak-ness. At least none he could manage to hide.

In truth, Raul Esteban was in no condition to chair the Sec-retariat, and he knew it. He belonged in a hospital. But he was determined to see this crisis through, to help ensure that the new order he had helped to develop survived long after he was gone. He told himself he would retire as soon as Taylor's army was destroyed, but he knew in his heart that wasn't true. They would take directly him from the Secretary-General's Seat to his grave. Men like Raul Esteban did not give up power willingly. Not ever.

*   *   *   *   *

Esteban stared right at Samovich, and for an instant a bit of the old strength was back in his voice. "Thank you for com-ing, Anton." The Secretary-General was dressed casually, sit-ting on one end of an enormous leather sofa. Esteban's villa was just outside Geneva, overlooking the lake. It was a massive structure, over a hundred rooms, built from pristine white marble imported from northern Italy. It was fit to take its place among the great royal palaces of European history yet, despite its appearance, it was thoroughly modern, both in terms of luxurious living and security.

"Of course, Secretary-General." Samovich bowed his head slightly. "I am, as always, at your disposal."

Esteban nodded. "It is easier for me to meet here than at my offices at UN Central." His voice was thin, only a shadow of the commanding tone Samovich remembered from hundreds of Secretariat meetings. Still, he sounded stronger than he had at the last conference. "Please, have a seat."

Samovich sat on the sofa, about a meter down from where Esteban was perched. "How can I be of service, Secretary-General?"

"Raul will do here." He paused. "A man as close to his end as I am cannot become too obsessed with formality." He glanced at Samovich. "Please, Anton, no feigned surprise. You know I am dying. The entire Secretariat knows I am dying, though you all feign ignorance with varying degrees of skill."

"Yes, Sec…Raul." Samovich spoke softly, a skillful facsimile of sadness in his tone. "I know. Yet, perhaps there is reason to hope that day may be postponed for some time."

A laugh escaped Esteban's lips, and it threw him into a coughing fit. When he recovered he looked over at Samovich. "A consummate politician to the end, Anton. I would have expected nothing less." He paused. "Though perhaps we can dispense with such nonsense. Especially since I suspect your intelligence sources have briefed you on my condition with rather more completeness than my own doctors have with me."

Samovich nodded again. "Yes, Raul. I am fully aware of your condition." There was a passing hint of emotion in his tone. Not sadness, but perhaps sympathy. The members of the Secretariat were like a pack of hungry wolves, constantly maneuvering and competing, each seeking to gain power at the expense of the others. Samovich was no different. He saw Esteban as someone who had been in his way for far too long, one whose approaching death he viewed, more than anything, as an opportunity. But he couldn't help but respect the success the Secretary-General had achieved. Samovich knew he could do worse than to emulate Raul Esteban in the ongoing struggle for political power.

"Ah, an honest answer. Perhaps it is the lateness of the hour in my life, but I find it refreshing. Honesty has not been a terribly useful tool during most of my career." Esteban smiled for a few seconds. Then his expression hardened. "I want to see this unfortunate business settled before I die, Anton." Esteban didn't feel anything akin to patriotism for UNGov. His outlook was far too practical and cynical for such thoughts to have much sway. But he felt a certain pride, a fatherly protectiveness for what he had helped to create. And he wasn't about to see some upstart soldier endanger it.

He looked at Samovich, his stare hard and intense. "The only priority is destroying Taylor and his army. Do you understand me, Anton? Any losses to the Black Corps or UN Force Juno, are acceptable. Any losses."

Samovich took a deep breath. "Yes, Raul. I understand."

Esteban held his cold stare. "This ends on Juno. No matter what it takes. If you need to transfer more forces, divert new recruits, requisition weapons and equipment, it will be done. Whatever you need, come to me. I will approve it myself." The strength in his voice was beginning to wane, and Samovich could see his energy fading. "We do not have time for the dithering of the Secretariat and their constant scheming. Whatever the cost, Jake Taylor must die on Juno, and all his soldiers with him." His eyes were becoming watery, but he maintained his hard stare. "See to it, Anton. I am counting on you."

Samovich nodded. "You can rely on me, Secretary-General. I will do whatever is necessary to crush the rebellion."

*   *   *   *   *

"Ah, come in, Anan." Samovich had summoned Keita, but he was surprised how quickly his fellow Secretary had come.

Theoretically, the two were of equal rank, the members of the Secretariat junior only to the single man who occupied the Secretary-General's chair. But both men knew their respective positions. Samovich was one of the two members of the Secretariat likeliest to succeed Esteban to the top position. Keita was a disgraced member of the top body, one with almost no political influence remaining. He'd retained his Seat only by Samovich's continued patronage.

"Have a seat." Samovich motioned toward one of the plush guest chairs in front of his desk. "We need to discuss the deployment to Juno...and the subsequent battle to be fought there." Samovich stared at Keita with a relentless intensity. "I trust you understand how vital it is to achieve a total victory on Juno...to UNGov, of course, but more specifically, to the two of us individually." Translation: if we lose they're going to find your body in a ditch somewhere, and probably mine too.

"Indeed, Secretary Samovich..." – Keita figured a little extra formality and respect couldn't hurt, especially since he was sure he owed his life to Samovich already – "...I am prepared to do whatever it takes to ensure that this destructive and dangerous conflict ends on Juno."

Samovich leaned back in his chair and smiled. "I am pleased to hear that, Anan. I expected no less from you." He paused for a few seconds. "I wanted to discuss the command structure for the expedition." He glanced down at a large tablet on his desk as he spoke. "The Black Corps units all have their own integrated commanders, of course, and General Samuelson is in command of the forces already on Juno." Another pause. "But I am thinking there should be an overall theater commander. Someone with the full trust and authority of the highest levels of UNGov."

Keita looked down for a few seconds, thinking. "What about General Ralfieri? He just returned from the successful conclusion of the war on Gemal." Keita nodded as he spoke. "Yes, I think he would be perfect. Highly competent, yet he only commanded on Gemal for three years, so I doubt he's gone native yet." Planetary commanders were carefully chosen from the higher ranks of the UN security forces. They were loyal to UNGov, or at least that was the theory. But there had been a few incidents of theater commanders resisting orders that were detrimental to the men under their command. The phenomenon had been common enough to acquire an informal name - going native.

Samovich thought for a few seconds. "Yes, I think Ralfieri would make an excellent choice for the overall theater commander." He looked over at Keita, amused at the confused expression on his colleague's face. "However, I'd like to have someone there in a position of supreme command, someone I can truly count on, no matter what is necessary to achieve victory. Someone with as much to lose as I have." A short pause. "You, Anan. I want you to go to Juno and assume the top command."

Keita sat silently. Samovich's words had hit him like a thunderbolt. He opened his mouth to answer then closed it wordlessly.

"This is your portfolio, Anan." Samovich was enjoying Keita's surprise and fear. He'd saved his associate out of political expediency – if nothing else, Keita was a vote he could count on when Esteban finally had the courtesy to die. But Samovich also blamed him for the whole mess, at least in part. Keita had overseen the Supersoldier program. Perhaps if he'd watched more carefully, kept a closer eye on the forces on Erastus, none of it would have happened. This time, Samovich would make certain that Keita supervised every detail. He had the best possible motivation. His very life depended on the success of the Black Corps in destroying Taylor's renegades.

"Yes, but my duties cover all of the Portal worlds, not just one." Keita was trying to think of something, anything else to say.

"There is nothing of greater importance than destroying Taylor. The battles on the other worlds will grind on without your close attention." Samovich's smile widened. "Indeed, you had a similar thought regarding the initial attempt to destroy Taylor on Erastus, did you not? You sent your man, what was his name? Kazan? Yes, Gregor Kazan. You dispatched him to supervise that operation."

The two men looked silently at each other. They were both aware Keita had sent his senior subordinate to oversee the battle...and they both knew Gregor Kazan never returned from Erastus.

Finally Samovich smiled. "This time we will not err in sending a man of insufficient stature and ability." He rose slowly, a signal for Keita to do the same. "You'd best go home and do some packing. Your plane is leaving for the Portal in..." – Samovich glanced at the chronometer on his desk – "...a little over 7 hours." He extended his hand. "Good luck, Anan."

Keita took a step toward the desk and grasped Samovich's hand. He looked like he might vomit any second, but he managed to maintain his composure, barely. He let his hand slip from Samovich's and, with a terse nod, he turned and walked shakily toward the door.

Chapter 8

From the Journal of Jake Taylor

Overconfidence...has there ever been so dangerous and damaging a force? How can confidence, the belief in yourself and your followers, be so vital, so utterly essential to success, yet too much of it is devastating? It is one of the hardest lessons a commander must learn...where that invisible line lies. Napoleon, Lee, Caesar...history is full of great generals who reached too far, sure in the knowledge that their skills and their soldiers could win any fight. It was sin I vowed to avoid, yet I too had to learn this lesson through bitter defeat.

I strive every day to understand this, to remind myself that my abilities are limited as are those of my soldiers. Yet, I do not delude myself that I am greater and wiser than these giants of history. Surely they, too, thought as I do...swore to themselves not to repeat the mistakes of those who had come before. Will I escape the doom that claimed them? Or will my crusade be just another broken cause in the dustbin of history?

"I want a quick, intense bombardment, no more than ten rounds. Then your boys go in." Taylor paused, staring out over the scrubby brown fields. "Hit them fast and hard, Bear. Don't stop for anything. You've got to get across the plain and up that hill as fast as you can. I don't want them to have time to even figure out what's going on." Taylor was micromanaging, as usual. He was a little worried about the enemy position. They were entrenched up on the heights, and his people would be coming in across a wide swath of open ground. It was just the kind of position he had turned into a killing zone more than once. But this time it was his people trying to get across, his soldiers advancing against the enemy's massed fire.

"No problem, Boss." Bear Samuels always seemed calm, even when combat was imminent. His slow Alabama drawl made it sound like he and Jake were discussing a day at the fishing hole instead of a brutal and dangerous fight about to begin. "I'll get 'em across the open ground before we take too many losses."

Samuels was a giant of a man, towering 20 centimeters over Taylor's own considerable height. For all his relentless calm and friendliness, he was an awesome warrior, almost unstoppable in battle. With his mods and exos amplifying his own natural strength, Samuels had the power of a Titan. He'd been wounded half a dozen times, but he'd never left the field until the fight was done. Taylor had even seen him lift a small armored vehicle and tip it over, a story no one who wasn't there ever believed.

"I know you will, Bear." Samuels was one of Taylor's oldest friends, a member of the trusted inner circle that had fought at his side for more than a decade on Erastus. Taylor knew he was lucky to have such close friends and comrades, but it was a curse as well as a blessing. It was hard enough to send his soldiers into the maelstrom of combat, never knowing how many would return. But ordering a comrade who was closer than any brother into the fight…it was the hardest thing he had to do. He'd gotten used to combat and personal deprivation over the years, and he'd learned to manage his own fear. But sending his friends into battle never got easier. It ripped at his guts every time.

Taylor stared out across the rugged ground to the enemy fortifications beyond. He knew his people would take the position. They always did. The Army of Juno was a fine combat outfit, but they didn't stand a chance against his own iron veterans. No soldiers, however seasoned, could face the warriors forged in the furnaces of Gehenna, the most hellish place men had ever tried to survive. Taylor's warriors were more than veterans – they had been surgically altered and enhanced, made into the deadliest killers humankind had ever produced. No normal army could face them.

He wasn't worried about winning the fight and taking those trenches. He was thinking about the losses his men would take. His Supersoldiers were irreplaceable, and if they beat the enemy and inflicted ten times the casualties they suffered, he'd consider it a defeat. UNGov could conscript a hundred men to fill the shoes of every soldier his men killed. He couldn't win a brutal, attritional war, and he knew it.

He'd planned elaborate outflanking maneuvers on the other Portal worlds where his men had fought, but the soldiers of Juno had pulled back toward their main base, into a mountainous region. There were huge rocky spurs spreading out to either side around the Portal like two outstretched arms. There was no way to hit them but frontally on the narrow open section, and he knew his men would pay in blood this time for their expected victory.

"Don'cha worry so much, Jake. We'll be OK." Samuels could feel Taylor's stress and his guilt at sending over 1,200 of his men into a bloody frontal assault. "It'll be rough on that plain for sure, but we'll be past it and into those entrenchments before they know what hit 'em." Samuels put his huge hand on Taylor's shoulder. It wasn't a very military gesture, but Jake appreciated it nevertheless.

"OK, Bear." Taylor's head was bent back, looking up at his enormous friend and subordinate. "You know what to do." Taylor turned to walk back toward headquarters. He took a few steps and stopped to look back. "And stay low, you big ox. Don't get that giant head blown off, OK?"

*   *   *   *   *

"You've got to do better than that, Major." Taylor was trying to restrain the exasperation in his voice. John MacArthur had been a pain in his ass for years on Erastus, and the two had engaged in countless verbal battles. But the wing commander had surprised him before their last combat on that hellish world, turning down an offer of free passage back to Earth for his squadrons and swearing to fight at Taylor's side against the invading UN army. MacArthur tended to be a little pompous, but he was a top notch pilot and air commander. And he'd turned out to be much less of an ass than Jake had thought. He'd seen the truth in what Taylor told him about the Tegeri and UNGov, and he'd made his decision. He joined the crusade without a second thought. To a man, his people followed.

Poom...poom...poom. Samuels' bombardment had begun. Taylor's head snapped around, looking back toward the front line. Poom...poom...poom. The shelling would only last a few minutes, maybe five. Then Samuels' boys would advance. Half an hour later Jake would know how many men that fortified ridge had cost him.

"General, I've only got two engineers, not enough techs... do you realize what a complicated piece of machinery a Dragonfire is? The parts situation is downright critical, and we don't have any kind of workshop. It's a miracle every time we get these things back in the air at all." MacArthur was tense, edgy. He and his tech teams had been working around the clock to get the army's air support element combat ready, and the fatigue was showing. The Dragonfire gunship was an awesome weapon, but it was fiendishly complex too. "We have to disassemble them almost completely to get through the Portals. It takes time to put them back together again."

Taylor sighed. He knew the pilot was right. His own tension was coloring his expectations. He wished the Ancients, whoever they were, had made the Portals a little bigger. Of course that would cut both ways, and UNGov would be pushing tanks and gunships through as well.

"Look, Colonel..." – Taylor's voice softened – "...I know your people are working like dogs, but I need you to push things even harder." He paused and sighed again, harder this time. "I'm worried about this one, John." Another pause. Taylor's mind kept drifting away from the gunships, back to Samuels and his people. The shelling had stopped. That meant they were beginning the attack, heading off across that deadly plain.

"I'm sorry, John. I know your people are working their asses off." Taylor took a deep breath and exhaled hard. "I don't know what it is, but something's wrong. Juno's the biggest army we've faced, and they're not behaving like the others. They're all concentrated in front of the Portal." He exhaled softly. "I can't figure out what they're up to. And I need that air support."

Taylor could hear MacArthur breathing on the other end of the com. Finally, the pilot sighed and said, "I can't promise anything, Jake, but I'll try to get a squadron mission capable in two days…and another one in three more."

Taylor felt a quick rush of satisfaction. That was a week earlier than the previous projection. Granted, MacArthur wasn't promising him the whole wing, but anything would help. Bear's people were going to have to deal with total enemy air superiority, but he didn't intend to let that go on a second longer than necessary. "Thanks, John. I knew I could count on you. Taylor out." He cut the connection.

Two days, Taylor thought…that was going to help a lot. Of course, he'd only have one squadron, and it would have to hold out against all the air power of UN Force Juno until MacArthur managed to get more of his birds ready for battle.

*   *   *   *   *

"Keep moving, all of you." Sergeant Singh waved his arm as he ran, urging his platoon forward. There wasn't a scrap of cover to screen their advance, and he didn't want anybody lagging. The faster they got up that hill, the fewer of his people would die. The troops didn't really need the reminder. They were all enhanced soldiers, seasoned in the inferno of Gehenna. But even veterans looked to their leaders for support, and Singh wasn't going to let them down.

He swung to the side, avoiding a small gully. He was running at 30 kph, and his troopers were keeping pace. The heavy mortar barrage had kept the enemy pinned down in their trenches, and their fire so far had been light and mostly ineffectual. But now the shelling had stopped. His people were less than 500 meters from the enemy, and General Taylor had made it clear he would tolerate no friendly fire casualties.

The enemy was still feeling the effects of the mortars, but now the intensity of their own fire began to increase. It was slow, a barely noticeable difference at first, but Singh's people started to take losses. He had 3 down. He was pretty sure 2 were just wounded, but Sanchez had taken two shots to the head. Singh didn't have any confirmation, but he was pretty sure the trooper was dead.

"Advance to the right." He barked his orders into the com, forcing himself to remain calm despite the increasingly heavy fire whizzing by him. "Forward right oblique at 45 degrees." His platoon's orders were to swing around and hit the very end of the enemy's left.

General Taylor was fond of flanking maneuvers, but this time the enemy line was anchored on a virtually impassable position, a thousand meter wall of sheer rock running all the way back to a mountain range behind the Portal. With no way to maneuver around the position, Taylor had placed 4 platoons of veterans on the extreme right. Their orders were simple: crush anything in front of them and separate the enemy line from the secure rock wall, opening their flank in the process. Then Samuels would unleash two fresh companies, and send them through the gap to take the enemy line from the rear.

Singh was a Ten Year Man, and most of his people had over five years' experience fighting on Erastus. They'd drawn the lead position among the 4 platoons in the assault. That was an honor, certainly. It showed the faith Taylor and Samuels had in them. It also meant they'd take the most punishment from the enemy fire, so they had every incentive to close the distance and assault the trenchline as quickly as possible.

He heard a loud crash behind him…the enemy was getting some of their own mortars into action. So far, taken by surprise by the speed of Singh's men, they'd overshot. But they were adjusting, and the explosions were getting closer.

"Prepare to open fire." Singh had ordered his men to hold their fire. The enemy trench was dug deeply into the top of the hillside. Shooting from the middle of the field would have been mostly ineffectual, and it would have slowed his advance.

The ground was becoming steeper as he got closer to the trench. The enemy fire was getting thicker, and he could see that another 5 or 6 of his men were down. "Fire!" he screamed as he whipped his assault rifle from his back and opened up on full auto, raking the top of the trench as he cleared the crest of the hill.

The incoming fire slowed as the enemy ducked back into their trenches, recoiling from the attackers' shooting. "To the trenches, men!" Singh flicked the lever and ejected his spent cartridge, grabbing another from his belt and slamming it in place. "Nobody gets away!"

He heard a muffled explosion in the distance behind. Enemy gunships were hitting the supporting units coming up behind the assault elements. Singh winced for the troops caught on that plain under air bombardment. His attack had been staged as quickly as possible specifically to minimize the risk from the enemy's air power. Surprise and speed were the only reasons his own platoon didn't get strafed in that open ground. But they were out of the reach of the enemy's air, at least for now. They were too close to the trench for the enemy to launch any airstrikes at them. But they had other things to worry about. "To the edge of the trench," he screamed into the com. "Full auto, boys. Give it to them hard!"

He ran up to the top lip of the trench, firing down into the panicking enemy soldiers. All along the line his men were doing the same, turning the fortification into a death trap. His platoon had taken heavy losses on the way in – at least a third of his men were down. Those still on their feet now exacted their revenge for fallen friends and comrades, mercilessly gunning down the confused and routing soldiers desperately trying to escape.

Most of the enemy troops died in the blood-soaked mud of the trenches, but a few managed to climb out and run for it. Singh coolly snapped in another clip as he raised his assault rifle and aimed at the fleeing troops. "Keep firing, men. And pursue." He blazed away, gunning down the men who had slaughtered his soldiers. "Nobody gets away!" he repeated.

*   *   *   *   *

"Second Battalion has taken the enemy trenchline, and they are pursuing the survivors." Captain Cho was rushing toward Bear as he spoke. "We are in complete possession of the heights." The aide was excited, elated at the victory.

Bear looked out toward the ridgeline his troops had just seized. There were heavy clouds of smoke everywhere, and the air was thick and acrid. He was pleased his men had taken the position, but his satisfaction was tempered. Bear Samuels didn't like killing. He did it when duty called, but it always left him troubled to see the death and suffering of war. He'd managed to adapt to killing the Machines, entities he had usefully, if mistakenly, viewed as inhuman monsters. But slaughtering humans, especially conscripts like himself - like all the men who'd fought on Erastus - was hard for him.

"Cease pursuit. Order them back to the trench line." His follow-up units had been hit hard by the enemy's gunships. He wasn't going to make it worse by exposing his victorious troops to unnecessary casualties. Cho hesitated, staring back with a confused look on his face. "Now," Bear roared. "All units are to occupy the trenches immediately."

"Yes, sir." Cho quickly repeated the command on the unit-wide com, ordering all pursuing units to break off and occupy the trenches they'd just seized.

Bear could see his aide was still confused. "You saw what the enemy air strikes did to us in the plain, Lin. Do you want the men coming out of the trenches to get the same thing after they fought their way up that hill?"

Cho nodded slowly as he began to understand Samuels' thinking. Their orders were to completely destroy the enemy, but Bear was one of General Taylor's oldest friends, and he wasn't afraid to take minor liberties with the commander's orders. The enemy air power was too strong for Bear to allow his men to run off in a disorganized pursuit across open ground.

"I understand, sir," Cho finally said. But he still couldn't imagine not obeying Taylor's commands to the letter, regardless of the cost.

Bear, of course, knew Taylor would have done the same thing. He wondered sometimes about the younger officers, the cult of personality they had built around the army's commander. Did they really think Jake would want his soldiers exposed to pointless losses just to take out the last few panicked men from a shattered formation? Would they just mindlessly follow the literal interpretation of his orders, regardless of the situation?

"Our losses?" Bear's tone was somber. He knew the figure would be high.

"Still coming in, sir." Cho was glancing down at a small tablet checking the latest data. "Looks like the lead elements lost at least a third of their strength. No data yet on proportions of killed and wounded." Cho paused, reading silently to himself.

"The supporting elements appear to have suffered lower casualties." Another pause. "Except the units on the extreme left. They were hit badly by the enemy air. A number of units there are reporting 50% casualties."

Bear closed his eyes for a few seconds. There would be a higher proportion of KIAs there too. The Supersoldier mods not only amped up a trooper's own internal injury response systems, they also flooded the bloodstream with billions of medical nanobots that assisted in rapid healing. The whole system was highly effective in saving a soldier even from a devastating gunshot wound, but it was far less useful to a man burned to a charred crisp by FAEs.

"I want those figures as soon as they are final." Bear started walking slowly toward the field his men had just crossed.

"Yes, sir." Cho watched Samuels for a few seconds. "Sir, where are you going?"

Samuels kept walking. "To the trenches, Captain." The fatigue and sadness were thick in his voice. "I'm going up to the trenches to be with the men who paid for this little victory with their blood."

*   *   *   *   *

"Goddammit!" Hank Daniels was pissed. More than pissed…he was absolutely livid. "You mean to tell me we can't penetrate that line with one drone?"

He'd burned seven of their precious reconnaissance birds, and every one of them had been shot down before it sent back anything useful. Daniels had originally thought the enemy was foolish to concentrate so tightly around their main base, putting their men into a dense formation that Taylor's army could easily destroy. Now he realized there were some benefits too. But the heavy AA presence still didn't make sense to him. They must have stripped all their units' anti-air capacity to protect their deep interior against surveillance. Why, he wondered… why would they be so determined to keep him from getting a good look at their support areas?

"The AA fire near the Portal is extremely heavy, sir." John Stavros stood next to Daniels, his hand held over his forehead, shielding his eyes from the bright midday sun. He had a passing thought about how much he'd changed and adapted. The sun on Juno was strong, but it was nothing compared to Erastus, especially when both suns were up. A year before he would have looked straight up at Juno's star and thought nothing of it. Now he was squinting and blocking the light with his hand.

"Our drone flights are not large enough to overwhelm their firepower. We'd probably need to hit them with a salvo of 20 or 30 to get one through."

Daniels sighed. His aide was right. He was wasting his ordnance popping them off one or two at a time. And 20 or 30 was out of the question. The Army of Liberation had the best soldiers humanity had ever produced, but its supply situation was precarious. The support crews had managed to get some limited ammunition production underway, but surveillance drones were out of the question. The army was dependent for most of its ordnance on what it could capture from the planetary armies it fought. That had worked well enough so far, but if the UN forces ever got their act together enough to destroy surplus supplies when the battle was lost, the army was going to be in big trouble.

"Alright, Captain…we've got no choice." Daniels' voice was determination itself. "We're going in with the intel we've got. We'll hold up the whole plan if we don't." Daniels was a true convert to Taylor's crusade. He was beyond bitter and angry over what UNGov had stolen from him, all because of a cynical, unjust war, a bloody conflict fought not to protect the people of Earth but to perpetuate the power of a group of self-proclaimed elites. To him, any costs, any losses, were acceptable if it brought UNGov a step closer to ruin.

"Yes, sir." Stavros' response was less convincing. He was a veteran, cool under fire and determined to follow Taylor to the bitter end. But he didn't like the looks of things, not one bit. It wasn't just the lack of intel. The enemy wasn't a match for Taylor's army, but they weren't stupid either. They didn't concentrate all their AA assets for no reason. There was something they were trying to hide, and that could only mean trouble.

Daniels' was looking over his assembled troops. They're ready, he thought…ready for whatever is out there. He knew as well as Stavros that the enemy was covering for something. They clearly had some asset positioned near the Portal, something they thought was worth hiding and protecting. Maybe they think it's a game changer, Daniels thought grimly, but there's nothing they've got – nothing UNGov has – that can stop us. Taylor's army had shattered a UN force of 50,000 on Erastus, a force four times the size of their own. He doubted UN Force Juno had anything that would change that calculus.

"No," Daniels whispered to himself. "There's nothing you've got back there that we can't take." He turned toward Stavros. "Order the men forward."

Chapter 9

UN Directorate of Internal Security
Special Order 721 – Level 3 Clearance

Upon receipt, all Regional Directors are to immediately increase reeducation assignments at a rate of 100%. Facilities have been instructed to increase the schedule of inmate liquidations by a comparable factor to create space for new inductees. Arrests are to be allocated as follows: 65% to previously identified targets under surveillance, 35% to strategically targeted sweeps. All Directors are authorized to utilize the 35% allotment on a discretionary basis to discourage overall dissent in their areas. No suspicion of guilt is required for arrest. – Anton Samovich, Secretary of Internal Security.

"We have an advance guard of the Black Corps on Juno as we speak. The rest of the force has departed Earth and is currently en route. We should be nearly at full strength in less than a week." Samovich sat back in a plush leather chair at the edge of Raul Esteban's bedside. The Secretary-General was propped up on a pile of white silk pillows, several IV lines connecting his left arm to a series of machines along the wall.

"Well done, Anton." It was clearly painful for Esteban to speak. His words came slowly, and he swallowed hard after every few. "Perhaps we will finally rid ourselves of Colonel Taylor and his troublesome followers." The Secretary-General closed his eyes and let his head fall back onto the pillows.

"Would you like to reschedule, sir? Perhaps you need some rest now." Samovich looked over at the effective dictator of the entire world, the shriveled remnant of a once powerful and energetic man. The top of Esteban's shaved head was wrapped in a fresh white bandage. It was obvious he'd had another surgery, one more attempt to hold off the ravaging cancer that was destroying his brain and spreading throughout his dying body.

"No, Anton." Esteban's voice was thick with exhaustion. "I am fine. As fine as I am likely to be, at least. Please continue."

Samovich took a breath. I need to keep his true condition from getting out, he thought, grimly. If Li and his allies knew Esteban was this weak, they might make a move to seize the Secretary-General's seat. Samovich had considered his own coup, but that was risky, and he knew the top position would be his for the taking once his enhanced soldiers destroyed Taylor and his rebels. However, if his enemies struck while he was pre-occupied with the war on Juno, they might just succeed. He was well aware the only thing holding them back was fear of Esteban and his lingering hold on power. If they saw how weak and close to death the Secretary-General was, there would be no stopping them.

"Secretary Keita is on his way to Juno to assume an overall command position." Samovich paused. "I felt we should have someone of the highest echelon on the planet." And I can't go myself, he thought, and leave that snake Li here unsupervised.

"He certainly has the incentive." Esteban's voice was a gravelly whisper. "Success will wipe away all his sins." A short pause. "And defeat will just as surely…" He let his voice tail off. Both men knew what failure meant for Keita…and probably for Samovich too.

They were both silent for a few seconds before Samovich continued his report. "I have also ordered increased crackdowns on the civilian population. We've had some minor problems with the families of the men lost in the final battle on Erastus. Nothing serious yet, but I don't want to take a chance on things getting out of control. I've ordered all immediate relatives of soldiers lost on the Erastus expedition sent to reeducation facilities." He paused, uncertain how Esteban would react. His action had been an aggressive and brutal one. It would send several hundred thousand people, most of them innocent of any offense, to their deaths in the camps.

The Secretary-General nodded slowly. "I concur. It is best to get ahead of this. We do not need problems from the civilian population. Certainly not until the Taylor situation has been resolved."

"I have also ordered targeted arrests among the population. I believe we are still at the level where we can control things with a moderate reminder of what is and is not acceptable behavior. We will be at escalated conscription rates for the foreseeable future, and we've seen some scattered civil disobedience as a result. A little extra fear might work wonders in getting people to accept the needed draft levels."

"You are handling things well, Anton. I approve of all your actions." Esteban took a deep, labored breath. He was clearly near the end of his stamina. "I believe, unless you have another topic, that is enough for today, but please return tomorrow with an update."

"Yes, Secretary-General." Samovich rose slowly from the chair, his eyes focused intently on the shriveled form on the bed. "I will be back tomorrow at the same time." He didn't get any response. Esteban had already fallen into a raspy, unsettled sleep.

*   *   *   *   *

"Ah...Alexi, come in." Samovich nodded, and the black-uniformed sentry at the door stepped aside, allowing a tall thin man to enter.

"Some added security, I see." Alexi Drogov was wearing a dark gray suit, exquisitely tailored and exorbitantly expensive. He walked toward the desk and, at a motion from Samovich, he pulled back one of the guest chairs and sat down gracefully.

"That will be all, Lieutenant." Samovich watched as the guard stepped outside and closed the door behind him. He turned toward the new arrival. "Yes, Alexi, I've become more concerned about Chang Li. He knows what is at stake on Juno as well as I do. I've tripled security on everything to do with the Black Corps and the combat operations, but I also figured the bastard just might skip all that and try to take me out."

Drogov nodded. The assassination of a Secretary would be a bold move, but he agreed that Samovich couldn't ignore the possibility. "Good thought, A, but what if they just bribe one of your new guards out there?" His tone said the comment was a joke, but Samovich knew there was a serious question there too. Drogov and Samovich had been friends since their days as two homeless teenagers living on the streets of Petersburg. Drogov had been calling his friend A as long as either could remember. He was the only person in the world who dared to be so informal with the feared Secretary of Internal Security.

"These aren't normal guards. I'm paying them a lot." Samovich grabbed a decanter and two glasses from the corner of his desk. "More than a lot. And I've got their families housed in a nice resort complex in the Caribbean. They're having a wonderful time, but if anything happens to me, they all get roasted by a bunch of FAEs." He filled the two glasses halfway and handed one to Drogov. "There's a completely different crew at those controls…and I'm paying them even more."

"You always were a fiendishly paranoid fuck." It was clear Drogov meant the remark as a compliment. "So I assume you called me for more than a chat about your enhanced security." He reached out and took the glass Samovich offered. "So what do you need, old friend?"

Samovich leaned back and took a sip from his glass. "Try the Cognac. It's a very rare bottle." He gazed across the table at Drogov. Samovich had thousands of subordinates and political allies, but only one true friend, one man he really trusted. He knew he owed his position to Drogov, and he was confident his oldest companion would never betray him. Fifty years of friendship was a powerful bond, but it was more than that. Samovich knew his friend had no interest in politics, no patience for the constant debates and arguments. There was only one thing Alexi Drogov liked, one skill where he was an unmatched expert. Killing.

"I need to deal with several problems, my old friend. Problems you can help me with."

Drogov took a gulp from his glass and smiled. "You want me to kill Chang Li."

Samovich smiled. "Yes, perhaps. Eventually. He's becoming too dangerous, and I'm far too distracted with the fighting on Juno to keep an eye on him. But, eliminating him won't be easy. No one can know I'm involved." The Secretariat had few rules binding its privileged members, but the biggest one was crystal clear. No assassinations of anyone else on the Secretariat. Not without an official sanction. "If anyone even thinks I'm behind it, I'll be in a shitstorm."

"So he needs to choke on a chicken bone?" Drogov laughed and took another drink, draining the glass in a large gulp. Samovich had never known anyone who could consume as much alcohol as Alexi Drogov and still remain perfectly lucid. And as dangerous as a viper.

"Something like that." Samovich slid the bottle across the desk toward his friend. "I'm not sure yet though. When the time is right, we'll figure it out." He paused uncomfortably. "There's something else."

Drogov had been about to pour himself another drink, but he stopped abruptly when he heard the change in Samovich's voice. Whatever his friend had in mind, he had a sudden feeling he needed to be stone cold sober when they discussed it.

"Esteban is much sicker than is commonly known." Common was a relative term. The population of Earth and the vast layers of the lesser bureaucracy knew nothing at all about the Secretary-General's illness. The members of the Secretariat – and probably a few other highly placed UNGov functionaries – knew he was sick. Some of them had incomplete details, but Samovich was fairly certain all the other Secretaries, at least, knew Esteban was dying. But he was pretty sure none realized just how much his condition had deteriorated. "I may need to make some kind move if I can't get things wrapped up on Juno quickly."

Drogov set his drink down on the desk. "You mean…" He let his voice trail off. There were some things you didn't say, even in a private office that was swept three times a day for listening devices.

Samovich nodded. "Maybe. Only if necessary."

Drogov's relaxed demeanor was gone. His expression was deadly serious. "It won't be easy to breach that security."

"None of it will be easy." Samovich leaned forward and lowered his voice. "But I need a plan, and it has to be ready to go on a moment's notice." He paused. "Just in case. Can you do it?"

Drogov sat silently, staring back across the desk at his oldest friend. He'd killed a lot of people to help Samovich reach the Secretariat, but this was something else entirely. It wasn't every day someone planned the assassination of the Secretary-General, the leader of UNGov and the effective dictator of all mankind.

He stared into Samovich's eyes wordlessly as the long seconds slipped silently by. Finally he took a single deep breath and answered. "Yes," he said softly. "I can do it."

Part Two
A Place Called Armageddon

Chapter 10

From the Journal of Jake Taylor:

I came to Erastus a boy, overwhelmed by my fate and scared of my own shadow. That hellworld, and the grizzled veterans who took me under their wing, forged me into what I have become...a man, a soldier. It has been many years since I felt as lost as I did when I first stepped through the Portal. I thought that part of me was gone forever, the frightened child replaced by the hardened warrior. But I was wrong.

Now I am a general, the leader of a crusade to right a terrible wrong, to free mankind from tyranny. My soldiers have rampaged across half a dozen worlds, shattering any army that dared to stand in our way. Until now.

We face something new, a reflection of our own might and power. The soldiers standing against us are enhanced like we are. They are faster, stronger, tougher than normal men. Cyborgs like us, they can see farther as we do, hear things normal men cannot. Our advantages are gone, many of them at least, yet we still face an enemy that greatly outnumbers us and a long and dangerous path to tread.

The child is back, scared and uncertain. I don't know what to do. My calm assurance is gone, and now I find myself questioning every judgment, every decision. Can my soldiers defeat this new threat? Or will our struggle for freedom end here, in the blackened and bloodstained fields of Juno, amid the broken wreckage of my army?

"General Taylor, this is Captain Stavros." The voice on the com was stressed, almost frantic. "The enemy hit us hard as we were moving into position." There was a pause on the com, the sounds of Stavros rasping for breath and gunfire loud in the background. "We fought hard, but we couldn't hold. They pushed us back, sir."

Taylor felt like he'd just been punched in the gut. His forces had never been defeated by any of the planetary armies, and the last force he'd expected to suffer a reverse was Hank Daniel's. Daniels was the most aggressive of his commanders, a true believer in the cause. Taylor couldn't imagine Spider Daniels retreating while he had a man left standing.

"Where is Major Daniels, Captain?"

Stavros hesitated. "The major was hit. It's bad, sir." Taylor could hear the emotion in Stavros' voice. Daniels was a very popular commander. "We sent him back to the field hospital."

Taylor took a deep breath. He realized that for all his planning and obsession over details, he'd never really believed the enemy could resist his soldiers. Now he wondered, was this his fault? Had he been too careless, too arrogant? Had he asked too much from his men?

"What's your status, Captain?" Taylor was worried about Daniels, but there was no point in asking more - he knew Stavros didn't know anything. And his friend wasn't his only concern. All the troops fighting were his responsibility, and those men were still out there, on the line and in extreme peril.

"After the major got hit, we pulled back about 2 klicks, sir. We didn't have a choice. The enemy was pushing around both flanks." Stavros' voice was apologetic, ashamed at reporting a defeat to Taylor. He paused, trying to catch his breath. Taylor could tell the captain was in the middle of some fierce action, even as he made his report. The sounds of battle were everywhere around him. "I can't explain it, General. They're fast... like us. Their fire is very accurate, even from extreme range. It's almost like..." He let his words tail off.

"Almost like what, Captain?" Taylor knew what Stavros was going to say, but he wanted to hear it anyway. "Speak your mind."

"Almost like us, sir."

Taylor nodded his head. Of course, he thought, I'm a fool. UNGov had created his Supersoldiers. Why should he be surprised if they made more to face his renegade warriors? But what to do, how to handle this new situation, that was the question. His mind was swimming with the implications of the enemy matching his troops' capabilities - and possibly outnumbering them too. "Captain, I want you to retreat immediately. Pull back to the trenchline and hook up with Major Samuels' men." He didn't know what to do yet, but he was damned sure he didn't want those men out there exposed until he had better intel.

"But, sir…we can hold here. I'm sure of it." His tone conveyed anything but certainty.

"You heard me, Captain." Taylor was yelling into the com. He'd let his overconfidence get the better of him once, and his men had died because of it. He wasn't going to do it again. "Get back to the trenchline now!"

It all made sense. There had been plenty of time for UNGov to produce another group of enhanced warriors. Taylor knew he was guessing wildly, but he was sure nevertheless. His people were facing something far deadlier than they had yet encountered. They were fighting soldiers with all the same capabilities they had. The game had just changed radically. Taylor had to rethink his strategies. But first he had to stabilize his lines. He had no idea how many Supersoldiers the enemy was sending his way, and he wasn't going to risk more of his troops until he had a better idea what was happening. Enough of his men had died already because of his arrogance.

*   *   *   *   *

Singh lay flat on the wet grass, looking out over the broken, scrubby ground in front of the ridge. His platoon was 200 meters from the trenchline, positioned to cover the enemy's line of approach. He'd have preferred to stay in the trench, but the fortifications had been built to defend against attacks from the other direction, and they were too far from the crest of the ridge to provide good firing positions against attackers approaching from the rear.

"Second squad, get your asses down now." Singh was keeping a close eye on his people. The top of the ridge was a strong position, but it was a lot more exposed than the entrenchments. Carelessness would get his men killed, and he wasn't about to let that happen, not if he could do anything about it.

"I want everybody 100% alert and focused. We've got trouble heading this way, and we need to be ready." Singh had seen a company of Daniels' force when they'd staggered back into the trenches. They looked more like a platoon than a company, but it wasn't the losses that hit Singh the hardest – it was the looks on their faces, downcast and vacant. They were stunned, covered in mud and blood. For the first time, Singh saw defeat in his comrades, and it scared him to the bone. Whatever Daniels' men had faced, it was something far more terrible than the planetary conscripts. And it was heading toward his position.

At least we have good ground, he thought, looking out over the rugged plain below his position. The enemy would have better cover coming in than his people had when they charged the trenches from the other side, but they'd still be in the open for much of their approach. And they'd have modified Supersoldiers shooting at them as they charged.

Singh rechecked his weapons. It was a pointless exercise. He'd done it three times already, and he couldn't forget any of them - his NIS recalled the exact time for each instance. Still, it made him feel better. Combat was hell, but sometimes waiting was worse. He knew the enemy was close, the same foe that had driven Major Daniels people back with heavy losses.

"Attention all units." It was Major Samuels' voice. Samuels almost always sounded calm, even in the middle of the fight. But there was urgency in his tone now. "Prepare for imminent enemy air attack."

Fuck, thought Singh. It made sense, he realized. The Army of Liberation had its own air wing, but the massive Dragonfire gunships had to be completely disassembled for transit through a Portal and reassembled on the other side. It was a process that took weeks and, until the work was completed, the army was completely without air cover and totally exposed to the enemy gunships.

Singh wanted to curse the engineers and technicians for taking so long while he and his men faced unopposed enemy air attacks, but he knew that was unfair. A nuclear-powered aircraft bristling with weapons and sophisticated tracking systems, a Dragonfire was an enormously complex mechanism. He'd seen the disassembled craft lined up by the Portal, thousands of boxes and crates for each one. Even the nuclear reactors that powered them had to be painstakingly taken apart, their radioactive materials stored carefully for transit. It was an immense job, and there was nothing anyone could do about it. Except grab some dirt and hold out until General Taylor managed to get them in the air and contest the enemy's control of the skies.

Singh caught a glint in the sky…then another, and another. The enemy had Dragonfires too, and they were heading right for his position. "Stay low, boys. We've got gunships inbound!" Singh had seen what the massive aircraft could do, and he didn't like being on the receiving end, not one bit. "Make like part of the ground." Staying down would help, but it wouldn't do much good if the attacking squadron dropped a FAE on top of his platoon. For all the skill and training and experience, sometimes all a veteran could do was hug the dirt and hope for the best.

*   *   *   *   *

"Hank, I'm so sorry." Taylor walked into the field hospital and dropped to his knees next to his friend's cot. "It's my fault this happened. All my fault."

The hospital was a makeshift affair, a combination of interlocked tents and portable structures. It was a loud, riotous mess now, overwhelmed with the wounded from Daniels' command.

The crazy pace of the hospital slowed for a moment, as nurses and orderlies dropped back, silently watching the general as he leaned over his friend. Taylor's legend was growing in the army, and more and more he was treated as some kind of avatar or spiritual leader rather than just another man – a man struggling to carry the massive burdens heaped on his shoulders. Taylor's interaction with the Tegeri was known throughout the army. His delivery of the message, that they had all been lied to and badly used by UNGov, had created an almost religious fervor around him, one that was fanned by his ability to project the images of the colonial massacres, courtesy of the strange device T'arza had given him.

Daniels turned his head slowly. He was propped up slightly, struggling to face Taylor. He was wan and pale, and his head had been partially shaved. The pillows behind him had once been pristine white, but now they were covered with crusted blood and fluids. There was an IV station next to the cot, but the tubes were hanging down loose, disconnected.

"Hey…Jake." Daniels was weak, his voice a slow, raspy whisper. "Nothing…to…be…sorry…about." He struggled to turn to the side, to get a better look at Taylor. "War…that's…all."

Taylor's eyes were moist, but he struggled to hold back his tears. Daniels was going to make it. The surgeon had already told him. It was the nanotech that had saved his life, not anything the medical staff had done. By the time he got to the hospital, the microscopic bots had repaired the immediately life-threatening damage. It had taken two emergency surgeries to fully stabilize him, but now he just needed rest. He wasn't even taking any more transfusions – the nanobots in his system were producing enough artificial blood cells to replace what he had lost.

"I shouldn't have sent your people out so far, Hank." Taylor took a deep breath, straining to control his emotions. "I should have been more cautious."

Daniels was shaking his head slowly. "No…Jake. Could…n't…have…known."

Taylor reached out and took Daniels' hand in his own. He forced a smile for his friend, but inside his spirit was grim. He knew damned well he should have realized UNGov would do something more than just leave planetary armies in his path. The easy victories had made him overconfident. And 700 of his men had paid for that arrogance with their lives.

"Were they like us, Hank?" Taylor was still working on conjecture, assuming UNGov had sent a new batch of Supersoldiers after his people. "Were they enhanced?"

Daniels nodded slowly. "Like…us. Fast…strong…acc… ur…ate." He closed his eyes for a few seconds, swallowing painfully. "More…of…them. Ma..ny…more."

Taylor closed his eyes. He'd hoped to get his army back to Earth intact, picking up strength from the planetary forces as they advanced. But that strategy had just become obsolete. The army on Juno had ignored his pleas to join the crusade…and now his people faced an enemy with all the abilities they possessed. The combat on Juno was just starting, and Taylor knew his people were in the fight of their lives. It was going to be a battle between giants, and he knew an ocean of blood would be spilled before it was done.

He squeezed Daniels' hand gently. "You rest, Hank." He forced a smile, though he doubted it was very convincing. "I'll take care of things."

Taylor rose slowly and took one last look at his friend before he turned and silently walked out of the tent and into the midday sun. He was deep in thought. For the first time in a long while, he didn't know what to do.

*   *   *   *   *

"Be ready to fire on my command." Singh was prone behind a small lip of ground at the edge of the ridge. His people had been lucky. They'd been strafed a couple times, but none of the FAEs had hit their position. He'd taken a fragment to his arm, but it wasn't too bad. He'd torn a strip of cloth from his jacket and tied it off to stop the bleeding. He didn't need to do anything else. He could already feel the strange tingling feeling of the nanos at work. They would mend the wound, close off any internal bleeding, and target any infection.

He'd lost 3 of his men to the air attack, and another 5 wounded. Two of those were bad – they were back about 300 meters waiting for evac. The other 3 were walking wounded, still able to take their place in the line.

Company D had taken the brunt of the enemy air attack. Singh could still see the columns of smoke rising off on the left, where the FAEs had ravaged the hillside. Singh wasn't in that line of command, so he could only guess at the losses, but he knew they had to be at least 50%, and possibly higher. D Company was most likely shattered as a fighting force, and that meant Major Samuels would have to commit most of the reserves to plug the gap. And that only increased the pressure on his people to hold the line on their own.

The enemy was moving toward them through broken plains, using the topography for whatever cover they could get. Singh flipped on the com. "Smith, Garibaldi, open fire." The range was still extreme for most of his soldiers, but the two snipers should be able to pick off some of the enemy as they approached.

He leaned forward, resting the barrel of his assault rifle on the small berm just in front of him. The enemy was staying low, using whatever cover they could find, but Singh could see immediately that his troopers were heavily outnumbered. They had the better ground, but it wasn't going to matter. If those troops heading toward his battered platoon were really enhanced soldiers like his own, there was no way his people were going to hold. It had been a long time since any of them had tasted defeat, and the prospect was bitter.

He could hear the distinctive cracks of the sniper rifles. Hyper-accurate and long-ranged, the weapons fired a heavy round that delivered an enormous amount of kinetic energy to the target. A hit anywhere vital would kill a man outright, even a soldier whose blood was full of medical nanobots ready to repair damage immediately. It was hard to confirm their hits at this range, but Smith and Garibaldi were two of the best, and every time Singh heard that crack, he was pretty sure there was one less enemy to fight.

Poom…poom…poom. He could hear the mortar rounds firing off to the left. The lieutenant had taken his platoon's mortar team and combined it with the others in one large company battery. Singh could see the explosions, the clouds of smoke and dust rising from the center of the enemy formation. The shells were taking a toll too, he knew, though a Supersoldier in full exos had a lot of protection. Still, anything that weakened the enemy on the way in helped.

"Platoon…" - Singh spoke clearly and firmly into the com - "…open fire!" He picked out a target and pulled the trigger, firing a five-round burst. All along the line, his troopers opened up. The advancing formation slowed slightly, and the enemy troopers began to return fire.

Singh crouched lower, ducking down between shots. His troops had the advantage, shooting from a fixed position, but the enemy fire was proving to be extremely accurate, despite their continued advance. The attackers probably wouldn't inflict too many casualties until they got closer, but they were keeping Singh's men down, and that reduced the rate of their own fire.

Singh exhaled hard and flipped a switch on his rifle. "Platoon, full auto, now." It was a waste of ammo at this range, but Singh knew his people had to take down as many of the enemy as possible. If that formation reached the crest of the hill intact, there was no way his people could hold.

He swung up over the berm and pulled the trigger, emptying a clip on the advancing enemy. Incoming rounds were zipping through the air and slamming into the dirt of the hillside. He could feel the adrenalin, the surging tension in his body as he kneeled there, partially exposed while his rifle spat death on the attacking enemy.

He ducked down again, pulling the release and ejecting the spent clip as he did. "Pour it into them boys!" he screamed into the com. Now was the time, he thought, now was the time to take down the enemy. He reached around his back, grabbing a new clip and slamming it in place. "Don't let up, men," he yelled as he swung back over the berm and fired again.

*   *   *   *   *

"Alright Yellow Squadron, let's take these bastards out!" John MacArthur spoke crisply and confidently into his com. "The guys on the ground have been getting pounded, and it's time to blow these fuckers out of the sky."

MacArthur was the overall commander of the army's entire air wing. He knew he had no place piloting the lead bird on a one squadron strike. But nothing short of Taylor's direct order would have kept him out of the pilot's seat. The troopers on the ground had been blasted to hell while his tech crews frantically rebuilt their disassembled gunships. Now he was going to make sure they got some payback.

The battle raging below wasn't going well. Hank Daniels' broken formation had pulled back, almost two-thirds of its number killed or wounded. Now it was Bear Samuels and his troopers trying to hold the line. They'd fought well and inflicted heavy losses on the attackers, but they were just too outnumbered. They'd pulled back in good order, their losses heavy, but nowhere near as brutal as those Daniels' people had suffered.

MacArthur felt the urge to push the stick forward, to dive down toward the battlefield and strafe the advancing enemy. But that wasn't his job now. Ground support would be useful, but first he had to take out the enemy air assets. Whichever side won air superiority would have an edge in the long and brutal fight MacArthur knew was ahead. There hadn't been any official confirmation they faced cyborg soldiers with the same capabilities they had, but rumors spread like wildfire through an army. If they really faced a force of enhanced soldiers, he knew Taylor's people had their hands full, especially if they were outnumbered. They had to control the skies. They simply had to.

But that was easier said than done. MacArthur had only one squadron ready for action. It was a huge risk committing it before he had more birds set to go, but the situation on the ground didn't give him a choice. The enemy air was pounding the AOL's soldiers all across the line. MacArthur knew he had to take some of them out.

His people had one edge – surprise. They'd gotten the squadron online faster than anyone could have predicted. The enemy probably expected unopposed control of the air for at least another week. Yellow squadron would be a surprise to them, a very unpleasant one.

"Squadron, arm all Avengers. Prepare to engage." MacArthur's birds were fitted out for aerial combat, armed to the teeth with one kiloton Avenger air-to-air missiles. The enemy had been inbound for an airstrike, and their bays were loaded with FAEs, devastating against ground targets, but useless in a dogfight. MacArthur had caught them with their pants down, and he was determined to make the most of it. He'd only get this surprise once.

"Full thrust, all ships." He was staring straight ahead as he pushed the throttle on the lead bird. "No way these bastards get away, Yellow Squadron." His voice was almost a feral growl as he thought of the destruction the enemy air had inflicted on the ground troops. "No fucking way."

The enemy ships had picked up his squadron on their scanners, and they were trying to revector, to arc away from their original target zone and flee back to their bases. But they were too late.

"All birds…open fire." MacArthur pressed the launch buttons, and the Dragonfire shook as a salvo of four missiles was released and blasted off toward the enemy. The Avengers were the most devastating weapons in his anti-aircraft arsenal, and he'd loaded Yellow Squadron with 10% of the army's entire stock. Like the rest of the army, MacArthur's gunships had been conserving ammunition, expending only the bare minimum to get the job one. But the situation had changed in an instant. Conserving ammunition was no longer the top priority. Surviving the battle was.

The ship shook again as MacArthur fired another volley. The air in front of the squadron was filled with the smoke trails of hyper-velocity missiles as they made their way toward the enemy formation.

"You can run, fuckers, but you're not getting away." MacArthur was whispering to himself, his hand clenched tightly on the firing controls as he launched a third volley...and then a fourth. The enemy gunships had savaged Taylor's ground forces over the past two days, killing hundreds. Now MacArthur and his people were here for revenge.

MacArthur could see flashes of blinding light as missiles began exploding in the distance. The scanners kept the tally. Two enemy gunships were destroyed almost immediately, and another two a moment later. The sky all around the fleeing squadrons was aflame as missile after missile struck its target or exploded nearby.

The enemy aircraft hadn't expected any resistance other than ground-to-air weapons, and they were almost defenseless against the attacking gunships. Flight was their only option. They might just outrun MacArthur's pursuing craft, but not the 120 air-to-air missiles they had fired.

MacArthur launched his fifth and last salvo. He watched the missiles zip away from his ship for a few seconds. Then he gripped the throttle and put his finger over the firing button. "All units, arm chainguns. Prepare for close action." He stared ahead, death in his eyes. "We're going in."

*   *   *   *   *

"Keep firing. All of you." Singh was peering out over the trench, firing at the enemy troops as they exposed themselves over the edge of the ridge. He knew they were preparing to advance toward the fortified line yet again. His people had held firm along the ridgeline, but they'd been forced back from the crest when the enemy punched through the lines closer to the center, where the FAE runs had devastated the defenders. Singh's men were compelled to withdraw or risk being flanked.

Now they were back in the trenches they themselves had taken just a few days before. The fortifications were strong, but the field of fire was short, only a few hundred meters from the reverse slope. Still, his people had repulsed two attacks already, though they had suffered heavy losses and burned through most of their ammo to do it. The third assault was coming, and he didn't see how his men could hold out again.

He only had 15 troopers left, and half of them were walking wounded. He'd taken a round to the shoulder himself, though the nanos had already started to repair the damage. He knew his troopers would fight to the last, but there was another problem. Supplies. He was down to 3 clips himself and, even after stripping the dead, most of his men only had enough to maintain a few minutes of fire. He had them all on semi-auto now, firing small, targeted bursts. But even at that rate of fire, they would be down to survival knives and rifle butts before long.

He was just about to tell his men to cease fire until the enemy charge got closer in, when his com crackled to life and Major Samuels' voice filled his helmet. "All forces are to withdraw from the trenchline at once and pull back to rally point A. Repeat, all forces are to evacuate the trenchline immediately and rally at point A." Samuels's voice was raw, hollow. "Withdraw by odds and evens, 300 meter intervals."

Singh exhaled hard. He'd been prepared to die in the trench, fighting with the last of his strength and ammo. But now there was a chance his people would live to take the field another day. He felt relief, and a knot of tension in his gut. They still had to successfully break off and get back to the rally point.

Rally point A, he thought…almost back where we started. Every meter of ground we fought and bled for, lost. He felt a wave of frustration, depression. So many lives lost for nothing. But there wasn't time for that, not now. His only priority was getting his survivors disengaged and back to temporary safety.

"Platoon, prepare to withdraw. Evens, covering fire – commence now." He heard the sounds of massed rifles, not only from his own troopers, but all along the line as half the force covered the retreat of the others. "Odds, withdraw 300 meters…now." He turned and added his fire to that of the 7 other men remaining in his section of line. The taste of defeat was bitter, and Singh vowed to stand and fight as long as he could. He was the last man to leave the trench.

Chapter 11

From the Tegeri Chronicles:

Long we have known of the humans, and it is written that they are the other children of the Ancients, our brother race, destined to share the Portals with us and explore the universe at our sides. But they are different from us as well as similar, and in this lies their peril...and ours. For where Tegeri seek individualism and freedom for personal reflection and the pursuit of intellectual growth, most humans crave, above all things, each other's acceptance. They are quick to subvert their own judgment and morality to those who would lead them, to recklessly surrender their most basic freedoms. We came to know of this strange susceptibility firsthand when we visited their world centuries ago.

Gods they came to call us, though we had gone to them as brothers and counsellors only, to guide them as they built their civilization, to hasten the day when they could join us and explore the Portals. Blind we were for centuries to the effect we had upon them, for such is utterly alien to the Tegeri mind. When at last we saw what we had done, we left them, returned to our world to allow them to grow and mature and build their civilization free of our influence. Yet never did they change, for their history is written in the blood of the victims as they rallied to one evil, unworthy leader after another. We shall never know, perhaps, how much blame we bear for exacerbating this trait... how much responsibility we carry for the centuries of tyranny and oppression the humans have suffered.

"Taylor has been opposed by human forces with the same enhanced capabilities his own soldiers possess." There was concern in T'arza's voice, and uncertainty. "I greatly fear he may be defeated before he reaches Earth."

The Council was assembled again in the Great Cavern, the ancient meeting place that had hosted such gatherings since the dawn of Tegeri civilization. The cavern was lit by hanging pots, filled with burning rocks, the red and yellow flames casting an eerie glow on the stone walls and dazzling crystal formations hanging from the ceiling far above.

The First of the Council bowed his head slowly. "Indeed, T'arza, your concerns have great merit. Yet, I do not know what we can do to assist Taylor. His mission is far more expansive than simply reaching Earth. He must enlighten his people to the truth about their leaders. He may utilize force in this effort, yet he cannot ultimately succeed only by strength of arms. He must persuade millions of his kind, a task that would become impossible if he were seen as our tool. Our overt aid would serve Taylor's enemies more surely than it would assist his forces."

T'arza bowed his head in acknowledgement of the First's wisdom. "All you say is truth, Honored First. Yet, I must then ask, what next if Taylor fails, if his forces are destroyed on Juno and the Earth government is triumphant and entrenched in its power?"

"Then, T'arza, we will have little choice." The voice came from the end of the table, from one of the Tegeri who rarely spoke in conference and whose words were always heeded when he did. C'tar was the Grandmaster of the Seminary, the closest thing the Tegeri had to a religious leader. C'tar was old, nearly as ancient as the First One, and his life had been spent in study and meditation. "If Taylor fails, we will be compelled to destroy the humans."

There was stunned silence in the Cavern. Such a proclamation from the likes of C'tar was unprecedented. The Seminary was an institution dedicated to peaceful study and enlightenment. Genocide was the last thing any of the Council had expected C'tar to suggest.

"C'tar, please enlighten." The First was as surprised as the others, and he bade the Master of the Seminary to elaborate.

"I speak harshly, for we are come to a time in our history where we must change who we are…or be destroyed without a trace." The ancient Tegeri spoke slowly, his voice soft and hollow with age. "I speak not of personal destruction, nor the death of any on this Council. Nay, it is nothing so trivial that besets us. I warn instead of the extinction of our entire race, and of the many others that grow and move slowly toward sentience and civilization in the vastness of space. For the Darkness is returning, and there is naught but our strength to stand against it." The room was silent, all eyes on C'tar.

"Long ago we sought to educate the humans, yet they are different from us, and our efforts met with little success. Quick to follow and pledge their allegiance to those who are unworthy and slow to question what they are told, they proved too susceptible to our influences. They styled us as gods, sought our direction in all things. They worshipped us instead of embracing us as brothers, as teachers. We saw this, yet perhaps too late. We left their world centuries ago, when we became aware of the extent of their malleability, yet we may never know how much blame for their continued susceptibility accrues to us."

C'tar paused, drawing a deep, raspy breath. "For all of this, I suggest it matters not. For our own actions, we must bear the blame that accrues to us. Yet we have another obligation, a greater one, not only to our race, but to those that will follow us in the ages to come. We must turn back the Darkness or all light in the universe will be extinguished. For all time."

T'arza felt his spirit sink. He, like all of the elders on the Council, held C'tar's wisdom above that of all others, even the First. The Grandmaster of the Seminary had spent the long centuries of his life pursuing knowledge for the sake of knowledge, wisdom for the sake of wisdom. He saw truth more clearly than any of the Tegeri…even when such true sight revealed naught but despair.

"The Darkness destroyed the Ancients many ages past, and for all our knowledge and science, we are but children compared to our old mentors. Yet, we must rise to the fight and face the challenge that is coming. We may do so with the humans at our side, as the Ancients intended, if providence so allows, or we may stand alone." C'tar paused, for it was no easier for him to pronounce a call for genocide than for the others to hear it. "But we cannot stand against the Darkness while the humans also fight us. What chance we have to prevail in the coming struggle, small that it may be, would be lost utterly if we allow ourselves to be caught between two enemies."

The emotion was heavy in C'tar's voice, and his gaunt face, gray in the flickering light of the firepots, betrayed his great age. "If we cannot win the humans to our side, if they persist in doing the bidding of their evil and despotic leaders, we must destroy them. To not do so would be to abandon any hope for the hundreds of young species to survive. That is too great a price to pay, even for our brother race."

The cavern was silent for long moments, each of the elders deep in thought, absorbing the words of C'tar. They all knew the Grandmaster was right, that his wisdom was true. But embracing such a reality was a nearly impossible task for the Tegeri.

Finally, the First spoke. "C'tar is out most learned scholar, our wisest counsellor. His words have reached me, and I concur with his findings." The First's voice was grim, the regret thick around his words. "Though I feel a spear stabbing at my soul at the mere thought of such a crime, we would be all the more damned, our guilt that much greater, were we to allow the Darkness to consume the galaxy because we were too weak to do what had to be done."

The First looked out over the assembled Council, his once dazzling eyes clouded with age and watery with emotion. "I put forth to this Council the proposal that we accept C'tar's words, that we resolve to do whatever we must, at whatever cost to our souls, to destroy the Darkness."

His head moved slowly, and he shared a long gaze with each of the elders present in turn. "Yet, I also believe we must do all that is possible to prevent such from coming to pass, that we take every action at our disposal to aid Taylor in his struggle, to provide whatever covert advice and assistance we may." He turned his head, his eyes resting on T'arza. "T'arza, my treasured friend and honored member of the Council, I propose that you go to Juno to advise Taylor and to assist him in achieving his victory. I know not what your counsel may achieve to aid his cause, yet I feel we must try."

Before T'arza could respond, the First held his arms before him and continued, "Are there any others who would speak before this Council?" He paused, but the room remained silent.

The First wore a grim expression. "Then we are resolved. T'arza will go to Juno to aid Taylor…with counsel only." A long silence. "If such aid is unsuccessful, if Taylor and his people fail and are defeated by their enemies…" The First hesitated again, so difficult were the words he'd resolved to utter. "…if Taylor's cause is lost then we have no choice. We will destroy the humans as a race."

The room was silent, every eye on the First as he spoke. After a long pause, he continued, "We find this action utterly repugnant. Our souls shall be scarred for all time if the blood of this brother-species should soil our hands. Yet, the obligation to stand against the Darkness, to hold back this blackest evil, is greater still and more sacred even than our kinship to the humans. Such we owe to those who came before us, the Ancients, wise and proud, who shepherded our race and left us the Portals. Such we owe to those who will come after us, the youngest children of the Ancients, still growing on their own worlds far away."

The First bowed his head. "Long have I lived, for I am the oldest of our people, and I would have gladly passed on to the Great Next before this fateful decision was forced upon us. Yet, such is unworthy of the First of our people, to seek to avoid responsibility and obligation. I do, therefore, what I must…and may the spirit of the Ancients have pity upon my soul."

He raised his head slowly, moving his gaze in turn to each of the elders standing around the great table. "It is therefore resolved that if Taylor's forces are destroyed, we shall unleash our true might on the humans, that the Earth shall be consumed by the fires of the atom and of anti-matter. That the humans shall cease to exist, and naught will remain to testify that they ever lived, save for the charred and radioactive ruins of their world."

The First gripped the polished stone sitting on the table in front of him. He raised it, and three times he slammed it down, the loud crash echoing through the cavern. "Such is resolved by this Council." He looked out over the table. "Are there any who oppose?"

T'arza felt the words trying to escape his throat, but he remained silent. The thought of destroying the humans was more than he could be, but they would all die anyway if the Darkness prevailed. It was the hardest thing he'd ever had to do, but T'arza, the 80th of his name and the master of his House, stood motionless and remained silent.

Chapter 12

From the Journal of Jake Taylor:

I remember the first time I saw a field hospital. It was on Erastus, about a month after I arrived onplanet. There had just been a particularly nasty battle, and the place was packed, every cot full and more wounded waiting outside, lying on the ground in the blazing sun.

The Machines had lured our forces into an attack that turned out to be a trap. We ended up surrounded on three sides, and we lost almost half our strength before we managed to extricate the survivors and pull back to our defensive line.

I can still recall the scene, the doctors working frantically, trying to save the most critically injured men. The first thing I noticed was the brightness of the lights. They were simple lamps, strung overhead along the roof of the portable shelter. They weren't quite as harsh as Erastus' two blazing suns, but they were close. For some reason that stayed with me. Most of the indoor facilities on Erastus were dimly lit, but not that hospital.

I always remembered that first impression and, when I rose in the ranks, I made sure to make time to visit the wounded. I went because the men in those beds deserved the respect and consideration, but there was another reason as well. A commander looks at maps and gives orders, but it is in the hospital, amid the cries and moans of broken men – and in the piles of bodies zipped up in nylon bags outside - that he gets the best reminder of what those commands and plans mean, what they will cost the soldiers asked to go into battle. The sight of broken

and battered men, is a something every general should experience often...so you never forget the cost of your orders.

"The last of Bear's people have pulled back as ordered." Black's hoarse voice revealed his exhaustion. He hadn't slept in at least three days, and it was beginning to show. "The enemy has reoccupied their original trenchline, but they haven't advanced from there. They surprised Hank's people, but Bear was warned and ready for them. They lost heavily retaking that position. Our best guess is around 2,000, maybe 2,500."

Taylor was nodding in agreement, though his expression was grim. "Any updated figures on our losses?"

Black hesitated. He knew Taylor blamed himself for the repulse, and for the heavy casualties. He understood, to a point. Taylor was the commander of the army, and the final decision to send the troops in was always his. But Black also knew that this was war – and men died in war. Expecting every battle to be an easy victory, quick and low-cost, wasn't realistic, not for any general.

"Blackie…" – Taylor looked up and stared at his friend as he repeated his question – "…what's the latest update?"

Black sighed. "OK, Jake. It looks like Hank's people lost about 62% killed and wounded." He glanced down at the small tablet in his hand, though the NIS implanted in his brain gave him total recall of the figures. "That's approximately 850 out of his total strength of 1406. About 400 of those were wounded lightly enough to return to duty within a week." The Super-soldier mods had completely changed the nature of battlefield medicine. Even troopers with serious gunshot wounds could recover rapidly if they survived the first few hours. Men who would have spent months in the hospital could walk out in days or a week.

"How many dead?" Taylor's voice was soft, quiet.

"As of last count, 363. The other 80 or so are critically wounded." He knew that number would have been much higher without the nanotech. "Most of those are expected to recover, but they'll be out of action for two weeks or more."

Taylor nodded. "And Bear's command?"

Black paused for a second. He knew Taylor was aware of the losses, and he wished his friend would stop punishing himself. "Lower than Daniels'. We're still finalizing the numbers, but it looks like about 585 from a total strength of 1334." He shot Taylor a quick glance then added, "They were closer in for evac, so it looks like we have a smaller percentage of KIA there too. Probably around 175."

"Thanks, Blackie." Taylor tried to imagine what the casualties would have been if he'd sent regular troops instead of his enhanced units. He doubted any of them would have returned.

Black opened his mouth, but Taylor knew what was coming, and he spoke first. "I know, Blackie. It's war. But I should have been more cautious. When we couldn't get any drones through…that should have told me we were facing something different." Black looked like he was going to interject something, but Taylor spoke again before he had the chance. "But it doesn't matter now. All that matters is what we do next." He looked off in the direction of the enemy trenches, the battlefield his men had fought over for the last two days. "I want the crews assigned to fortification construction tripled immediately. They're not taking us by surprise again."

"I'll take care of it, Jake." Conversations between Taylor and Black were always informal, regardless of rank. The two had been closer than brothers throughout their years of service on Erastus, though Taylor's near-total focus on the crusade had created a distance between them that hadn't been there before. General Taylor was becoming a larger than life figure, and though he retained the loyalty and affection for his old friends and comrades, there was less of Jake, the man, remaining than there once had been.

Taylor knew he couldn't dig in and hope the enemy attacked him. His army couldn't fight a defensive war, regardless of what they were facing. Time was not his ally. UNGov had enormous resources, a whole world's population and industry to draw upon. The longer the battle lasted, the greater their strength would grow. They could replace ammunition, troops, and equipment, while his army would only grow weaker, his logistics more perilous every day. But he still had half his men out digging trenches. He wasn't about to underestimate his enemy again. He would borrow some strategy from the Romans. Everywhere his army went they would dig in, prepare as if the enemy was about to attack. He didn't know what was going to happen - his army might lose the battle for Juno, wiped out to the last man. But no more of his men would die because of his overconfidence or carelessness. He promised himself that much.

*   *   *   *   *

Keita moved slowly down the narrow gravel path, a tall slim man in a set of dusty camouflage fatigues walking alongside him. There were 3 silver stars on the man's collar and his name was stenciled on the front pocket. General Antonio Ralfieri was the commander-in-chief of all UN forces on Juno.

Keita himself wore an exquisitely tailored uniform, ornate and jet black with silver trim and a single large gold star on each shoulder. If he had to be here taking charge in the field, he was determined to look the part – though to the hardened veterans of the Black Corps, he looked like an absurd fop. There were a variety of amusing nicknames circulating among the rank and file, any one of which would have sent the arrogant politician into an apoplectic rage if it reached his ears.

He'd tried every way he could to get out of the assignment, but in the end he couldn't refuse. He kept his Seat – even his life – only because of Samovich's aid and continued sponsorship. There was no way he could say no to his patron. As a member of the Secretariat, he was essentially the UN's viceroy on Juno, and the one man ranked higher than Ralfieri.

"The first battle appears to have gone well, General. The enemy has been thoroughly repulsed and has fled ignominiously back to their base camp." There was satisfaction in Keita's voice, and disdain for Taylor's forces.

"We did reclaim the fortified positions the enemy seized

from the Juno forces, Mr. Secretary, though I wouldn't characterize their withdrawal in such terms." Ralfieri was a veteran of combat on other Portal worlds, and he'd fought dozens of battles against the Machines. He'd never experienced anything like fighting Taylor's troops, and he was still a little shaken by the tenacity and coolness under fire they had displayed. "I will remind the Secretary that we had 2-3 times the losses of the enemy and that we outnumbered them four to one at the critical position." Ralfieri stopped walking and turned to look at Keita. "I would not expect a quick or easy victory here, and I strongly recommend that you do not promise such to UNGov."

Keita felt a rush of anger. As far as this arrogant general was concerned, he *was* UNGov. He'd been a highly placed government minister even before he'd been named to the Secretariat. He was used to craven, obsequious fools, gathering at his feet, begging for his favor. People didn't speak to him in so blunt a manner. But he was realizing the soldiers, the veterans especially, were different. They obeyed their orders, but there was a gruffer, more direct manner to them. Keita didn't like it, not one bit - but he'd resolved to put up with it. The sooner Ralfieri and his men could wipe out Taylor's traitorous bunch, the faster he would get back to the comforts of Earth. And tomorrow wouldn't be soon enough for him.

"So what do you propose now, General?" Every word out of Keita's mouth dripped with impatience. "When do you attack the enemy base camp?"

Ralfieri suppressed a sigh. He'd been excited at first at his new command, but that was before he realized he'd have a pompous windbag whining in his ear every second. Keita wasn't military, but he was the Secretary of Off-World Military Affairs, the top bureaucrat in charge of all the forces fighting on Portal worlds. Ralfieri was stunned at how little the politician seemed to understand about soldiers and combat, despite years of supposedly supervising the war effort. He wondered if every top official at UNGov was so ignorant of the areas he supervised. "We must be cautious, Secretary. The enemy is extremely capable, as we just learned, even in our small victory."

Putting up with Keita was a pain in the ass, but Ralfieri admitted to himself he'd still have taken the job, even if he'd known he'd have to deal with a Secretariat babysitter. It wasn't wise to turn down an honor bestowed by the Secretariat itself, no matter what the reason. And the Black Corps was the most prestigious force UNGov had ever put into the field. A victory on Juno would likely bring considerable rewards, a plush retirement among them.

He hadn't been given much background on Taylor or the cause of his rebellion, only that the first batch of enhanced soldiers had mutinied and were rampaging across the other Portal planets, slaughtering the UN armies they met along the way. He suspected that wasn't the whole truth, but he was a soldier, and he followed his orders.

"General, we must conclude this battle as quickly as possible." Keita wanted to get the hell off Juno, but he also realized Samovich needed a short war. The longer things dragged on, the more time Chang Li had to plan his move for when Esteban died. And it would be a disaster for Keita as well as Samovich if their mutual rival succeeded.

He'd considered approaching Li, offering to sell out Samovich in return for a promise he'd keep his Seat. But he'd come to the sad conclusion that he simply didn't have enough to offer. Samovich had kept Keita out of the most crucial aspects of his plans, keeping him busy with an endless stream of trivial jobs. No, he thought, I'm Samovich's man, like it or not. I will live or die with his success or failure.

"Secretary, you must understand." Ralfieri's face was red; holding back his frustration was driving his blood pressure through the roof. "We are still waiting for almost half our strength to arrive. It will be another week before the entire corps is assembled here." He stopped and turned to face Keita. "We can't even think about a large engagement until we are at full strength."

"But you have the entire Juno army available as well as your people, General."

"Secretary, our latest drone surveillance indicates that General Taylor is entrenching his forces. An attack against such a fortified position would be pointless. We would lose two to three thousand men and end up back where we are. And while the corps outnumbers Taylor's forces, we won't for long if we launch suicidal attacks and whittle away our strength." Ralfieri had a bad feeling in his stomach. Keita didn't strike him as the kind to listen to advice from those he considered beneath him. And he knew an attack on Taylor's lines with half the corps assembled was a recipe for disaster.

Keita returned Ralfieri's gaze. "Use the Juno forces as a screen, General. Have them assault the enemy trenches while your enhanced warriors move up behind. The regular soldiers will absorb the casualties, and your men can seize the fortifications."

Ralfieri was silent for a moment, trying to hide his shock at Keita's monstrous suggestion. "Secretary…the regular troops will be massacred coming in. They are far slower than the enhanced soldiers, and it will take them twice as long to reach the enemy position. Thousands will be killed…many thousands." He could feel his heart sink as he looked into Keita's eyes. It was obvious the slaughter of thousands of men was nothing to him, nothing at all as long as he got what he wanted.

"This war will not be won without loss, General, and the regular forces are far more expendable than your troops." Keita spoke calmly, almost like he was conducting everyday business in his office.

"But my men will suffer losses on the approach too, even if they are positioned behind." Ralfieri had lost hope, but he was still trying. "And the Juno forces may break and rout before they reach the enemy. It will be a disordered mess, a perfect opportunity for Taylor's forces to slaughter my men wholesale."

"There is a line, General, between caution and timidity." Keita's voice was firm, confident. "You are ordered to organize the operation for tomorrow. Advance and assault the enemy's line. Let us finish this without further delay." Keita stared at the general with a look of pure arrogance. "There will be no further discussion.

Ralfieri's gaze dropped to the ground. "Yes, Secretary. As you command." He wanted to argue, to scream in frustration, but he knew it was pointless. A lot of men were going to die in the next 24 hours, and it wasn't going to accomplish a thing.

The general snapped a quick salute. "If you'll excuse me, Secretary, I have a considerable amount of work to do."

Chapter 13

From the Journal of Jake Taylor:

I've never commanded in any fight where I didn't come away carrying massive feelings of guilt. In the end, it doesn't matter if the men were volunteers, if the battle was essential, if you stood with them in the line...all you see are the dead and broken men, and you know they are that way because they followed your orders. It's impossible to stop the wondering and second-guessing. If you'd tried harder, if you'd studied the field more carefully...would some of those boys still be alive?

But since we left Erastus, there's a different sort of guilt, one about the enemy troops we kill. I know those men are conscripts, just like my own soldiers. They were taken from their homes, stripped from parents and girlfriends and siblings, sent to a distant world, never to see home again.

They may fight us, but only because they've been lied to and conditioned...just like I was. Their situation is virtually the same as mine had been for 14 years...a decade and a half during which I ruthlessly slaughtered the Machines, driven by duty and an overwhelming self-assurance I was fighting an evil foe. I finally discovered the truth, but only after the Tegeri contacted me and showed me proof that all I'd fought for was a lie.

The soldiers on the Portal worlds have no such proof, just my impassioned plea for them to abandon all they've believed and fought for and join my soldiers. I wonder if I would have responded to such a call, if any of my officers and friends would have.

I understand how the men of the Portal world armies react, how most of them choose to ignore my pleas. There is no evil in that choice, no complicity with my enemies. They are told I am crazy, that my people are traitors, renegades. They act rationally with the information they possess, and I would probably do the same in their place.

But that doesn't matter. I give the orders and we cut them down anyway, leaving none alive in our path. They never feel quite like the enemy, these soldiers we massacre, but that doesn't stop us. My cause is a good and noble one; I believe that with all my heart, with a surety I never knew existed until I finally felt it. Why, then, must I do such terrible things to achieve that goal? Can any cause, however true and worthy, justify so much horror invoked in its name?

Is there good and evil in the universe? Or only different kinds of evil?

"Move your asses, all of you." Captain Horace Jahn was walking down the front of the trench, watching his men shoving heavy logs in place along the front of the fortification. "We've got nasties on their way, and you don't want those trenches caving in on you when they take a few hits now, do you?"

Jahn was in command of one of Major Young's two battalions. With Hank Daniels still in the hospital and Bear Samuels' command all shot up, Young's people drew the assignment to man the front line position and to hold the new fortifications if the enemy attacked. And the enemy was on the way.

Jahn had questioned the logic of going to so much trouble to build fortifications, but now that the drones had spotted thousands of the enemy less than 10 klicks away, he was grateful to have them. He wondered how Taylor could have known. What strange gift did the general have, what clairvoyance that allowed him to lead the army to victory after victory?

The army's confidence in its leader was unshakable. Even after the recent battle, despite the heavy casualties, the troops refused to call the engagement a defeat. All estimates suggested

Daniels' and Samuels' battered forces had inflicted at least 2 to 3 times the losses they suffered, against a force many times the size of their own. The morale of the Army of Liberation was as strong as ever, the troops ready to follow any orders Taylor issued, even if that command was to march through the fiery gates of hell.

Jahn stared down into the trench as he walked, watching his men continuing to fortify the position. He was going to keep them working until the enemy was in range. Every beam shoved into place, every rifle pit dug, could save a trooper's life. He wasn't going to waste a second of prep time.

He saw two of the men struggling with a heavy log. They weren't his; they were from one of the new battalions, recruits from the Portal worlds they'd already taken. He jumped into the trench and grabbed onto the massive tree trunk, adding his enhanced strength to that of the two unmodified soldiers and slamming it into place.

"Thank you, sir." The trooper was exhausted, and he gasped for breath as he spoke.

"You're welcome, soldier." Jahn nodded and hopped out of the trench with a single massive leap. "You boys report back to your unit now. We're going to be in action soon." The unmodified soldiers had no place on the front line, not when they were expecting an attack from the enemy's Supersoldiers.

"Captain Jahn…" It was Major Young on the com, and there was urgency in his voice. "Prepare for action. We've got enemy forces less than 8 klicks out."

"Yes, sir." Jahn turned and started back toward his command post. "We're ready, sir." He felt the tension building inside him, the excitement and stress he always felt before battle. There was something else too…anger. He and his people owed it to Samuels' and Daniels' men to make the enemy pay. And they were going to do precisely that, no matter what it took. "Don't worry, sir. None of them will get past us."

*   *   *   *   *

"Frantic's units should be engaged any minute." Black was staring at a map displayed on a small tablet as he spoke. "The latest drone reports show the enemy moving into mortar range." He looked up at Taylor. "Should I order him to open fire?"

Taylor looked off in the direction of the front line. He couldn't see it from HQ – there was a large hill blocking the way – but he had the picture of it in his mind anyway, every centimeter. Taylor had been up there most of the last few days, walking among the men, even helping to build fortifications. After what had happened to Daniels, he'd been determined to position himself dead center in the forward trench line when the enemy attacked, but his officers had unanimously intervened and insisted he return to HQ.

He was the one man the army could not afford to lose, not only its heart and soul, but also the single human being the Tegeri had chosen to contact. If Taylor fell, the crusade would fall apart – they all knew it. Even Taylor realized that was true, though he was intensely uncomfortable thinking of himself that way.

The troops were well aware their only hope for survival lay in total victory. True believers or not, they all realized there was no going back. UNGov had started the war against the Tegeri by killing its own civilians; they imprisoned hundreds of thousands in thinly-veiled death camps; they consigned their soldiers to a lifetime on war torn Portal worlds with no hope of going home. There was no way they were going to allow a group of surrendered traitors to survive. No, it was victory or death for the Army of Liberation. Even the rank and file realized how much they needed Taylor alive.

"Yes. His people are to commence firing." Taylor's face was twisted into a frown. He was troubled by the scouting reports on the approaching enemy. They were moving too slowly, too sluggishly. He had something in the back of his mind, a thought so dark he suppressed it at first. "However, please advise him to conserve ammunition as much as possible." He looked up at Black. "And get Denisov's people in supporting position in case we need to plug any holes."

"Sure, Jake." Black had a confused expression on his face. The trench position was a strong one, and they already had local reserves in place. "What is it? What are you worried about?"

Taylor sighed. "It's just a hunch, Blackie, but I don't like the look of that approach. It's too slow." He glanced up at his friend. "I'm afraid those are unmodified troopers in front, conscripts from UN Force Juno. And I'm worried they're human shields for Supersoldiers advancing directly behind them."

"But the regulars will get slaughtered charging that trench…" Black's voice trailed off as realization set in. "And UNGov doesn't give a shit how many men die as long as we're destroyed." His urban Philly accent came out, as it always did when he was surprised and angry.

"Just a hunch, Blackie." Taylor's voice was grim. He knew it was more than a hunch. He was sure he was right. "So let's make certain we're ready, just in case they get some undamaged Supersoldier units close enough to overrun a section of trench."

"I'm on it, Jake." Black turned around and walked a few steps, pulling out his com as he did.

I have to remember, Taylor thought as he listened to Black relaying the commands, what we're dealing with…and stop underestimating what they are willing to do to defeat us.

*   *   *   *   *

"Sir, with all due respect, I strongly urge against this attack." Colonel Roberts stood at attention, his eyes focused tightly on Ralfieri's. He was holding his helmet under his arm, and the wind was blowing thinning wisps of hair in front of his face. "The position is very strong, and the approach is mostly through open ground. We can still call it off." There was obvious tension in the colonel's voice. He was clearly working himself up to something he was hesitant to say.

"General…attacking them here is doing them a favor." It finally burst out, like a dam breaking. "Time is on our side. We should be engaging in scattered hit and run attacks, making them expend supplies they can't replace." Roberts was beyond checking himself, and he continued to pour out his concerns. "If we attack here, the losses among the unmodified troops will be enormous. Please, sir, I urge you to reconsider."

Ralfieri felt his hands clenching into fists. He wasn't angry at Roberts, but the frustration had become almost overwhelming. "Yes, Colonel, I understand all of that."

He paused, taking a second to suppress his rage toward Keita. "I do not disagree with your assessment of the enemy position, however I have been expressly ordered by higher authority to launch this attack, and my objections have been ignored. So let's not waste time debating the wisdom of an assault neither of us can stop."

He paused, allowing his words to sink in. "I suggest you focus on your tactics instead of wasting time on futile arguments, Colonel."

He saw realization in Roberts' eyes, then acceptance. "You and I both know the only chance for this attack to succeed is to get your Black Corps units into those trenches as soon as the regular forces rout." There was no question in Ralfieri's mind that the Juno forces would break. Any normal troops would. And if they didn't, they'd be wiped out.

"Yes, sir." Roberts nodded, but his tone was still uncertain. He paused for a few seconds then looked at Ralfieri. "General, those regular units in the front are going to be slaughtered."

Ralfieri felt his stomach tighten. He knew just how badly the lead elements would take it. He could see it in his mind, though it hadn't happened yet, men falling in their hundreds as they pushed forward into the maelstrom of enemy fire.

"There is nothing to be done about that, Colonel. You have your orders." He turned to leave, but he stopped and looked back at Roberts. "We can't prevent this attack, so focus on trying to make sure the sacrifice isn't in vain."

He took a deep breath. He couldn't imagine a worse feeling than being forced to order an attack you know will fail, realizing you are sending thousands to a pointless death. He grasped at a small glimmer of hope, his mind trying to convince himself there was a chance the enhanced soldiers in the second line would seize the fortifications. But he just didn't believe it.

"You may attack when ready, Colonel."

*   *   *   *   *

Jahn was firing on full auto, and he'd have sworn every projectile that left his weapon found a target. The enemy was coming straight at his position, charging across open ground into the concentrated fire of his battalion. They were falling in clumps, entire lines disappearing in the withering firestorm. It was the most perfect killing ground he'd ever seen.

He had to admire the courage it took those men to continue to advance, pushing forward, climbing over the bodies of the fallen. They were moving slowly, and their incoming fire was less accurate than Jahn had expected. He pulled out his com with one hand, holding his assault rifle in the other. He continued to fire while he punched the code for HQ.

"This is Captain Jahn reporting."

"Jahn, this is Colonel Black. Report."

"Sir, I don't believe the forces we are facing are enhanced troopers. I think they are regulars." Jahn was confused. The normal troops didn't stand a chance of breaking the trenchline. Why would the enemy launch an attack that couldn't succeed?

"We're aware of that, Captain. Reports are coming in from other positions as well. Be on alert for a force of modified soldiers positioned directly behind the regulars."

Jahn felt his stomach flip. There were at least a thousand of the enemy down already, just in front of his section of the line. "Sir? You mean the troops in the front are a...a shield?"

"They may be, Jahn." Black's voice was crisp, professional. He'd had time to get over the shock of the enemy's tactics. "So stay sharp up there, and don't let them take you by surprise. Black out."

Jahn heard the click as the com line went dead. He was staring out at the enemy, watching his unit's fire rip into the advancing lines. He swung his rifle around, gripping it tightly and slamming another clip in place. He flipped down to semiautomatic and started firing aimed bursts. The enemy was less than 200 meters out, but their advance was slowing. The bodies were piling up all across the field, and the men behind were beginning to waver.

Jahn's people kept up their fire, raking the shaken enemy troops. Dozens more fell, hundreds. Then they started to run. Jahn couldn't see where it began, but in a few seconds the formation started to melt away, like ice on a hot day. Clumps of soldiers were dropping their weapons and running for the rear. Jahn watched the slaughter for a few seconds then he grabbed his com again. "All personnel, cease fire." He stared out of the trench, fixated on the massacre taking place out on the plain. There was still scattered shooting up and down the line. "Cease fire! Now!" He stared out as the routing troops ran, slowly revealing the checkerboard formation deployed behind. There were fresh enemy soldiers there, thousands of them. The fleeing troopers flowed through the gaps between units as the new line began to advance.

"Prepare to repel another attack." He shouted into the com, reloading his rifle as he did. He stared at the approaching columns for second. He had no way of knowing for sure, but there wasn't a doubt in Jahn's mind. They were Supersoldiers. All of them.

"Open fire. Target the units in the second line!" He felt the sweat pouring down his neck, the tightness in his chest, as fear and stress built within him. Those troops were just like his – stronger, faster, and more capable than normal soldiers, and ge could see immediately they heavily outnumbered his force. And they were barely 200 meters away."

"Fire!" he repeated. "Now! Full auto. Target the new formations." He brought his rifle down and opened up, as the attackers moved forward, hosing down the trenchline with their own extremely accurate fire.

*   *   *   *   *

Lucius Vanderberg stood behind a line of emplaced autoguns watching the fleeing troops stream down the hillside, directly toward his position. He wore the plain black uniform and body armor of an Inquisitor in the field. The man was built like a bull, his massive neck protruding from his shirt like a tree trunk. Everything about him radiated fear and intimidation. "All guns...open fire."

The Inquisitor was motionless, impassively watching his deputies gun down the panicked troops as they came over the ridge. The formations were already shattered, and the withering fire sent the soldiers fleeing in every direction in a mad panic. Hundreds fell, and Vanderberg stood silently, staring at the nightmarish scene without a shred of pity or mercy. His com was clipped to his belt, and he made no motion to order the line of heavy autoguns to cease fire. He intended to give the rest of UN Force Juno a lesson in the price of cowardice. One they would not soon forget.

The targeted soldiers were torn to shreds by the heavy projectiles, and men in the primary fields of fire were hit five and six times, their bodies seeming to explode into grotesque red mist.

Vanderberg spoke softly to himself. "They run from the enemy to flee the risk of heroic death as soldiers of the United Nations of Earth, but they reap a bitter harvest. They shall not escape. None of them. Now they shall die as traitors, cowards." There was no pity or hesitation in Vanderberg's voice as he stood and watched his men mow down the panicking soldiers. Inquisitors were among the most zealous of UNGov's security forces, true believers, sadistic men who crushed the government's enemies with a quasi-religious fervor. And Vanderberg was one of the best.

His eyes glistened as he stared out at the killing zone. "So shall it be for all who fail their duty to UNGov."

*   *   *   *   *

The fighting in the trench was hand to hand, as two forces of enhanced warriors battled it out with knife and pistol and rifle butt. The attackers had lost heavily on their approach. Jahn's men made them pay for that last 200 meters, and the plain in front of the trench was littered with the dead and dying. But the assaulting troops kept coming, and their accurate fire took a toll on the defenders too. Now they were streaming over the edge of the trench, and their numbers were beginning to tell. Slowly, grimly, the defenders were losing the fight.

Jahn raised his rifle to shoot at an onrushing enemy, but he was an instant too late, and his adversary fired first. He felt the pain in his side, and he lost his footing in the slick mud of the trench, falling back hard, his rifle slipping from his grasp. The melee in the trench continued all around, a confused mass swirling about, as his men rallied and redoubled their efforts to drive the invaders out.

Jahn lay back, catching his breath as enemy soldiers raced by all around. He reached to his belt, grabbing the heavy survival knife from its sheath and plunging it into the leg of an enemy soldier standing next to him. The trooper fell hard into the muddy bottom of the trench, and then Jahn was on him, trying to bring the blade around to stab his adversary, gritting his teeth against the agony from his wound.

The two struggled, his enemy grabbing his wrists, trying to force the blade away, back toward its wielder. The pain in Jahn's side was almost unbearable, and straining muscles pumped blood from the wound as he put all that was left of his strength into the fight. Finally, he managed to get on top of his enemy and force the blade toward the pinned soldier's neck, shoving it steadily downward. Slowly, relentlessly, Jahn pushed with all his strength and, finally, the razor point slipped into the flesh of his victim. The enemy soldier fought with a last burst of desperation, but then his strength left him. He choked and spat blood as Jahn shoved the deadly blade home.

Jahn rolled off the dead enemy and gasped for air. He'd put everything he had into the fight, and now he felt weakness flood his body. He tried to get to his feet, gritting his teeth and pushing as hard as he could, but he didn't have the strength, and he slumped back down to his knees. His shirt was soaked in blood, and he felt lightheaded, dizzy. He fell back, sucking all the air he could force into his tortured, aching lungs. He'd lost too much blood. He knew the nanos would begin producing artificial blood – they probably already had. He didn't know if it would be enough to replace what he'd lost – was still losing until the nanos managed to seal the wound. But he suspected he wouldn't live long enough to get an answer.

He knew the enemy had taken this section of trench. He was trapped, separated from his men. He didn't have a chance in another fight, but he gripped the knife with the last of his strength anyway. If he died, he promised himself, it would be fighting...not lying helplessly in the mud.

*   *   *   *   *

"What?!" Ralfieri was apoplectic with rage, his fists clenched, his body shaking. His enhanced strike force was assaulting the enemy line. They'd lost heavily despite getting within 200 meters of the fortifications before taking any direct fire. Now they were in the trenches, fighting their death struggle with the defenders. The last thing he needed now was a new disaster.

"Inquisitor Vanderberg and his men are firing upon the flee-ing troops from the first line's attack." Major Evans managed to keep his tone cool and professional, but not his expression. With one look into Evan's eyes, Ralfieri could see the aide shared his own rage.

Ralfieri pulled out his com. "Colonel Roberts, you are in command of the attack. Send in the final reserves immediately."

"Yes si..." Ralfieri cut the connection before the stunned colonel could complete his acknowledgement.

"Evans, I want 6th Battalion assembled immediately." The 6th was the newest arrival, and the men had just transited the Portal the day before. "They are to march to Vanderberg's coor-dinates immediately. I will meet them there."

Evans hesitated. He felt the same anger and outrage as his commander, the same urgency to put a stop to the travesty tak-ing place. But Vanderberg was a UN Inquisitor, empowered to act as judge, jury, and executioner – even with an army commander. Ralfieri was the general of the combined forces on Juno, but Evans didn't know if he had the authority to override an Inquisitor. And from the look in the general's eyes, he had something far more final in mind than overriding Vanderberg.

"Now, Major. I want 6th Battalion on the move in five minutes."

"Sir…" Evans held Ralfieri's gaze for a few seconds. "Yes, sir." The major punched the code into his com and connected with the battalion's commander. "Major Marks, you are to assemble your battalion at once and march to the coordinates I am transmitting. Your men are to be fully-armed and ready for battle. These orders are from General Ralfieri."

"Yes, Major. Understood."

Evans remembered Marks from the Black Corps training facility. He was a veteran of Santoro, a Portal world known for the ferocity of the war that had been fought there for more than ten years. Santoro wasn't Erastus, nothing matched the reputation of that hell world, but Marks' combat credentials were strong.

"Evans out."

Ralfieri was walking briskly toward his transport, his hands balled into tight fists. Evans chased after him. "Sir, please." The major easily caught his unmodified commander and positioned himself between Ralfieri and the transport. "General, think about what you are doing."

"Get out of my way, Major." Ralfieri's tone was as cold as death.

Evans didn't know what to do. He could have easily restrained the enraged general. His enhanced muscles gave him three times the physical strength Ralfieri possessed. It was a court martial offense, one that could easily land him in front of a firing squad. But if Ralfieri got to Vanderberg in his current state…Evans didn't even want to think of what would happen.

He tried to will himself to grab the general, to stop him from getting on the transport. But he couldn't. All he could think of was the general's order – "get out of my way," over and over again in his head. He couldn't keep himself from stepping aside.

He didn't understand what was happening. The conditioning was buried deep in his psyche, in the subconscious of every warrior of the Black Corps. He could think about disobedience, but he couldn't actually make himself do it.

"Stay here, Major." Ralfieri climbed into the transport and slammed the door.

"Yes, sir," Evans said helplessly, trying without success to force himself to follow, to open the door and stop the general. He was still trying when the truck pulled away, spitting up a dust cloud and leaving him in stunned silence.

*   *   *   *   *

Jahn heard the shouts, but he thought he was imagining it all. He lay in the mud, holding his blade with a single shaking hand. He was done; he knew that much. He might survive the wound, but he had no strength to fight – and he was surrounded by enemies. They'd ignored his still and prostrate form so far, but eventually one of them would notice he was still alive. And that would be the end. But the shouts…they were getting closer. Or was he dreaming it all?

He saw the troopers rushing around, a new urgency in their movements. Then he heard the sounds of fire, and he saw half a dozen enemy fighters fall to the ground. Those who were still standing were firing too, shooting at something along the back rim of the trench.

He tried to raise his head, to get a look at what was happening, but he didn't have the strength. Men were falling all around him, their bodies ripped apart by hypervelocity rounds fired from close range. The survivors fled toward the front edge of the trench. They were leaping out, enhanced leg muscles propelling the retreating soldiers the two meters in a single leap.

The whole thing had a dreamy, unreal feel to it. Jahn felt himself drifting into unconsciousness, still unsure what was happening. He struggled to remain aware, summoning all the strength that remained to him. The fighting around him was fierce. In some areas the attackers, now on the defensive, fled the trenches; in others, pockets of resistance developed, and they held firm, at least for a while.

Jahn felt an impact on his legs, a body falling on top of him. Then another. He lay, partially covered, watching the battle with failing eyes and fading awareness. Then he slipped into blackness.

"Captain Jahn?"

He saw a dim light, then a hazy form in front of him. He was weak, so weak. He had no idea how long he'd been out. But he heard the voice. Someone was calling to him. Then he heard the quiet. The sounds of battle were gone.

"Captain Jahn, sir." The voice was urgent, it's tone one of concern. "Sir? This is Sergeant Hind. Captain Denisov sent me to find you, sir."

Jahn tried to focus his eyes, to zero in on the voice. "Ser… geant?" he whispered.

"Yes, sir." He felt hands on him, pulling, lifting. "Just relax, sir. We've retaken the position. The enemy is gone. We're going to get you the field hospital. You're going to be OK, sir."

*   *   *   *   *

"They're pulling back all across the line, Jake." Black was fully clad in body armor and exos. He'd been up to the front himself, and he'd just returned. "They hit Jahn's people hardest. The fighting was heavy in that sector, but Denisov's reserves cleared the enemy out. It looks like Jahn's down. They're looking for him now."

Taylor took a deep breath. He remembered Jahn from Erastus. Good man. Was he dead somewhere in that nightmarish trench, or was he just wounded? He didn't know.

He sighed. Another fight, a victory this time. But the difference wasn't as stark as he'd hoped. His people held the ground this time instead of losing it, but that didn't seem so important. Both sides had lost heavily, and the war was no closer to a conclusion.

"How bad did we get hit, Blackie?"

Black was reaching around behind him, unlatching the heavy harness he was wearing. Part armor, part weapon, the exos amplified the already considerable combat power of an enhanced soldier. A private stood behind Black, holding the heavy rig while the short, muscular officer contorted his way out.

"I don't know yet, Jake, but it was pretty bad. We lost a lot of good men today." Black was pulling off the smaller parts of his exoskeleton and handing them to another aide. "We should have some hard data soon." He paused. "The enemy took it worse, at least. Much worse." Black had been up to the front line, and he'd seen the results of the carnage firsthand. "The field in front of the trenchline is covered with bodies."

Taylor nodded, a somber look on his face. This was carnage like he'd never seen before, even in the hell of Erastus. He was beginning to realize the battle between his men and the UN Supersoldiers would be apocalyptic. The two armies would savage each other in a horrific fight to the death, and the winner would have nothing left but a few stunned and exhausted survivors.

He took a deep breath, but he didn't say anything. He was sinking into dark thoughts, facing the prospect of his army being torn apart. And he had no idea how to prevent it.

Chapter 14

From the Secret Files of Raul Esteban:

As I write this, I know I am nearing my own death. It is a so-
bering when you finally realize the doctors have done everything
possible, that your remaining time is measured in months,
perhaps weeks. I don't think a man can describe how this feels
to another who is not experiencing it. Death is an adversary we
all must face, and one we cannot defeat. Yet it is a stark reality
when you know you can no longer delay it, that its victory is imminent.

My life has been an extraordinary one, and I have spent the
last 40 years at the very seat of power in the world. I was born
into a fragmented world, carved into nations based on ethnicity,
on geography, on past wars. Nations that fought each other,
competed economically. I was part of a movement that ended
all of that and brought unity out of man's chaos.

It is natural for me to ponder not only what I have achieved,
but also the future and what it may bring after I am gone, to
imagine what will become of the new order my allies and I
forged so long ago. I am the last of the original Secretariat, and
when I am dead, the reins of power shall pass fully to the next
generation.

Our government has maintained order throughout the world
for four decades; it has largely erased the vast differences in
wealth between the citizens of the world. We have controlled
harmful speech and dangerous, unsupervised freedom. The
state we created is supreme. Men in every corner of the globe

are subject to its laws and regulations, and those who would upset the system are tirelessly weeded out.

We have eradicated the foolish notions that allowed disruption and violence in the name of freedom. Freedom is a foolish dream, a philosopher's construct, beyond the ability of the masses to appreciate. The people want food, security, physical safety...not amorphous concepts like freedom. Our government has given them what they craved and taken from them the responsibility that was beyond their capacity to understand and appreciate.

But can this government survive? Can it maintain its control over the people indefinitely? Or will it be dragged down by infighting and power struggles from within? Will it splinter, fragment again into competing and warring nations?

The greatest challenge we face is arrogance. There is a point in the development of any government where pride replaces judgment, when disputes over the inconsequential attain greater import than debates over vital affairs of state. There are always more aspirants craving power than positions for them to occupy.

It is a natural progression, and one we must make every effort to restrain. We must not only contain the harmful impulses of the population at large, but we must look to control the power struggles of those within the government. The battle for my Seat will be the first test, I fear. Will the Secretariat come together and peacefully select a successor? Or will the parties descend into bloodshed and destruction, striving against each other to grasp the highest power? My death will be the greatest test for this government, the most difficult obstacle for it to clear.

I like to think my work will last long after I am gone, but I'm not sure I believe it will. I will strive, at least, to see that this renegade Taylor and his traitors are destroyed before I die...for the danger they represent is real, and if they reach Earth in strength they can cause massive damage. UNGov is strong, but Taylor's people represent an idea. And ideas are dangerous.

Oddly, Taylor, so great a danger, may also aid us. If Samov-

ich is successful in defeating the rebel forces, he may achieve
enough momentum to succeed me without a major struggle. A
strong Secretary-General with broad support on the Secretariat
can take UNGov boldly into the future. A long and bitter power
struggle could destroy it.

"Inquisitor Vanderberg is hereby ordered to do whatever
General Ralfieri commands." Samovich was livid, his face red,
his fists clenched. He still couldn't believe the reports. His commanding general and the UN Inquisitor almost getting into a
firefight in front of an entire battalion. And they did it in the
middle of a major offensive, an attack that crumbled without
Ralfieri's close supervision. "Please assure Vanderberg that if
another matter like this comes to my attention, I will feed his
miserable carcass to the people he's crushed under his boot for
so long."

Inquisitors were highly placed operatives, but the position
required blunt brutality rather than heavy thinking. They had
a tendency to become arrogant and inflexible, especially when
they'd held the position for as long as Vanderberg had. Their
job was to instill fear, and the individuals appointed as Inquisitors tended to be angry and sadistic by nature.

They were usually employed in situations where incor-
rect thought or outright defiance had to be rooted out from
the population, but this was the first time Inquisitors had been
dispatched to the war zones. Samovich made the decision in
response to reports of increasing recruitment by Taylor from
the planetary armies. He realized something had to be done to
stem the flood of desertions to Taylor's army and, with no idea
where Taylor's people would next appear, dispatching an Inquisitor team to every Portal world seemed to be the best solution.

Indeed, the plan had been extremely successful, at least
at first. Vanderberg's quick action had minimized defections
on Juno before the Black Corps even arrived onplanet. But
Samovich hadn't considered the potential for conflict between
the Inquisitor and the commander on the scene. The officers

in command of planetary armies understood the limits of their authority, but they weren't used to cowering at the roar of UNGov thugs like civilians did, especially not generals like Antonio Ralfieri. UNGov had learned early in the war that trying to control its generals too closely was a recipe for lost battles and shattered armies, and they'd allowed their senior officers to exercise considerable independent authority in the combat zones.

Ralfieri was a skilled commander, one of the best on any of the Portal worlds. There weren't many others as capable, and Samovich didn't want anything to interfere with the destruction of Taylor's army, especially not a contest of egos between a pompous Inquisitor and his handpicked military commander.

"Yes, Secretary." Colonel Farrier was typing the message, a response to Anan Keita's urgent communique. Samovich had always thought of Keita as a clueless fuck up, a warm body to fill a Seat and give him another sure vote on the Secretariat. But he had to admit, his delegate had handled the near-fight between Ralfieri and Vanderberg very well.

Keita had been warned by a Major named Evans, and he'd managed to get to the scene just as Ralfieri and Vanderberg were about to start shooting at each other. The hierarchy between the general and the Inquisitor was fuzzy, a gray area each man interpreted to his own benefit. But Anan Keita was a member of the Secretariat, and he clearly ranked above both of them. The two men were both livid, furious almost past the point of reason. But, however grudgingly and resentfully, they both obeyed Keita's orders.

The conflict could have been a disaster, but Keita put a stop to it before any serious damage was done. He ordered both men back to their quarters, and each of them barely managed to suppress his rage enough to obey. Samovich reminded himself to congratulate Keita in the communique for a job well done. He'd gotten used to his ally being a burden, but now he remembered why he'd chosen Keita in the first place. He was a fool, but not a total fool, and from Anton Samovich, that was a compliment.

He thought about Ralfieri's aide, Major Evans. There was

no question Evans had prevented a catastrophe by calling Keita. Samovich considered rewarding the officer, but then he remembered that none of the Black Corps soldiers were coming home anyway. It was a shame. Evans seemed like a smart officer, and he'd certainly done good service. He deserved better. But the Black Corps had been created to destroy Taylor, and it would exist only as long as it took to attain that goal. The modified warriors were far too dangerous to keep around. Taylor himself had proven that. The soldiers of the Corps were heavily conditioned, unlike Taylor's people, but Samovich wasn't taking any chances. No, there was no way he was going to let his new modified warriors long survive their victory. He couldn't imagine the chaos men like that could cause back on Earth.

Ralfieri wasn't coming home either. The general hadn't been modified, and Samovich had originally planned to allow the commander to return to Earth and retire. But things had gotten too messy, and he felt it was better to cut all ties with the entire sorry episode. He sighed. It wasn't fair, none of it. But he'd never let that interfere with his decisions. Fairness was a quaint concept, the stuff of weak minds and fantasy, but good governance required ruthlessness. Individual people didn't matter when the good of the state was involved. Except for those at the top, of course, the ones who made the decisions.

He would probably let Vanderberg do it when the time came. That would salve the Inquisitor's bruised ego. But he promised himself it would be quick and painless. Ralfieri was serving UNGov well, and if he defeated Taylor he would deserve a parade through Geneva and a king's ransom as his reward. Since none of that was going to happen, Samovich figured the least he owed his general was an easy death.

Like any despotic government, UNGov was suspicious of successful generals, and the systems and procedures they employed were designed to prevent any rebellion arising from the military. Rank and file soldiers and junior officers got one way tickets to the Portal worlds where they fought. Most died in the fighting, but those who survived remained where they were, never to see Earth again. The last thing UNGov wanted was a bunch of veteran soldiers wandering around, seething with discontent or rallying to some old general.

The senior officers and commanders did get return trips to Earth, and sometimes reassignment to other Portal worlds. But their soldiers always remained behind. Forever. The very idea of allowing a victorious general to transit back to Earth at the head of his army was anathema to the paranoid political minds that ran the Secretariat. The men in charge of UNGov believed in secret police, surveillance, and draconian laws, but they were always uncomfortable with the military.

"Send that communique at once, Colonel." Samovich wasn't going to take any chances. He didn't want Antonio Ralfieri interfered with, not until he had destroyed Taylor's forces. "That should settle things between Ralfieri and Vanderberg." And if it doesn't, he thought angrily, Lucius Vanderberg will come home in a box.

"Send a second message, Colonel, this one under Secretariat Seal to Anan Keita." He paused. "If Vanderberg causes any more trouble, Secretary Keita is authorized to have him summarily executed. Along with any of his men who resist." It was a superfluous message, he knew. As a member of the Secretariat placed in charge of the operation on Juno, Keita already had the authority to execute anyone on the planet at will. But Samovich wanted to reassure his beleaguered political ally, to stiffen his spine. The unspoken message was clear – I'll support anything you have to do to keep the operation on track.

Samovich waved his hand, dismissing the colonel. "Send those immediately."

The messages would be hand carried through the Portals and then transmitted across each planet by the fastest available communication. Arleon was already pacified, and its permanent infrastructure was under construction. There were active communications satellites in orbit, so the messages would be transmitted to the Oceania Portal almost instantaneously.

Oceania was still contested by the Machines, though the battle there was progressing satisfactorily. The communique would travel by aircraft to the Juno Portal, which was on a small island far from the main landmass. Overall, it would take about 9 hours for the communique to reach Juno. Less than half a day. With any luck, he thought, there won't be any other disasters in that time.

Chapter 15

From the Journal of Jake Taylor:

Is there anything as stressful as command? I am a veteran with 14 years of service on the most violently hostile world where men have tried to fight. I am the commander of an army on a crusade to free mankind from tyranny. I have seen thousands of men die and killed vast numbers of my enemies. I was turned into a cyborg, half machine, my enhanced biotech implants making me one of the deadliest warriors in history, if somewhat less human.

Yet I constantly question my judgment, second-guess the orders I issue. I try to rely on my experience, but my confidence fails me. Every command, every strategy leaves me uncertain, questioning if I made the right choices, wondering how many men will die as a result of my orders.

I must keep my uncertainty to myself, look to no one for my own reassurance. Command is the loneliest of all things, and I will burden none of my people, not even my top officers, with the doubts I feel. My soldiers, even my closest friends and toughest veterans, look to me for strength. They have made me into an unstoppable force, a resolute commander, sure of every decision, never doubting the right course of action. It is a fiction, but it is one they need, so I must maintain the façade.

The responsibility is overwhelming. So many men die. I tell myself they do not give their lives for me, that my soul doesn't bear the weight of so many good men dead. They die for the cause, to free the world, to fight against the evil that represses

mankind. I tell myself they don't die for me, but I don't really believe it.

"General Taylor...I'm sorry to wake you, sir..."

Taylor was lying on his bed, futilely trying to sleep. "You didn't wake me, Lieutenant." If only he knew how little I slept, Taylor thought. "What is it?"

"Um, well, sir. You have a visitor." Lieutenant Warne's head was poking through the tent, and the expression on his face was as bewildered as his tone.

"Visitor? What the hell..."

"He refers to me, General Taylor." Another figure, clad in a gray hooded robe, slid past the canvas flap and entered the tent. He stood silent and still for an instant then he reached up and pulled back the hood.

"T'arza." Taylor sat up, staring at the new arrival, his eyes wide with surprise. "What are you doing here?"

Taylor had only seen the Tegeri once, but that day had been a turning point in his life, one he could never forget. He'd been hostile at first, regarding himself as a POW and the alien as an enemy. That changed quickly when T'arza began to show him what had really happened on the early colony worlds, how the war had truly begun.

Taylor had resisted at first, but somehow he'd known everything the alien showed him was true, that all he'd been told his whole life was nothing but a series of lies. He would never forget the feeling. In an instant he lost the only belief that sustained him, the thought that his sacrifices, UNGov's despotic rule, all of it, had been necessary to save Earth. Not only had that been a lie, but the responsibility for the death and destruction of 40 years of war did not rest with the Tegeri as he'd so long believed. Taylor realized it had been him – and all his men – who were the murderers, the aggressors, not the Machines and the Tegeri. It was overwhelming, a realization that shook him to his core, and he was still struggling to accept it all.

The Tegeri moved forward slowly. "I have come to offer

you counsel, General Taylor, if you will take it." He nodded. "Among my people, encouraging an individual to action, as I have done with you, creates an obligation to assist. Honor demands that I help you in any way that I can."

"You can send an army of Machines to help us." Taylor knew it was a foolish thing to say. There was nothing he needed less than to give UNGov the propaganda tool of his soldiers fighting alongside aliens the people of Earth still considered murderous monsters.

An odd expression came over T'arza's face. Taylor didn't recognize it, but somehow he knew it signaled guilt and frustration. "Indeed, General Taylor, I wish such a simple expedient could aid your task." The Tegeri spoke softly, gently. "However, I believe such an action would decrease your chances of success, rather than aiding you."

"You are right, T'arza." Taylor stood up and walked toward his visitor. "Which is unfortunate, because we are facing a serious fight here, and we could use all the help we can get."

"I have received some data on your battles to date." T'arza stopped short of disclosing that the Tegeri had monitoring devices watching every step Taylor's army took. The omission caused him discomfort. Tegeri could lie when necessary, but it was a stain on one's honor – and T'arza was one of the most honorable of his race. Failing to disclose information wasn't exactly lying, but Tegeri culture frowned upon such hair-splitting technicalities, considering them unworthy of a great race. "It would appear that your adversaries have deployed forces with the same modifications as your soldiers." The Tegeri spoke calmly, evenly. There was something oddly soothing about his voice, despite the grave nature of the topic. Taylor had noticed it back in the cave on Erastus too. There had been no trace of anger or resentment toward Taylor or any of his people, not even after more than 40 years of war provoked by the humans.

"They have, T'arza." Taylor exhaled loudly. "I should have expected this, but I let myself be taken by surprise." He forced a weak smile. "Perhaps you should have chosen someone more capable as your point of contact."

"You were the correct choice, General Taylor. I remain sure of the decision to approach you. Your willingness to assume the responsibility not only for your actions, but for your failure to anticipate your enemies' reactions, verify that our choice was correct." The alien fell silent for a few seconds, judging what he should and should not say to Taylor. "I can see the inner torment your responsibilities cause you. I was, perhaps, remiss in not warning you that your destiny as the leader of this rebellion is not necessarily coincident with the path offering you the greatest personal happiness."

"You did not ask me to take on UNGov, T'arza. You merely gave me the truth and allowed me to make my own choice."

T'arza nodded slightly. "Indeed, General Taylor, it would be unthinkable for us to command you to attack your own kind, even to seek, against all odds, to destroy the government that holds your people in bondage." There was a strange tone to T'arza's voice. Taylor didn't understand Tegeri speech patterns, but he was sure the alien was uncomfortable about something. "However," T'arza continued, his voice slow and deliberate, "it would be intentionally misleading for me to suggest we did not know what you would choose to do. You were not selected at random, General Taylor, nor without long and careful consideration. When I confronted you in the cavern, there was no doubt in my mind what you would do with the information I provided."

"You mean you picked me because you knew how I would react? That I would try to destroy UNGov?"

T'arza gazed intently at Taylor. "You were chosen very carefully, General Taylor. Very carefully indeed. We selected you as our point of contact for many reasons, but it would be a breach of honesty to suggest that your hostility toward your own government was not one of these. Your relationship with your superiors was troubled even before we made contact with you."

"If your people wanted UNGov destroyed, why didn't you take steps to win the war rather than holding back your true capabilities?" Taylor's eyes met his visitor's. "We both know your race has greater technology than you've deployed on any of the contested Portal worlds. You could have swept our forces away at will any time you chose." He paused. "Isn't that true?"

T'arza gestured with open arms and nodded slowly. "Indeed, General Taylor, I can see that our choice was indeed wise. If any of your race can succeed in this difficult quest, it is you." The Tegeri paused and held his palms out, signifying truth. "Yes, General. My people possess sufficiently advanced technology to defeat your armies. We have not done so for several reasons."

Taylor watched and listened intently to his guest's words. He wanted to learn more, to know and understand the whole truth, and the history of human and Tegeri contact.

"Your people are a brother race to mine. We do not know the precise history of this relationship, for its roots lie in the distant past, long before my people attained civilization. Surely you have noticed the similarity between our peoples. There is great diversity in the life forms we have encountered on the Portal worlds, but our people are so alike, in genetic terms we are nearly identical."

Taylor nodded but remained silent. There were differences in appearance between humans and Tegeri, certainly, but they were all superficial, almost meaningless in a universe of infinite diversity. He stared at his guest. He wanted to hear what T'arza had to say. All of it.

"Your people know little of how the Portals came to be, of the race we call the Ancients. They were gone before your people became civilized, but my ancestors knew of them. As gods they walked among us, teaching us, bidding us to grow, to step through the Portals they had created and explore the universe. They told also of our brothers on another world, and they charged us to shepherd your people, to lead them to the stars as they did us."

T'arza's words were slow, his voice almost lyrical. The knowledge of which he spoke was the most sacred lore of the Tegeri race, and he passed it to Taylor with the greatest reverence.

"Of how our races, so similar, came to develop on two different worlds, I know not. If the Ancients shared this knowledge with my forefathers, it has been lost through the ages. Yet we know they bade us watch over humans, and so, for many millennia, we did just that. We saw your people come together in small groups, to learn to grow food, to create bricks from mud and build walls to defend their first, tiny settlements. Then we came to your planet, to guide, to aid your development. It was on your world that we came to realize just how genetically similar our races were, yet how vast were the differences in our psyches."

T'arza's voice changed slightly, as though he were attempting to hide disapproval. "Your people warred with each other constantly...for land and food, yes, but also for the vanity of your leaders. The vast majority of your people stood ready to follow kings and emperors, to bend their knee in servitude. Thousands died so one king could wrest control of a valley or stretch of forest from a rival. They warred with each other at the behest of their masters, existing in squalor and deprivation while those who ruled them built palaces and lived in opulence.

"This willingness to blindly follow leaders, with scant regard to their fitness to command, was alien to us. For centuries we did not understand; we did not realize we were contributing to this behavior. Apollo, Ares, Zeus, Odin, Thor, Anubis, Anu, Marduk, Quetzalcoatl...all were names your people gave to us. They began to worship my people, to sacrifice animals – and even other men – to us, begging for our favor, for us to smite their enemies and grant them dominion over their neighbors."

T'arza paused. His voice had become softer. Taylor found Tegeri expressions difficult to read, but he knew T'arza was uncomfortable with what he was revealing.

"My people were horrified when we realized what was happening. We had come as teachers, not masters, and the thought of humans invoking our aid to destroy other humans was incomprehensible to us." T'arza closed his eyes for a few seconds. "We saw that we could only worsen your tendency for blind obedience. We abandoned the task the Ancients had set for us and fled your world, leaving you to develop on your own, hoping you would mature and that your people would discover their individuality." T'arza gazed directly at Taylor. "We rejoiced when you stepped through the first Portal, and we planned the day we would renew contact and teach you all we knew of the legacy of the Ancients."

His eyes dropped. "Alas, your people hadn't changed. In thrall again to an unworthy leadership, you began a war with us. Humans came, arrayed for battle, and they killed your own colonists, massacring even the youngest. They slew also our emissaries, members of our greatest houses, for the honor of meeting the first humans to leave Earth was supreme, and only our most worthy were allowed to go. Many of those you later came to call Machines were also killed, as they had accompanied our greeting parties. Our people had no weapons – we had come as friends and ambassadors, not invaders. Yet all who could not flee were slain."

"T'arza…" Taylor spoke his visitor's name, but his voice faltered. The words didn't come.

T'arza held up a single hand. "I say this not to insult you, General, nor to disparage your people as a race. It appears they cannot easily control this behavior. You have followed inferior men as long as your race has existed. You have grown, learned much, become educated, developed advanced technology, reached out to explore the vastness of the universe. Yet still you rush to heed the commands of those not fit to lead, those who promise you security, who offer you baseless platitudes in exchange for your self-determination." T'arza paused for a few seconds. When he continued, his tone was serious, grave. "This must end, General. It must end now. With you. You must lead your people to greater wisdom, whatever the cost."

Taylor's stomach heaved. He could feel the gravity in T'arza's voice. There was something else, something menacing there. "What are you not telling me, T'arza?"

The Tegeri paused. "I have told you of the Ancients, General, those who built the Portals. Have you never wondered where they are?"

Taylor stared back quietly. Finally, he nodded. "I guess I assumed they left, that they lived far away."

"No, General. The Ancients did not leave." T'arza's spoke

slowly, his voice grim. "They were destroyed."

Taylor stood silently, a look of shock on his face. He looked like he might speak, but he said nothing.

"The Ancients had an enemy. We call them the Darkness, though we know little of them. They waged war until the Ancients were destroyed then they departed. The Tegeri and the humans were too primitive to draw the attention of the enemy, and the Ancients, with their last strength, hid our existence, and thus saved us. Where the Darkness went, we know not.

"The Ancients left us clues, scraps of information hidden in our oldest lore, for they knew that one day the Darkness would return…and that we would have to face it. My race and yours. It was for this purpose the Ancients nurtured us, guided our races. We are destined to fight the Darkness together, your people and mine. Thus is the legacy of the Ancients."

Taylor was stunned. He stood rigid, still, his silvery eyes boring into T'arza's.

"You understand now, why my people did not destroy yours, why we have allowed the beings you call Machines to fight a losing war against your armies while thousands died on both sides. You are our brothers, born to stand with us, to fight side by side against the evil that destroyed the Ancients." T'arza spread his arms wide as he spoke. "The Portal network is vaster than your people imagine. There are many sentient races on the distant worlds to which it leads, young peoples, primitive beings tentatively striving toward civilization. We must protect them as the ancients protected us. That responsibility has now fallen to us."

T'arza stepped toward Taylor. "If we fail," he continued, "all shall be destroyed. The Ancients sacrificed themselves to protect our races, and that duty is now ours, General. It is our sacred obligation. And the time is almost upon us. For the Darkness is returning."

Taylor stood still and silent, feeling the weight of the universe pressing down on him. One thought kept going through his head, again and again…T'arza's words. "The Darkness is returning."

Chapter 16

Transmitted Under Secretariat Seal
From Anton Samovich to Anan Keita

I repeat my congratulations on your handling of the Vander-berg-Ralfieri Affair. Your prompt intervention prevented potentially enormous problems and did much to preserve our position. I must now urge you to more actively utilize your overall command authority to force the matter to a hasty conclusion.

Matters in Geneva are progressing more quickly than I had hoped or expected, and it is essential that we complete our expected victory on Juno in the shortest time possible. I have received numerous communiques from General Ralfieri advocating a defensive campaign to maximize our supply and reinforcement advantages over Taylor and his army.

As you are aware, such a strategy is politically impossible at this time. I suggest you assume more direct command of the field forces, deferring, of course, to General Ralfieri's tactical decisions (to the extent they support our political objectives and requirements).

It is of crucial importance that the battle on Juno be completed, and Taylor's forces destroyed, in no more than one month. If the campaign lasts any longer than that, our plans will be placed at grave risk.

I trust you understand the importance of this communication.

"This is the third operative to disappear, Alexi." Samovich sat behind his desk, his face twisted into a frustrated grimace. His plush office offered sweeping views of the Swiss countryside in three directions, but he wasn't noticing any of it. All he could see was trouble brewing everywhere. The final dance for the Secretary-General's Seat had begun, and he knew he had to be at his best. Every second. It was the highest stakes game imaginable. The prize was the ultimate power over all mankind. The alternative to victory was almost certainly death.

"Is it possible they are being bribed rather than killed?" Alexi Drogov sat opposite Samovich, his hand wrapped around a heavy crystal glass. The drink was seltzer water with a large slice of lemon. Drogov was a world class drinker, capable of downing enough vodka to kill most men, but he realized as well as Samovich that he and his old friend were in the opening stages of a deadly battle. One that required him to be at his sober best.

Drogov didn't seek political power. His wants and needs were far baser and simpler. When he wasn't killing someone, he preferred to spend his time bedding Swiss girls, preferably blonde and, when possible, 2 or 3 at a time. He didn't want the political position Samovich craved, but he knew his life of comfort and decadence was guaranteed only as long as his close associate was on the Secretariat. Without Samovich's power, Drogov would have a much harder time living his chosen lifestyle. He'd have to waste time seducing his women, rather than simply picking them out and dispatching security forces deliver them to him, pliant and willing under pain of their families being sent to reeducation camps. And he'd have to find a way to pay for the priceless truckloads of the very best vodka and brandy that pulled up to his compound on a frighteningly regular basis.

If Samovich's rival prevailed, Drogov knew it could quickly get worse than losing his supply of expensive liquor and captive women. He might find himself on the run, fighting to survive in a world turned suddenly hostile rather than drinking and fucking the days away in his lakeside villa.

"Anybody can be bribed, my friend." Samovich leaned back in his chair and sighed. "But these were agents with top clearances, long-service men I hand-picked. Li might have gotten to one of them, but I find it difficult to believe he flipped all three." His expression was hard and angry, but Drogov could see the frustration and bewilderment there too. "I am not a fool. I employ the usual guarantees of loyalty. They all have weaknesses, families. None of them could doubt how I would respond to betrayal."

"Still, whether he killed or flipped them, his people exposed three of your top agents in short order." Drogov's tone was grimly serious. "Even if none of them were turned, the effectiveness of his security is worrisome." He paused. "Perhaps it is time to eliminate Secretary Li once and for all."

Samovich sat quietly, staring back at Drogov. "I don't know," he finally said. "It's a risky move. If it gets traced back to me, I'll lose most of my support on the Secretariat." The one inviolable law of UNGov was the sanctity of its ruling class. Killing a member of the Secretariat would be an unprecedented move. "Worse, if we got caught in a failed attempt, it would hand the Seat to Li. And probably send both of us to an unpleasant execution."

Drogov let out a loud exhale. "You're gambling either way. If the fucker's catching all your spies, it means he's on full alert, and then some. It's only going to get tougher to get to him." He paused. "And what are you going to do if the battle on Juno drags on? Stalemate is almost as bad for you as defeat."

Samovich sighed. "I don't know." He put his face in his hands and rubbed his temples. "It feels reckless going after him directly. If Keita and Ralfieri can get me a victory soon, I'm sure I can get a majority on the Secretariat. I can bring Li up on charges, even if they're bullshit, and get him expelled from his Seat." He looked up at his friend. "Then we can take him out with no real consequences."

"It comes down to the fight on Juno." There was heavy skepticism in Drogov's voice. "And wars tend to drag on longer than expected, especially when the other side is a veteran force under the command of a military genius." He stared right into Samovich's eyes as he spoke.

No one on the Secretariat had dared to speak of Taylor's true abilities before, for fear of sounding disloyal. But Drogov put it right out there. Jake Taylor was a natural leader, and now, courtesy of UNGov and the Supersoldier program, he was one with superhuman abilities and total recall. Samovich imagined Caesar or Alexander or Napoleon, but with iron constitutions and absolutely perfect memories. Instant recall of every soldier under his command, each scrap of ground he'd passed, the capabilities and weaknesses of every weapon system. Could he be beaten? Even by a force more than twice the size of his own?

"We need to pour everything we can into the fight on Juno. Damn the rest of the Portal worlds. I need to strip the veterans from the other planets and send them to support the Black Corps. I will bury Taylor and his people with enemies, however many it takes to destroy them, whatever the losses. All that matters is victory on Juno."

Drogov sat impassively. Certainly, more resources sent to Juno would increase the chances of overwhelming Taylor and his people. But there would be damage too, losses on other worlds - lower order disasters than a victory by Taylor certainly, but still reverses Samovich's enemies could use against him. Could pouring forces through the Juno Portal win the battle there before the damage elsewhere became too problematic? Drogov decided it would probably be a close race. He was just about to say so when he heard a deafening crash.

The explosion ripped through the wall, sending chunks of debris flying around the office and shattering the floor to ceiling picture windows. Drogov reacted first, diving over the desk and pushing Samovich to the floor. "Under the desk," he shouted as he shoved his friend with one hand and pulled out a machine pistol with the other. "Stay down, Anton. Don't move."

The reflexes of a career assassin took over. This was an attempt on Samovich's life; he was sure of that. He whipped his head around to both sides, scanning the room. Fuck, he thought, the windows...they're coming through the windows. An instant later he saw the shadows outside, descending rapidly from above.

He jumped up, grabbing the desk and pulling hard, tipping it over to shield Samovich from the approaching assassins. He jumped over the desk himself, but too late. Three cables had dropped down outside the shattered windows, and the attackers were already leaping in the room, firing as they did.

Drogov caught a round in the leg as he leapt behind the desk. He felt the adrenalin coursing through his bloodstream as he pulled himself up, ignoring the pain from his wound. He held the auto-pistol over the desk, emptying a clip to spray the area with fire. The assassins were in the open. He knew that advantage would only last a second, and he intended to make it count.

He didn't dare raise his head to see if he'd hit anyone, but there was only one gun returning fire. I must have gotten two, he thought. His satisfaction was short-lived, though. There were shadows descending from above the window again, more assassins about to leap into the room. He slammed another clip into the auto-pistol and fired just as they came into view. He watched as all three slipped from the cables and dropped, one of them making a brief effort to grab onto the window frame before he too slipped and fell almost a kilometer to the ground below.

There's one at least still out there, he thought, just as he saw the grenade sail through the air and land behind him. He dove to the side, shoving Samovich harder into the space under the desk as he tried to take cover himself. He heard the doors swinging open, Samovich's security firing on full auto as they poured into the room. An instant later there was a deafening blast...then pain. He tried to raise his head, to see what was happening. But he couldn't. Then the blackness took him.

*   *   *   *   *

"I cannot express my joy at seeing you safe, Secretary Samovich." Li's words sounded sincere, his voice tinged with equal parts sympathy and outrage. "We have had our differences, but when the Secretariat itself, or any of its members are threatened, we must stand together as one."

Samovich nodded to his rival. "Thank you, Secretary Li."
You lying motherfucker, he thought, but he kept it to himself.
"I appreciate your support, and I agree with you completely.
Whatever our disagreements, we must stand together when the
sanctity of this great body is at stake." He held up his neatly
bandaged arm. "Fortunately, my injuries are quite minor." He
stared directly at Li. "And my security was able to capture one
of the would-be assassins alive. They are questioning him now."
It was a bluff – all of the attackers were dead. He watched Li's
reaction carefully, but his rival was silent, maintaining a solid
poker face. Samovich wondered if he could read anything into
the lack of a response.

"When I find out who is responsible for the attempt on my
life…" – his voice became emotional and he paused an instant,
sucking in a mouthful of air – "…and for the murder of my
very good friend, Alexi Drogov, I will make a full report to this
body along with my request for a Secretariat Warrant of Execution against all conspirators."

There was a flurry of nods rippling around the room. Li
bowed his head toward Samovich and stared across the table, his
expression one of apparent sympathy. "Of course, Secretary
Samovich. An attack on any of us is an attack on all of us. I
will be the first to sign the Warrant when the perpetrators of this
heinous act are found."

Damn, he's good, Samovich thought, forcing himself to
offer a smile to his enemy. No wonder he's given me so much
trouble. He hadn't expected Li to confess, but there wasn't a
glimmer of guilt or doubt in the Chinese politician's expression,
not even an instant of hesitation. It was going to take a lot of
digging, and probably some luck too, if he was going to expose
Li as the mastermind behind the assassination attempt.

"If you are feeling well enough then, perhaps we should
begin the session." Li's eyes glanced to the empty chair at the
head of the table. It was the first meeting of the Secretariat
he'd attended without Raul Esteban presiding. Unavoidably
detained…that was the word from the Secretary-General's staff,

and his absence was driving them all to wild speculation. Was Esteban just having a bad day? Or was he near death? Would the final power struggle begin sooner than they had all expected?

"By all means, Secretary Li, let us begin. First on the agenda is the status of the combat on Juno."

"I have heard our forces there suffered a severe reverse." Li spoke up before Samovich had a chance to continue. "Also, I am told there was some dissension among our own personnel." He stared across the table at his rival. "Is the campaign experiencing difficulties, Secretary Samovich?"

"Indeed no, Secretary Li." Samovich could play the game as well as Li. "There was no reverse, merely a diversionary attack intended to cause enemy attrition. A successful operation by any measure." It was a lie, but Samovich's voice was utterly convincing. He knew no one really believed what he was saying, but his performance was strong enough to deflect any open challenge. For a while.

"What of the dispute between General Ralfieri and Inquisitor Vanderberg?" It wasn't Li this time; it was Simon Yardley, one of his cronies.

They're well-rehearsed, Samovich thought, holding back a sigh as he did. "I believe the reports you may have seen are in error, Secretary Yardley. Indeed, the general and the Inquisitor were simply discussing strategy, and it was misinterpreted as a conflict." It's going to be a long afternoon, he thought wearily. A long afternoon.

*   *   *   *   *

Samovich stepped into the brightly lit room. He was deep beneath his villa, in a sub-level that didn't officially exist. No building plans anywhere showed the subterranean complex, and only Samovich's most trusted subordinates and henchmen had ever seen it. It was his secret refuge, accessible only through a heavily camouflaged entrance, one shielded against all detection devices.

He turned and looked at the large bed at the other end of the room, positioned near a bank of machines. "You look pretty good for a corpse." Samovich smiled as he walked toward the bed. Alexi Drogov was propped up on a pile of pillows. He was ghostly pale, and he had heavy bandages on his chest and head. Two IV lines were attached to his arm. One was filled with clear fluids, but the other was attached to a strange machine, and it was filled with a sickly yellow liquid. The patient looked like he was in rough shape, but he was very much alive. Contrary to the belief of everyone in UNGov.

"If you think this is good, you need to get out more." Drogov's voice was hoarse with fatigue, but otherwise he sounded normal.

"Well, the entire Secretariat thinks you're dead, my friend." Samovich smiled as he walked toward the side of the bed. "Everybody thinks you're dead. Except a well-chosen few... and none of them will leave here until we're finished with what needs to be done."

"I have a pretty good idea of what has to be done, but I'm not exactly in top condition right now. You've got to deal with this situation long before I'll be back on my feet." He swallowed hard before continuing. "Who's your second stringer for pest control?"

"Don't be so skeptical of modern medicine, my friend. We live in wondrous times." Samovich smiled. "Do you feel a tingling feeling?"

Drogov nodded. "Yeah, as a matter of fact I do. What the hell is that? It feels like it's coming from the IV."

"It is. It's nanotech, the same stuff the Supersoldiers have. Although your nanobots are being produced outside your body and manually injected. It's fixing you up...a hell of a lot faster than anything else could. You'll be on your feet in two days and almost 100% in a week."

"That's amazing." There was surprise in his voice, and some disbelief. He'd believe the prognosis when he saw it happen. He forced a tired smile. "And my captive doctors? They must be some serious specialists. I hope they don't mind being stuck down here 24/7."

"Oh, don't worry about them. They'll walk out of here wealthy men and women. It's all been arranged." Samovich shot his friend a devious smile. "They have a lot to gain from your complete recovery. And a lot to lose if you're not ready for action in time."

Drogov nodded slowly. "I hope you're estimates are right. Then I will take care of that fucking worm, Li. I'll have him in a hole in the ground in no time." Samovich's rival was more than just an enemy now. Drogov knew how to respond to a failed assassination attempt.

"No."

"What?" There was genuine surprise in Drogov's voice. "After what he tried to pull?" He paused for a few seconds. He knew Samovich's political scheming was moving at full speed. But this was more than politics. It was life and death. And that was Alexi Drogov's game. "Anton, it's too dangerous to leave him alive. What if he tries again?"

"That's a risk, Alexi, but one I think is manageable. My security has been tripled, and Li has to lay low for a while. He's already suspect, and he can't risk getting tied to another assassination attempt." Samovich sat on a small chair next to the bed. "No, we'll take him out if we don't have a choice, but only if we have no other options. What I really want you to do is try to get me some proof he was behind this attempt. If you manage that, he's done. I'll have a Secretariat Order for his execution in a day. And that will be the end of Mr. Li."

"I'm not a detective, Anton. You know what I do, what I'm good at."

"I know indeed. And don't underestimate the value of your skills. You can grab as many of his people as you want, roast them on spits if it helps. Just leave Li himself alone. Every eye on the Secretariat is looking my way, waiting for a revenge attempt. But they're not going to see one. I'm going to turn this back on that piece of shit…and I'll lock up the votes I need to succeed Esteban." A wicked smile crossed his lips. "And then we'll escort Mr. Li to a shallow grave somewhere."

Drogov nodded. He always enjoyed watching Samovich think. His friend had a master politician's mind; he was a manipulator without compare. But Drogov had the expertise in understanding threats, and he knew if he was Chang Li, he'd try again. As soon as possible. The Secretariat might dislike attempts on its members' lives, but that didn't mean they were immune from fear. If Li managed to get rid of Samovich, Drogov didn't doubt he'd quickly seize total control, and no one would dare challenge him on anything. They might whisper in the shadows, but they wouldn't do anything. If his friend had a weakness, it was giving his colleagues credit for more intellect and courage than they possessed. Drogov knew Samovich and Li were the only two on the Secretariat with any real balls, other than Esteban. And the present Secretary-General was a dead man walking, no longer a factor in the struggle that had begun for the succession.

Drogov pulled himself up higher on the pillows, wincing at the pain the motion caused. "That all sounds good, old friend." He paused, taking a deep breath as he fixed his gaze on Samovich. "As long as he doesn't manage to take you out before we get it done." He figured the odds on that were a coin toss.

Chapter 17

From the Journal of Jake Taylor:

My army is being destroyed. The battle we fight is one to the death, against an enemy well-equipped to face us. The easy victories are a thing of the past, and my soldiers die now...they die in the thousands.

I knew when this crusade began that we faced an almost impossibly difficult road, that few of those who followed me would survive the journey. Nothing happening on this field of battle should be a surprise to me, yet it always is. There are some horrors you cannot prepare yourself to endure, some nightmares that shock and scar your soul no matter how much you expected them.

But there is no choice, no alternative I can embrace. I am the only one who knows the doom of which T'arza spoke, and I will shoulder that burden myself for now. But UNGov must be destroyed and Earth united to face another challenge, the Darkness that is coming from the depths of space.

I must get my people back home, back to Earth. But I cannot leave live enemies behind me. I will not. I must find a way to end this battle, to destroy our adversaries before they do the same to us.

The black, moonless sky was lit every few seconds by blinding flashes, as the battle continued unabated deep into the night. The ferocity of the fighting hadn't ebbed, not a bit. If anything, darkness had brought an increase in intensity as both sides, exhausted and bled white, threw in their last reserves, hoping to maintain their effort, to outlast the enemy.

The ridgeline in the distance was alive with explosions and the sounds of war. The two sides had been fighting since dawn, when Taylor's army launched an all-out attack on the main enemy positions. The front was vast, over 20 kilometers, and battle raged over every centimeter of that bloodsoaked ground. But the ridge was the key. If the enemy held on, the attack would falter. If it fell, Taylor's troops would break through into open country and have a chance at victory.

"Get your battalion forward now, Sanchez." Tony Black shouted into the com, his voice barely audible over the din of battle. He was exhausted and wracked with stress, and his urban Philly accent was thick as he barked out commands. "You are to reinforce and support Major Young's forces." Young's men were advancing steadily, but Black knew their losses had been brutal. They'd need reinforcements to keep their forward momentum, and Sanchez's group was all he had left to give them.

"Yes, sir." Sanchez's reply was crisp, immediate. His people were still fresh, the last of the uncommitted veterans from Erastus. Now the army's reserve was down to a few battalions of unmodified soldiers, formations assembled from the men who'd responded to Taylor's recruiting on the other worlds. Black knew they were good soldiers, but they were unmodified, and he couldn't have the same confidence in them he did in men who'd fought on the burning sands of Erastus. Black knew, almost better than anyone, just what it meant to be a veteran of Gehenna.

He stared out over the darkened plain, at the grim silhouette of wrecked vehicles and abandoned weapons. He could see the devastation in the flickering light of the fires, the shattered and pockmarked ground where the Army of Liberation had been fighting a horrific battle of annihilation for almost 18 hours without a pause. Soldiers were battling on that line, low on ammunition, with empty water bottles and parched throats. He knew the men of the army, and he was sure there were hundreds still fighting with wounds that should have sent them to a field hospital. One thing he knew for sure – if the battle was lost, it would not be for lack of good men giving all they had.

Taylor had surprised him with the orders for the attack. Black didn't understand what had gotten into his friend. He knew as well as Taylor that time wasn't on their side in this fight. The enemy would only grow stronger and they weaker and lower on supplies. But Taylor was possessed now, insistent the attack continue without stop until the enemy forces on Juno were completely destroyed. He kept pushing more forces forward, driving his men past the breaking point. Black had tried to talk to him, but he'd gotten nowhere. Taylor had been adamant. The battle would continue without pause until the enemy was defeated.

Black watched as Sanchez's soldiers began to file past his position. Young's people were about four klicks forward, assaulting the fortified enemy positions on the ridge. Black didn't like releasing his last real reserve force, but he couldn't see how Young's 1,300 troops – how any 1,300 men – could take that position. And smashing through on that sector was crucially important. A breakthrough there would open up the battlefield and get some maneuver back into the operation. Black knew there was no way they were going to win the battle charging fortifications nonstop. Maybe, just maybe, if they could punch through on a wide enough frontage, they might break the stalemate and gain the upper hand.

"And then what?" he whispered grimly to himself. The enemy will just fall back to another position, he thought. Yes, they would take heavy losses in the retreat, but they could afford the casualties, and they could always get more reinforcements from Earth. Black was well aware that the men Taylor had brought to Juno were all he had, all he could get. Every casualty was irreplaceable. They were pushing forward, driving the enemy back, meter by meter. But they were losing too many men in the process.

"Too many," Black whispered to himself, watching the last of Sanchez's people jog by.

*   *   *   *   *

"You outnumber the enemy 2-1, and they are attacking your prepared positions." Keita was angry, and it was apparent in his tone. "Yet your forces keep yielding ground, General." Keita stared at Ralfieri, his eyes ablaze. The political disasters of the past year had tempered some of Keita's arrogance, but now he was on Juno, the only member of the Secretariat on the entire planet. Far away from his political rivals and clearly the highest ranked individual present, his pride and ego were waxing once again. He spoke to Ralfieri, veteran commander of two victorious Portal world campaigns, almost as if issuing commands to a servant.

Ralfieri bit back on his anger, trying to ignore the heat building around his neck. He wanted to grab the loud-mouthed politician by the throat and choke the life out of him. But he'd served too long to allow himself to give in to such desires. He understood the arrogance of politicians, and he also realized it was they – not the soldiers, not the citizens – who truly held power. Dealing with them was a necessary evil, and he was too seasoned a veteran to let his temper lead him into an argument with a member of the Secretariat.

"But, Secretary Keita, the situation is far more complex than that." Ralfieri paused. He, too, was shocked at the fighting ability of Taylor's men. The Supersoldiers of the Black Corps were the physical equivalent of their adversaries, but Taylor and his warriors had been forged on Erastus. Throughout all the Portal worlds, the name Erastus had been synonymous with hell itself. On a dozen planets, grim warriors prodded each other with sayings like, "At least we're not on Erastus." But for all the token acknowledgements of the brutal conditions faced by the soldiers who'd actually been sent there to fight, Ralfieri hadn't realized just how hard and grim those veterans had become. Until now.

"No excuses, General. You have numbers, better supply and, currently, the advantage of defending." Keita was motivated by more than self-entitled arrogance. There was fear too, the dread of what would become of him if the battle on Juno was lost…or even won too late. He was on shaky ground already on the Secretariat, and he knew he'd never survive if his sponsor lost his long power struggle with Chang Li. Indeed, if Keita returned from a defeat on Juno, he had no doubt Samovich himself would have him killed, before Li even got the chance.

"Secretary, these soldiers we are fighting are veterans of the harshest place men have ever fought. Even my Black Corps troops cannot match them evenly." Ralfieri's voice was becoming softer. He knew he wasn't getting through to Keita, and he was starting to give up the effort. "It is more than just the experience of Erastus. They fight with a spirit I cannot explain. They have a motivation, some kind of inner fire than drives them to push beyond normal human endurance."

Ralfieri was grasping at an understanding of what truly drove Taylor's men. Belief in a cause was something that had largely vanished from human culture. The war against the Tegeri was driven by fear, not by inspiration. The feelings of patriotism and pride soldiers had felt in some of the old nation states had been largely forgotten in the decades of UNGov rule – and the idea of men sworn to fight tyranny had been lost utterly, brutally eradicated by years of reeducation camps and terroristic internal security.

"Nonsense excuses, General. Yes, these men were hardened by their years on Erastus, but your soldiers are veterans also. Your numerical and supply advantages should be more than sufficient to counter whatever X factor you assign to service on Erastus."

Ralfieri was just beginning to comprehend what his forces were facing, but he knew Keita was beyond understanding any of it. The politician was a creature of the system, and he would never be able to rationalize that there was more to success on the battlefield than numbers and equipment. Keita knew only the UNGov way, that of self-serving expediency, of constant politics and maneuvering for personal power. He was ill-equipped to understand what drove fighting men, the sense of brotherhood that gave veterans their true strength. The spirit and camaraderie that made men rush back into the killing zone they had just escaped to carry a wounded comrade back to safety.

Anan Keita could never comprehend what made Taylor's soldiers so formidable. But Antonio Ralfieri was beginning to see…and he started to wonder if his people were fighting on the right side.

*   *   *   *   *

Aaron Jamison crept forward, holding his assault rifle at the ready. It was dark, the battlefield lit only by explosions and fire. Jamison's mechanical eyes adjusted to the low light levels, and he was able to see well enough to get around. He kept reminding himself the enemy had the same ability. Jamison and his people had fought in all of Taylor's battles, but they hadn't faced a foe with their own capabilities until Juno.

He heard a gunship approaching. His enhanced ears picked it up kilometers away, but it sounded like it was heading his way. It was coming from behind, which probably meant it was one of theirs. But not definitely.

"On your guard, boys." Jamison spoke with a heavy Irish accent, but his men were used to it, and he knew they all understood what he was saying. "Airship incoming." There was no way to know for sure if the aircraft was friendly or not, and if there was any chance the enemy was about to drop a batch of FAEs on his position, he wanted his men ready.

He looked ahead, but it was still quiet. The enemy had pulled back on this section of front. There was no knowing how far, or where they would stop and form another defensive line. For all he knew, they could be hiding just over the hill he was climbing, waiting on the reverse slope to ambush his men. The scouting reports from the drones had come pretty frequently earlier in the battle, but now they'd slowed to a crawl. He knew the captain had requested a flight three times, but the high command had to conserve its supply of the recon devices. And that meant Jamison had no idea what was waiting over that hillside. That's where I'd be if I was them, he thought warily.

"Conover, Gupta...scout forward and check out the downslope of this ridge." Gupta was the platoon's scout, and Conover was its most experienced enlisted man.

"Yes, Lieutenant." The two replied almost simultaneously.

Jamison turned again, looking at the sky behind him. The sounds of the gunship were louder. Indeed, now it sounded like at least two craft incoming.

He flipped his com to the platoon frequency. "I want everybody to take cover now." He wasn't taking a chance of his people getting caught out in the open by an air attack. He still figured the gunships were friendlies, but he'd started to doubt his judgment when there was still no contact.

Just then his com crackled to life. "AOL ground units, this is Red Squadron Leader inbound. You are instructed to take cover. We are bombing enemy units 600 meters forward of your position." Jamison still wasn't used to the Army of Liberation designation, but he sighed with relief that the birds were friendlies.

So there are enemy troops over that hillside, he thought. "Everybody down. We've got FAEs coming in just over the ridge." Six hundred meters was close, very close.

Fuck, Jamison thought an instant later. "Gupta, Conover, return to your former positions immediately." On the unitwide com: "Repeat...everybody get down. We've got friendly air about to bomb enemy positions on the other side of the hill."

He jogged toward a small crater and jumped into it. "Gupta, Conover," he repeated, the urgency in his voice increasing.

He heard the gunships streaking across the sky, coming in low. It sounded like they were just over his head, but he knew they'd be at least 100 meters up.

"Order received, Lieutenant. We're on the way..." It was Conover, and his report stopped abruptly, just as the top of the hillside erupted into billowing flames.

Jamison dove down into the crater, shouting into his com as he did. "Gupta? Conover? Respond!"

He felt the wave of heat surging down from the hillside, and he tried to imagine the inferno raging just over the crest. The whole area was as bright as day for half a minute before the roiling flames began to subside, and darkness slowly crept back over the field.

Jamison was still crouched in his crater, shouting madly into his com. "Gupta? Conover? Respond!" But there was no reply, nothing but the static.

*   *   *   *   *

"Charge!" Bear Samuels' shout ripped through the com lines and, as one, 975 enhanced soldiers leapt over a small rise and ran toward the enemy position half a klick away. The enemy was withdrawing, retreating from the ridge they'd held for the past 6 hours. Samuels was determined to hit them hard before they got away. He was as uncomfortable as ever with the killing, but he knew the only way to end the fighting was total victory. Taylor's actions and orders were clear. The fight would continue without a stop until the battle was won. And anyone Samuels let escape here would only come back to fight his men later. Mercy now would only condemn more of his own men.

He ran across the field, leading the charge himself. He and his Supersoldiers would cover the distance in less than a minute, and then they'd have a clear field of fire on the flee-ing enemy troops. If his people stayed close, if they exacted a heavy enough toll, maybe they could extend the breakthrough and bring this nightmare of a battle closer to an end.

The enemy fire was light and sporadic. Most of the defend-ers had already fled, many of them dropping their weapons as they ran for their lives. Samuels pushed himself, running as hard as his enhanced muscles could manage, and he bounded over the top, firing as he did. There were enemy soldiers all across the plain ahead, fleeing. It was a wholesale rout, and when Sam-uels stopped to look around, he understood what had finally broken these Supersoldiers. The entire ridge was blackened, the result of repeated FAE attacks. The AOL gunships had pounded this position, dropping load after load of fiery death on the defenders.

The airmen had paid heavily to punch this hole for Samuels' people. He could see the wreckage of at least four of the giant airships, blackened smoldering hulks lying silently on the great plain. It didn't take more than one look for Samuels to realize that none of the crews had made it out of those birds. They had paid a heavy price, and he'd be damned if he'd allow that sacrifice to be in vain.

"Pursue, men. Pursue and maintain fire." He reached around and pulled a fresh clip from his belt, ejecting the spent cartridge as he did. "Let's go, boys. Forward to victory!" He slammed the clip in place and ran down onto the plain, gunning down the fleeing enemy as he did. He knew he'd hate himself later, recount all the helpless, fleeing men he'd massacred. But there was no time for that now. Bear Samuels had a gentle soul, one the soldier side of him caused constant torment. But nothing was stronger to him than loyalty. Loyalty to these men he led…and to Jake Taylor. "Let's go, boys. Pour it into them!"

*   *   *   *   *

"Jake, this is insane. We're pushing the men forward without a break, without a chance to regroup. Even the enhanced troops are becoming exhausted." Black was upset. He'd been holding his tongue, but the dam had broken, and it was all pouring out. "Friendly fire incidents are up 350%." He stared at Taylor as he spoke, his hands clenched in frustration. "We're so disorganized and tired, we're gunning down our own men."

Taylor stood quietly, impassively, listening to his friend's protests. Finally, he just said, "Blackie, we've got no choice. We need to destroy the enemy, and we need to do it now."

"I'm not saying not to attack, but I don't understand this sudden urgency. We're sending in FAE strikes as quickly as we can turn the surviving birds around. The crews are exhausted. It's so rushed, we're not even getting notice to ground units of incoming strikes." Black paused. "Does it make you happy that we're incinerating our own men in some of these attacks?" Black was immediately sorry for the last comment, wishing he could take it back. He disagreed with Taylor's orders, but he didn't for a second think his friend didn't ache for all the soldiers he lost.

"Colonel Black, I am sorry you don't agree with my tactical judgment." Taylor's voice was cold, unemotional. It was taking all his strength of will to keep it that way. He was mourning every one of his men who'd been lost. Every one. But there was no place for that now, no time to indulge emotions. Not after what T'arza had told him. "However, my orders stand. We will not let up the pressure on the enemy no matter what. All units are to continue to attack, and they will do so until we have utterly destroyed the UNGov forces on Juno." He paused an instant, his mechanical eyes staring into Black's. "Is that understood, Colonel Black?"

Black hesitated for an instant, returning Taylor's hard gaze. "Yes, sir," he finally snapped out, his voice hard and brittle.

"Then I suspect you have work to do, Colonel." Taylor struggled to keep his voice firm. "Dismissed."

Black raised his hand in a perfect salute and spun around on his heels. Taylor watched the man who had been his closest companion through the years on Erastus as he walked crisply from the room, and he tried to imagine what was going through his friend's mind. It tore at Taylor's insides not to confide in Black, not to tell him all he'd discussed with T'arza. But he had resolved not to burden Black or any of his officers, with the terrible truth. All men had a breaking point. Taking on UNGov, resolving to free Earth from tyranny – that was enough for any man to bear. How could he tell them their sworn mission, as impossible a task as it appeared to be, was just the beginning? That if they somehow managed to liberate Earth, they would have to rally humanity to face another, graver threat.

Taylor wanted to tell Black, he wanted to share the burden with his friend. But he'd decided this load was his and his alone, and he was determined to stand by that. His men faced enough hardship and loss, and he wasn't going to add to it. If they survived, if they managed to free Earth…then he would tell them. But not before.

Chapter 18

From the Journal of Jake Taylor:

How much can one man bear? How much pain and anguish? How much guilt? I watch my soldiers suffer and die, faithfully following my orders. I see the survivors drive themselves forward, through hunger and exhaustion, enduring unimaginable suffering, and all I do is push them ever harder. I watch my officers, my friends, look at me as if I'm some kind of monster, a cold-blooded killer with no soul.

It is one thing to swear to a quest, to acknowledge the pain and suffering it will inflict on those involved. It is another to actually live it, to force yourself to take each bloody, exhausting step. I sit alone in the darkness, feeling lost, hopeless. Then the rage comes, the self-hatred for wallowing in such self-indulgence. Do my soldiers suffer less than I, fighting against overwhelming odds, bleeding to death on the cold ground of an alien world? Is the sacrifice of a private, dead on the field, never to see another sunrise or feel the embrace of a friend, less than my own?

How dare I feel sorry for myself or shrink from the responsibilities I have undertaken? Let my friends hate me, let my soldiers feel I have forsaken them if that is what must be. For I do what I do for them, and for the oppressed millions on Earth. If I must become a pariah, hated and feared, then so be it. But giving up, running from my responsibilities, that would be the ultimate betrayal. And that is something I cannot do. Not ever.

"Stand fast. You've got 30 minutes, boys, so try and get a breather and something to eat." Jamison crouched behind the shattered tree, now little more than a charred stump, shouldering his rifle as he addressed his men. He'd had his weapon set on semi-auto during the last firefight, trying to conserve ammunition. They'd gotten one batch of supplies since the battle began, but that had been late on the first day. It was day three now, and they'd seen nothing since. If he hadn't ordered his men to start stripping the enemy dead, they'd be throwing rocks by now.

His original platoon was down to half strength, but he was commanding the whole company now. Captain Wallace had been caught out in the open during a gunship attack. Jamison had been watching as he raced toward a crater, looking for a place to take cover. He never made it. Jamison was staring right at him just as he disappeared into a mass of billowing fire. He ran over after the firestorm subsided, frantically looking for his CO. But there was nothing. No body, no remains. Nothing.

He didn't have time to mourn Wallace. The company had lost its leader, and he was the senior lieutenant. He took over immediately, reorganizing a battered force that had been hit hard by the enemy air assault. A few minutes after he started barking out orders on his own initiative, Major Young's voice blared through his com and made it official. The company was his.

He looked around at the blackened and ravaged ground his people had fought over for the last six hours. They'd advanced a little more than ten kilometers in three days. Ten klicks of broken, tortured hills and blackened, lifeless plains. Not a tree stood unscorched over that ten kilometers, nor a blade of grass. Just the savaged, blood-soaked ground. And the unburied dead.

Half his men. That was the price of ten kilometers. And he knew other units had suffered even more heavily. Jamison had served in the brutal, burning hell of Erastus, but he'd never seen combat as intense as that of the past three days. He was exhausted, having trouble focusing, staying sharp. He knew the nanotechnology inside him was producing adrenalin and flooding his bloodstream with amphetamines, but it wasn't enough to stave off the crushing fatigue. He wondered what was keeping the non-modified troopers on their feet.

He glanced at his chronometer, though it was a pointless exercise. The NIS in his head kept perfect time, and it was available to him with just a thought. Thirty minutes. That's how long a rest his people had drawn. Now they had less than 20 minutes of that left. Then they'd be back on the line.

"Eat up, boys." He spoke loudly into the com. "We're moving out soon." He kept his voice upbeat for the benefit of the men. They didn't need to hear his own exhaustion. Jamison had served under Taylor for years, through many battles against the Machines on Erastus. He'd been one of the first to rally to the general after he'd returned from his encounter with the Tegeri. He'd never doubted Taylor, not for an instant. Not until now. He couldn't understand why Taylor was pushing his soldiers brutally forward, without rest, without adequate supplies or provisions. A last ditch defense, he would understand. But they were attacking. Why weren't they pausing to regroup, to bring supplies forward? How long did Taylor think his men could continue to fight with no rest, no hot food, stripping the dead for ammunition and half-empty water bottles?

Jamison realized he hadn't eaten anything himself since the day before. He pulled a nutrition bar from his sack and tore open the wrapper. He knew he should be starving, but he wasn't. Fatigue was overcoming hunger. Still, he needed all the energy his aching body could get. He took a bite and washed it down with a deep drink from his canteen.

He looked around at the men of his company. They were exhausted, caked in filth, many of their faces blackened with soot from the fires and FAEs. Some of them had minor wounds. There were battered men sitting all across the plain, torn sections of shirts and jackets serving as makeshift bandages, now bloodstained and tied haphazardly around injured arms and legs. But they remained in the line, ready to move as soon as the orders came. Jamison felt proud to lead such men.

There was something in his mind other than the pride, something darker. He thought of the men who should be sitting out there with their comrades, soldiers who now lay dead across the ten kilometers of bloody battlefield behind them. Broken men in the field hospitals, struggling to survive their grievous wounds. What a waste, he thought, what a pointless sacrifice of good men. Is this how it has always been? How it always will be?

He tried to understand the sequence of events that brought him to this battlefield. The lies, the great fraud that sent him to an alien world not to defend mankind against a bloodthirsty alien enemy, but to provide propaganda to allow a worldwide coup to succeed. To put a cabal of evil men in total control of the human race. And now he and his brethren were fighting other men like them, misinformed conscripts of the totalitarian regime that ruled the world.

My God, he thought grimly, we are wretched creatures, men.

*   *   *   *   *

"You must counterattack now, General." Keita was furious, waving his arms wildly as he shouted at Ralfieri. The two were alone in Keita's makeshift office, and the politician had lost all restraint. He was unnerved by the ferocity of Taylor's attack, of the gains his troops had made, and he was terrified that news would reach Samovich and the Secretariat. "We have been pushed back all across the line. Ten kilometers. Your pathetic soldiers have turned tail and run ten kilometers from an enemy with less than half their strength. It must stop. It must stop now. You will order an attack, General. At once."

Ralfieri was sick of Keita's non-stop, mindless pressure. The politician had no idea of the realities of combat, no understanding of what his men had endured over the past several days. He was tempted to drag Keita out to the front, to show him the battered remnants of units that had lost half their strength or more, the field hospitals overflowing with shattered men. Maybe then, he thought, the pompous ass would stop using words like pathetic to describe the soldiers fighting and dying for him. But probably not. Politicians like Keita considered the men who fought for them to be tools, nothing more.

"Secretary, with all due respect, my forces are in no condition to attack. We've lost over 10,000 men in the last three days, more than half of them from the Black Corps. The rest of my forces are exhausted and demoralized." Ralfieri's own self-control was wavering. Fatigue was wearing down his ability to deal with Keita and his constant harangues. "We are in no condition to go on the offensive right now."

"And what condition do you suppose Taylor's forces are in after their constant attacks? Have they not suffered losses too? Are their men not tired and worn down by the fighting?" Keita didn't know a thing about combat, but he spoke with the arrogance of an expert on the subject.

"Of course they are tired too, Secretary. And low on supplies. But they have momentum. It is a wiser strategy to withdraw slowly, to allow them to expend the last of their strength and ordnance. When their attack has finally exhausted itself, when they have no energy left to continue to advance and they have used up their supplies…that is the time for a counterattack." Ralfieri knew from Keita's expression his argument wasn't getting anywhere, but he wasn't finished trying. Not yet. "I don't know why they are attacking so aggressively, Secretary. It seems to me they are taking unnecessary chances. But we will do them a favor if we attack now."

"Nonsense, General." Keita's voice dripped with arrogance. "Your timidity does not serve you well. You are to launch a counter-attack across the line. It is time to end this battle, to destroy this outlaw and his rebels. Now."

"Secretary, most of our units in the line are disordered. They need time to reorganize and resupply." Ralfieri couldn't imagine the confused mess if he ordered all the retreating units to turn and attack. He wasn't even sure how many of them would – could – obey such a command. And the only reserves were…

"Then commit your reserves, General. At once."

"Secretary, those troops are protecting our lines of supply. If we commit them and the enemy gets around our flank, they could cut us off from the Portal." Raflieri's stomach was clenched into a knot. He knew Keita wasn't listening.

"That will not happen, General, because our attack will destroy the enemy utterly." Keita's face turned down to look at the tablet on his desk. "You have your orders, General. That will be all."

*   *   *   *   *

"Lieutenant, we've got a large body of enemy troops heading toward us, company strength at least." Sergeant Brand's voice was calm and professional as always, but Jamison could sense the concern the veteran was hiding. Brand's platoon was out on point, about a klick forward of the rest of the company.

Jamison turned instinctively to look toward their position. His people had advanced through the remains of a section of woods. There wasn't much left of the forest, just a few charred and splintered trunks still standing, but there was a small hill beyond, and Brand's people were on the other side of it.

"Pull back to the hill and form a defensive line. I'll bring the rest of the company up."

"Yes, sir."

"Fuck," Jamison whispered under his breath as he cut the connection. "What the hell is going on?" The last thing he expected was a counter-attack, even a localized one. As battered as his forces were, the enemy was even worse off. His people had been doing nothing for the last day but chasing routing and withdrawing enemy formations.

He felt a flash of anger over the lack of drone reconnaissance. He understood the army's logistical limitations, at least in theory. But when his men almost ran into a major enemy force with no warning, frustration overwhelmed understanding. He knew General Taylor couldn't launch drones he didn't have, but that didn't stop Jamison from feeling anger and resentment.

He flipped on the companywide frequency. "Company C, we are moving forward to the hilltop, now. Prepare for action." He'd thought his men were finally going to get some time to rest, maybe even time to eat a hot meal. But it didn't look like it was in the cards. "Move out."

He jogged forward slowly, reminding himself as always just how fast and high his enhanced leg muscles could propel his body. He was about halfway to the hill when all hell erupted.

"Lieutenant, we've got at least two companies attacking, and it looks like they've got a second line coming up." Brand's cool demeanor was gone, replaced by the hurried report of a combat commander in the heat of battle. The sounds of gunfire and explosions were almost drowning out his words.

"Find the best ground you can and hold out, Danny. I'm bringing the rest of the company up to your position now." Jamison flipped the com back to the company line. "Let's move it, people. We've got enemy coming in just beyond the hill."

Jamison ran up the slope, diving to the ground as he reached the crest. Brand's men were already there, at least the ones who'd made it back up the hillside. At least ten of them were dead on the slope below.

"Open fire, everyone." It was a superfluous order – most of the company was already firing on full auto. They'd seen the same thing Jamison did. Hundreds of enemy soldiers, racing across the plain and up the hill, right at their position, firing up at them as they came on.

Jamison crawled toward a large rock, a spot that offered decent cover and a good vantage point for shooting. He stared out at the approaching enemy forces, firing at those closest to the hill. The field was already covered with dead. Brand's men had made their fire count. But there were hundreds of fresh troops behind those in the front, and more moving up in the distance.

"Keep firing, boys," Jamison yelled in his thick Irish accent. "They're not taking this hill. No fucking way." His voice was confidence itself, but his mind was full of doubts.

*   *   *   *   *

"Jake, we've got enemy counter-attacks coming in all across the line." Black was tense and out of breath as he rushed into the headquarters tent. "They're hitting us in strength everywhere."

Taylor looked up from his makeshift desk. "I'm monitoring the company commander reports now. They must be committing the last of their reserves."

"I'll issue the orders to pull back. We can retreat to Grayhill Ridge." Black walked over to the desk and held out the tablet he was carrying so Taylor could see the map it displayed. "We can build a strong position there and…"

"No." Taylor's voice was like iron. "We're not falling back. Not a centimeter." Taylor stared at Black, his mechanical eyes focused on his second in command. "We'll fight it out on the current line."

Black stared back at Taylor, his mouth open in surprise. "But, Jake," he finally said, "we've been pursuing the enemy as they withdrew. Our forces are strung out all across the battlefield, disordered and low on supplies. If we regroup…"

"No." Taylor slid back his chair and stood up. "Our goal is to destroy the enemy army. Falling back will only give them time to reorganize their own shattered units. A pause will make them stronger, not weaker. We'll shake out some disorder, nothing else. They'll get reinforcements and supplies through the Portal. We'll get nothing." There was no emotion in Taylor's voice, none at all. "We must maintain the pressure until they surrender…or until they are destroyed."

Black stood stone still for a moment, looking at Taylor wordlessly. Finally, he said, "Have you completely forgotten what's it's like for the men out there, Jake?" He tried to stop, to hold his tongue, but once he started, it all burst out. "Whatever cold, inhuman logic you've got rattling around in your head, remember we're still talking about men out there, human beings. Your men. Those boys have been fighting nonstop for over a week. We've got units up there at 25% strength, and still they're pushing forward." Black's voice was hoarse, angry. "Don't you care about the men anymore, Jake? Don't you give a shit how much they suffer? How many of them die?"

Taylor felt each of Black's words like a knife cutting into him, and the pain welled up inside. But he maintained his emotionless façade, his grim countenance. He was determined to keep what T'arza had told him from Black and the rest of his men. That was a burden Jake would bear himself. If Black and the others blamed him so be it, but they didn't need the distraction and demoralization the truth would cause them. Telling them would only put them at greater risk, take their minds off the current battle. And they were in a fight to the death already.

"I'm sorry you feel that way, Colonel." Taylor was struggling to hide his emotions. "I thought you understood that the crusade itself was more important than any of our lives, than all of our lives." He stared coldly at Black, every bit of his will struggling to maintain his determined façade. "Nevertheless, despite your personal feelings, I expect you to obey my orders to the letter. Is that understood?"

Black looked back at Taylor, and his gaze hardened. "Yes sir, General." He turned and walked toward the exit. He pushed open the small door and stopped. "I had a friend once, closer than a brother."

He paused for a few seconds then continued without turning around. "My friend was named Jake Taylor, and he bled inside for every man he lost. He agonized over every plan, struggled to save as many of his soldiers as possible."

Black finally turned, looking over his shoulder as he went on. "But my friend is dead, gone. And all that is left in his place is a cold-blooded butcher, deaf to the cries of his soldiers." Black turned and stepped through the door before Taylor could respond.

Taylor walked over and closed the still-open door. Then he sat down and put his face in his hands and sighed. Black's angry words had hit him like spears, slicing into him, tearing at his soul. He wanted to chase his friend, to tell him why he was pushing everyone so relentlessly. But he just sat there.

He'd known from the start the Crusade would take all he had, every last bit of his endurance, but now he was beginning to doubt his strength, his ability to do what had to be done. It was too much, too heavy a load for any man to carry. But still, he had to try, he had to find a way to go on. And he would.

Later. For a moment he just sat there, replaying Black's words again and again in his head.

Chapter 19

From the Tegeri Chronicles:

The Ancients left us more than the Portals, more than the ability to explore the worlds of the galaxy. They left us all they had taught us, the wisdom they shared with our ancestors. They left us also a great responsibility. For we and the humans are not alone, not unique. The Portals lead to thousands of worlds, and upon many of these, far away, lie the seeds the Ancients planted.

The Other Races are younger than we, than the humans. They still reach toward true sentience, striving to take the first steps toward civilization. Primitive and helpless, their survival is in our hands, for the Darkness will not repeat its error and allow the lesser races to survive as they did millennia ago.

We Tegeri know our race is slowly dying, that we will one day follow the Ancients into the next plane of existence. But first we must rally to face the Darkness, to answer the Ancients' charge to us to stand in their place, alongside our human brothers, to protect the younger races, those who have not yet come of age.

To fail those we regarded as mentors, as fathers, would be a great dishonor. The coming struggle will determine if the Tegeri race departs this universe slowly, gracefully, having honorably defended those destined to come after us or if we are destroyed quickly, in failure and disgrace everlasting.

"I have returned from Juno to address this Council." T'arza stood at the ancient table, speaking to the other elders of the Tegeri. "Taylor and his army are engaged in a massive battle with the forces of the Earth government. Both sides are suffering enormous losses, yet the struggle continues. If we do nothing, Taylor's force will be destroyed, or they will be too battered to meaningfully challenge the authorities on Earth. His quest will fail, even if he is ultimately victorious on Juno."

The First nodded. "Indeed, T'arza, I believe all gathered here understand the situation. Yet, as before, I see no meaningful way we can assist Taylor without doing more harm than good." The First gazed at T'arza with ancient eyes. "Have you any actions to propose that we have not previously considered?"

"Yes, Honored First. I would not waste the time of this Council if I did not." T'arza looked down the table, at the heads of each of the great houses of the Tegeri. "You are all aware that I feel the Kzarn'ta to the human Taylor, for though I acted at the direction of this body, I was the instrument by which his current path was chosen. Yet, all here have known me for many an age. Never would I seek to influence the Council's wisdom simply to alleviate my own dishonor."

T'arza paused and turned his gaze back to the First. "I believe there is a way we can assist Taylor without damaging his quest." He stood at the table, his gray robes hanging loosely about him.

The First nodded. "Please, T'arza, share your reasoning with the Council, for all here are united in our hope that Taylor succeeds in his quest and we are able to renew our brotherhood with the humans."

T'arza returned the First's nod. "My thanks, Honored First. I shall." He paused and inhaled deeply. "The human government is supplying their forces and sending reinforcements to Juno through the Portal from the world they call Oceania. The struggle on that planet continues, though our forces have been retreating for several years, yielding territory to the humans."

T'arza glanced down the table again and then back to the First. "I propose that we commit additional resources to Oceania and launch a major offensive there, with the goal of materially interdicting the human supply line between Juno and Earth. Such an action will not appear to be directly connected to Taylor, yet if we are able to slow or eliminate the flow of supplies and reserves to his opponents, we will substantially increase his chances of victory."

T'arza looked at the First, awaiting his reaction. But a voice came first from down the table, from C'tar, the ancient Grandmaster of the Seminary. The spiritual leader of the Tegeri spoke softly, but there was certainty and assurance to his words. "T'arza's plan is wise." C'tar stood at the far end of the table opposite the First, clad in the unadorned robes of a teacher. He looked down the table at his fellow elders. "It is a way we may aide the human Taylor and his soldiers while remaining, to all appearances, uninvolved in their conflict."

All eyes were on C'tar. He had surprised the Council at the last meeting with his proposal to destroy the humans if Taylor's crusade failed, and now, once again, he was taking an unexpected position.

"All here know that I proposed the destruction of Earth if Taylor failed in his mission. Such a course of action would be a horrendous crime, a stain on the honor of our race for all time. Yet to allow the war with the humans to distract us, to meet the Darkness with less than the total force we can muster, would be an even worse offense. For we stand against this nemesis of the Ancients not only for our race, but for the many others only now struggling to attain sentience and to move down the path toward civilization. The Darkness overlooked us ages ago, when we were a young and primitive race and the Ancients shielded us. They will not make such a mistake again. If we fall, so too do all those races, children of the Ancients as are we, and in all the galaxy there will be naught but the silence of death."

C'tar nodded slowly, and he held up his ancient and withered hands to the Council, a gesture of sincerity. "Such is my counsel."

The cavern was silent, everyone present slowing turning their gaze from the Grandmaster of the Seminary toward the First, awaiting the word of the eldest and most senior of the Tegeri.

"I thank you for your words, C'tar, on behalf of this Council. Your wisdom, as always, lights our path." The First was the closest thing the non-hierarchal Tegeri had to a head of state, but the Grandmaster of the Seminary was considered the wisest of his race, one whose entire life had been devoted to study and contemplation. The First bowed slightly toward C'tar, followed by each member of the Council in turn.

"C'tar's wisdom, as always, offers us a lantern to guide our way." The First looked out over the assembled Council. "T'arza has proposed a course of action to this body, one the Grandmaster of the Seminary has endorsed." He paused, his ancient, hazy eyes staring out at his colleagues. "I, too, support T'arza's plan. Such action would be warranted, if only to reduce the chance that we might be compelled to destroy the humans. This Council has already approved such an action as a last resort, but any effort that may allow us to avoid such a travesty is worthy.

"Yet there is more reason still for us to take such action. For our hope of defeating the Darkness rests heavily on meeting the enemy with the humans at our side. It is clear to see that they are more suited to conflict and war than we, that their very nature gives them an advantage in battle. Indeed, I begin to see and understand the designs of the Ancients, how our two races, so similar and yet so different, were groomed to stand together to face and defeat an enemy the Ancients knew they themselves could not.

"Yet for all their wisdom, the Ancient were not omniscient. For I venture they did not anticipate the human susceptibility to suggestion, their propensity to follow unworthy leaders and support evil causes. Indeed, when the Ancients were destroyed, the men of Earth still roamed in small bands, hunting with sharpened sticks. If it is possible to save them, to bring them to stand with us in the final confrontation as the Ancients intended, we must make every effort available to us. We cannot intervene directly, for reasons well debated on this Council. Yet here is a chance to aid the human Taylor and his followers without direct involvement in their battle. It may indeed be our only way to aid him. Our effort may yet be in vain, but I feel that we must, at least, try."

The First was silent, allowing any who dissented to speak. He moved his gaze around the table, pausing to focus at each of the elders. There was not a sound, not an objection. Just a series of slow nods as the First's eyes fell on each Tegeri.

"It is decided then." The First looked toward T'arza. "We will dispatch a large force of New Ones to the planet the humans call Oceania, and they will launch an offensive designed to interdict the human supply lines leading from Juno to Earth. We will do nothing to arouse undue suspicion of collusion between our forces and Taylor's. Indeed, we will not even disclose our efforts to the general. The New Ones sent to Oceania will be armed and equipped in exactly the same manner as our forces already deployed there and on other Portal worlds."

He nodded slowly to T'arza. "You, T'arza, are the architect of this plan, and you shall have the authority of the Council to execute it as you see fit within the scope of the Council's decision."

T'arza bowed slowly. "My thanks to you, Honored First…" – he turned his head and looked down the table – "…esteemed Grandmaster, fellow elders. I shall endeavor to act honorably, as directed by this great assembly."

Chapter 20

Official Announcement
The Office of Raul Gabriel Esteban
Secretary-General of UNGov

The Secretary-General has had a minor surgical procedure to address a chronic health issue. The condition is not danger-ous, and the procedure was completed without complications. Secretary-General Esteban is resting comfortably and expects to return to a normal schedule shortly. He is gratified by the outpouring of support and good wishes from around the world.

"The Secretary-General has now missed three consecutive meetings of the Secretariat." Chang Li sat behind his massive wooden desk, his face twisted in a concerned frown. There was a floor to ceiling window behind him with a view of his gardens and the lake beyond. Chang's villa was a magnificent structure, equipped with every imaginable luxury, but its privileged owner wasn't enjoying any of it. He was too worried.

"We have tried to get updated intelligence on his condition, but his security is impenetrable." Zhao Min sat opposite Li in one of the plush leather guest chairs. He was bald with a long scar down the right side of his face, giving him an imposing look despite his neutral expression. "Anton Samovich met with him several times in private, but it appears that he too has now been shut out."

Li leaned back in his chair and sighed. "Could they have

planned something?" His hand tapped nervously on the desk top. "Esteban was supporting Samovich in the last few meetings he attended." He sat silently, pondering the possibilities. None of them seemed appealing. "Is it possible Samovich has secured the Secretary-General's support?"

"Perhaps it is time for more aggressive action." There was a deep current of menace in Zhao's voice.

"How much more aggressive can we get than trying to assassinate Samovich?" Li's voice softened noticeably. Even in the confines of his heavily guarded chateau, he was uncomfortable speaking of the attempt. "I've had to do considerable damage control from that. Even my allies are concerned now." He looked up and stared at Zhao. "And for all the risk involved, the operation was botched."

Zhao returned Li's gaze. "That was probably the doing of Alexi Drogov. It was just bad luck that he was with Samovich when the attack occurred." Zhao paused briefly. "At least Drogov was killed while foiling the plot. That is a considerable achievement. He was an extremely dangerous man, and completely loyal to Samovich. His death removes many risks."

Li snorted. "Yes, I would expect one professional killer to admire another. But Samovich is the true threat, and if he is able to find any evidence linking this attack to me, we are in deep shit, my friend."

"I planned the entire thing, boss. There is no trail leading back to you."

"I hope you are right." Li looked back at Zhao, his expression uncertain. "Samovich claimed to have captured one of the assassins." A pause. "If that is the case, I can assure you that no one has greater resources for interrogation than Anton Samovich and his internal security apparatus." His eyes bored into Zhao's. "If he has a prisoner, he will break him. There is no doubt."

"He does not have a prisoner." There was an unsettling smile on Zhao's face. "I told you, I planned every aspect of the operation. The assailants were all poisoned before they even launched the attack. None of them had more than an hour to live."

Li's eyes widened. This was the first he was hearing of Zhao poisoning the operatives. "Are you certain none of them could have survived?"

"Absolutely. There is no antidote." Zhao's smile grew. "You can be certain that Samovich has no prisoners. If he says otherwise, he's trying to play you." Zhao paused for a few seconds then added, "I would have briefed you fully, but you said you wanted no connection to the operation."

"That is very interesting, Min." Li returned Zhao's grin. "Very interesting indeed. If Samovich was trying to rattle me into giving something away, he must not have any real evidence. Or at least he didn't then." His smiled widened as he spoke. "And if anyone should have been able to turn up something damning, it would be Samovich." Not for the first time, Li pondered the inconvenience of squaring off against a man who controlled a worldwide intelligence and enforcement operation.

"As I said, Chang, they don't have anything. They can suspect all they want, but they can't prove a thing."

Li nodded. "Perhaps you are correct, perhaps it is time for us to consider a bolder strategy." He looked down at his desk, and the smile faded slightly. "I've been unable to get any real intel from Juno. I have no idea how the battle is progressing there, but if Samovich pulls off a win, it's going to be too late." The smile disappeared completely. "I'll be as good as dead. And you too, my friend."

"Then we can't let things come to that." Zhao had a bloodthirsty streak, one he didn't try very hard to hide. "And with Drogov dead, the time couldn't be better for a move. He was a very dangerous man, and a highly unpredictable one. There may be a hole in Samovich's security now, an opportunity that won't last long."

Li sighed. He had no problem with killing to get what he wanted, but he didn't particularly enjoy it. He knew his associate thrived on it, rejoiced in the artistry of the kill. Alexi Drogov had been like that too, Li knew. Perhaps, he thought, all the truly great killers share that trait. Maybe now was the time to hit

Samovich, while he was still reeling from the loss of his long-time associate.

"We would have to attack Esteban and Samovich simultaneously, or at least close to it." Li spoke softly, the tension in his voice obvious. "And we would have to move quickly to seize power. There is no way to predict how the remaining members of the Secretariat will react to the assassination of two members, but it won't be good. We need fear and speed working for us. We need to present them with a fait accompli. I must be in firm control of the vital branches of government before I call upon the Secretariat to confirm me as Secretary-General."

"We will have to plan it well. We'll need key members of the bureaucracy involved. If you control the vital functions of government, the other Secretaries will be helpless to oppose us." Zhao paused. "Samovich's internal security apparatus is a concern. There is no way to know how they will react. I wouldn't want to begin to guess at what methods he has used to ensure loyalty from his top operatives, or how well these will continue to function after his death. Will his top people seek revenge, or will they move to secure their own futures?" Zhao didn't expect an answer. Li didn't know any more than he did.

Li leaned back in his chair and stared at the wall. His stomach was clenched into a knot, and his head pounded like a hammer on an anvil. He couldn't believe he was even considering a plan like this. The risks were incalculable, but the rewards... the rewards were beyond measure. All his life he'd dreamed of reaching the pinnacle, the ultimate power. Now he was just a single step away. It was a dangerous plan, but he was in no less peril if Samovich's forces defeated Taylor, and his enemy ascended to the Secretary-General's Seat. He took a deep breath and summoned all his courage.

"OK, put together a plan. I want this ready to go as soon as possible."

*   *   *   *   *

Alexi Drogov walked across the polished marble floor of the

main gallery and into the study. He still had a small limp, but otherwise he felt remarkably strong for someone who'd been near death 9 days before. Drogov wasn't much of a scientist, but that didn't stop him from appreciating the miraculous nanotechnology that had saved his life.

"You look good, my friend. For a dead man. I have received numerous condolences." Samovich was sitting in a plush leather chair next to the fireplace, a small tablet laying on his lap. It was snowing lightly outside, and the manicured grounds of Samovich's villa covered with freshly fallen snow created a perfect winter image. It was a peaceful scene, soothing and beautiful. But the serene vista was lost on Samovich and Drogov. Both men knew the current situation was anything but peaceful.

"That nanotech is amazing." Drogov walked toward a chair next to Samovich and gently eased himself down. "I'd swear I've even got less pain in places I had old injuries."

"I'm sure you do. The nanobots are programmed to fix anything in your body in less than perfect condition. They are quite an amazing development. I've kept the wraps on their true capabilities, but their capacity to extend human life is incredible. With the right programming, they can cure any disease, even rejuvenate body parts subject to age-related deterioration."

"That's amazing. A step toward immortality." Realization hit Drogov. "They could cure Esteban, couldn't they?"

"Almost certainly." Samovich nodded as he spoke. "The nanobots can easily be programmed to seek out and devour cancer cells anywhere in the body. Indeed, if the life-extending capabilities live up to expectations, they could not only cure his illness, they could keep him alive another 50 or 60 years, at least." He paused for a few seconds. "Of course, that would be an intolerable situation. The old fool has stood in my way far too long as it is."

"That is why you have kept this technology secret."

"That…and other reasons too. First, it is still being developed. You are the first non-modified soldier to have the nano injected." He glanced up at his Drogov. "Sorry to use you as a lab rat, my friend, but there was no choice. It was the only way to save you."

"I've never been happier to be used in an experiment."

"I'm thrilled it worked. We will need to think long and hard about how to handle this technology in the future. We certainly can't afford to have it become common knowledge. It is far too expensive to be used on most people, and the demographic and economic realities of significantly extending the average person's life span are problematic anyway. However, if the population is aware of it, they will want it. It's one thing to take their freedom; it was something they didn't use much anyway. But they're all scared of death, and they will riot in the streets if they think there is a way to extend their miserable lives. It could be a source of dangerous unrest."

Samovich picked up the tablet and set it on the table next to him. "But we have other things to deal with first. I've been keeping close tabs on our friend Chang Li, but I haven't been able to find out much. I'm afraid he's gone completely dark. As far as I can see, he hasn't left his villa in over a week." There was concern in his voice. "I think you were right. He's plotting something. He's a miserable piece of shit, but he's not stupid. We can't underestimate him. And I can't tell what's true and what's bullshit in Keita's reports, but the battle on Juno is certainly not over yet."

"You want to move against Li?" Drogov leaned back in his chair, enjoying the warmth from the hearth. He was still a little sore, and the heat from the fireplace was soothing.

Samovich nodded gently. "I don't think there's a choice. I haven't been able to get any evidence to prove he was behind the attack on my office. And I don't think we have time for you to start poking around now that you're up and about."

"You know I agree." Drogov tended to favor any plan that included riddling an enemy with bullets. He paused, staring right at Samovich. "And Esteban?" Even Drogov lowered his voice when discussing the assassination of the Secretary-General.

Samovich sat silently for a few seconds. Finally, he sighed and said, "I just don't know. I was giving him regular briefings, which was a good way to stay close to him, but that stopped about ten days ago. He looked like shit when I last saw him. He could die any day now, and we wouldn't have to take the risk of getting involved."

"Or he could linger near death for weeks, months even." Drogov leaned in toward his friend. "And if he found out about your nanotech and that you withheld it from him...we'd be screwed all kinds of ways then, wouldn't we? I know you're keeping it under wraps, but you know better than anyone, no secret is totally safe."

Samovich sat quietly, his eyes drifting to the fire. He stared into the flames, his mind analyzing every aspect of the situation. No matter how he considered it, he was making guesses, gambles. Samovich liked facts; he always tried to make decisions based on solid information. But there were too many variables now, too much he couldn't predict. He'd just have to make his best guess on how to proceed.

Finally, he turned toward Drogov. "Yes, Esteban too," he said softly.

Drogov just nodded, and the two sat quietly in front of the fire for a long while.

Chapter 21

From the Writings of T'arza, Elder of House Setai:

The humans are our brethren, so it was written by the
Ancients. They are like to us in so many ways, yet still there is
a gulf between us. For they are unlike us also, many of their
behaviors and philosophies completely alien to the Tegeri mind.

Nevertheless, despite these differences, despite decades of
war between our races, despite the unconscionable behavior
of their leaders, I find myself drawn to them. I experience a
strange feeling of kinship, particularly with the human Taylor. I
see in him what his people can be, the strength and ability they
can at last achieve if they choose to stand for their own, to truly
think for themselves and shed their dependence on those unfit
to lead.

The humans have not yet chosen their final destiny. The
time of that ultimate determination is now upon them. Will
they finally stand for their own, basking in the light of freedom
and enlightenment? Or will they continue to be slaves, their
liberty and self-determination willingly surrendered to those
who would be their masters? The first path leads to the light, to
wisdom and a place as the guardians of the universe. The latter
leads to servitude and despair, to darkness...and ultimately to
destruction.

I have thought and meditated many long hours, yet even I do
not know what will happen, how this ultimate fate of man will
be settled. They have the capacity for greatness, the humans,
yet they are easily distracted and misled too. They may yet

**throw away their destiny. Only the passing time will tell. And
the fate of the galaxy may depend on the path man chooses.**

T'arza stepped through the Portal, ignoring the brief feeling
of disorientation that accompanied a transit. Centuries before,
when he was young, he had traveled through many Portals,
exploring numerous worlds, each different and enlightening in
its own way. He pursued knowledge and enlightenment for their
own sake, and his restless heart drove him onward, seeking to
learn the secrets of the universe. He relished the gift of the
Ancients, the paths they left to the universe.

It was obligation that ended his travels, not boredom, not
the quelling of his thirst for knowledge. The duty to assume the
eldership of his house was not a responsibility he could refuse.
He returned sadly to Homeworld, abandoning the adventurous
spirit of his youth to take up his new role. There he'd remained
for many years, wisely tending to the affairs of his house. Until
he journeyed to Erastus at the behest of the Council to initiate
contact with Taylor.

He had almost forgotten the strange feeling of a transit,
and the wondrous experience of stepping through the gateway
and emerging instantly on a world far away. He'd always been
amazed at the notion that he could look at a star, seeing light
that had begun its journey to him a century before then, with
a few simple steps, he could be on a world orbiting that sun,
staring up at Homeworld's star, seeing the past again, light that
began its journey 100 years before.

Tegeri science was highly advanced, far beyond anything
humanity had attained, yet man was next in line among all the
children of the Ancients, his technology ages ahead of the other
races. On the other worlds where life had been nurtured slowly
toward intelligence, beings still struggled to master fire and till
the ground with blunt tools.

Yet the humans, even the Tegeri, were children compared to
the Ancients who had come before. Tegeri science, unimaginable wizardry though it would appear even to man's greatest

minds, couldn't begin to explain the Portals. They were the masterwork of the Ancients, a wonder that defied all of the Tegeri's comprehension of the universe.

How, he wondered, can we possibly stand against the Darkness when the Ancients could not? What could the Tegeri and the humans do that those who came before, the great beings who built the Portals, could not? Was it violence and war? Were the Ancients too peaceful, too completely devoted to knowledge and scholarship that they simply could not adapt to warfare? Could it be that simple?

Is that it, he wondered; is that what the Ancients foresaw, that we would be better able to fight, to kill, than they? The Tegeri weren't warlike by nature, but they understood conflict and they could defend themselves when necessary. They valued personal liberty above all things, and they would fight, individually or as a race, to defend it. The more he considered it, the more convinced he became. And he saw the importance of the humans with far greater clarity, for they were vastly more aggressive and warlike than his own people, seemingly willing to fight for virtually any cause.

Indeed, he wondered if mankind's role in the coming battle wasn't meant to be the greater of the two races. Had the Ancients foreseen the violent nature of men and prophesized that they would be the primary force capable of defeating the Darkness? Perhaps the Tegeri's purpose was to shepherd the humans, to prepare them for the greatest war the universe has ever seen. If so, Taylor's quest was the most important thing in the galaxy, a matter of vital importance to every sentient race just beginning to grasp at civilization.

T'arza felt his burden growing heavier. If Taylor fell, if his army was destroyed, the future would be lost before the battle even began. His people would fight alone if need be, but now he was sure they had no chance, not without the men of Earth. If Taylor was destroyed, so in turn would all light in the galaxy be extinguished. There would be nothing left. No illumination, no joy, no knowledge. Only the silent Darkness.

It was midday on Oceania, and the planet's yellow sun was

high in the sky. The Portal connecting Oceania with Sisara was on a small island, far from the single large continent the humans and Machines had battled over for two decades. T'arza had commanded the New Ones fighting on Oceania to dispatch all available transport to the island. If his efforts were to succeed, there was no time to be wasted. He had to rush his reinforcements to the primary combat areas as quickly as possible.

Unfortunately, the battle on the planet had been winding down for several years, the New Ones pushed into an ever smaller defensive perimeter. The available transport assets were inadequate to the task, and that meant it was going to take longer to ferry the thousands of New Ones streaming through the Portal to the battle lines. And every day that went by meant more men and arms would get through to Taylor's enemies.

T'arza shed his cloak as he walked out into the bright sunshine. Oceania's climate was almost perfect for humans, though the Tegeri found it a bit warmer than optimal. Homeworld was a chilly place, its equatorial zone not unlike Taylor's own home in the New England region of Earth. He imagined what Erastus must have been like to the young Taylor, accustomed as he was to cold breezes and winter snows. The Tegeri could not survive the heat of Erastus unprotected, not for more than a few minutes, and the New Ones that had been sent there were surgically modified to increase their endurance. But the humans just stepped out of the Portal into the brutal heat, and they adapted. Even men like Taylor, from one of his world's cooler regions, acclimated quickly, their bodies changing, become used to chronic dehydration and constant, searing heat.

Yes, T'arza thought, perhaps it is the humans, and not my people, who are equipped to defeat the Darkness. Taylor must prevail. He must.

                    *   *   *   *   *

"What the hell is going on?" Colonel Marcus Halston stood on a large rock outcropping, staring off into the distance with his binoculars. Columns of smoke rose into the sky, the massive black clouds blocking the slowly setting sun and casting a dark haze over the field. The battle was raging all across the line, with an intensity the commander of UN Force Oceania had never seen before.

His positions were getting pounded, the field hospitals already overflowing with casualties. He'd rushed supplies and reserves to the front, but they'd barely managed to slow the enemy's sudden advance.

"Where are they getting the strength to launch these attacks?" The Machines were advancing all along the line, pushing his overwhelmed soldiers steadily back. They'd been coming at his people non-stop for three days, massive assaults, one after the other, ignoring losses. General Jonas had been killed in one of the first attacks, caught by surprise and trapped with a cut off battalion. By the time his men had managed to relieve the beleaguered unit, it had lost two-thirds of its strength, including Jonas. Halston had been in the rear, supervising support services for the supply line to Juno, when he got word he had inherited command of the army. He rushed to the front lines to take charge, and he'd been running from one trouble spot to another ever since.

"I've ordered a complete recon of their rear areas as you commanded, sir." The Tegeri entry Portal was on an island in the center of the World Ocean, thousands of kilometers behind the front lines and hard to reach with surveillance assets. Major Igor Sandrian stood behind the CO, holding a large tablet. "We're having trouble penetrating their AA near the Portal. It looks like they beefed up their defenses there. We've lost at least two dozen drones, but we haven't been able to pick up anything except vague reports of increased transport traffic from the entry zone to the front lines."

"They're bringing more troops onplanet, substantially increasing their deployed strength. That much is clear." Halston's voice was edgy. "But why?" The Tegeri typically replaced casualties up to a point, but he'd never heard of an instance of them increasing force levels in the middle of a campaign. Until now. He was sure of it. There was no other answer. "I want all offensive operations canceled immediately."

"But sir, we're in the middle of three major offensives. UNGov has given us progress guidelines, and if we…"

"I said all operations are to be terminated immediately, at least until we've got some fucking idea what's happening." Halston didn't know what was going on, but he was damned sure he wasn't blundering forward into some kind of trap. "We have no idea how much force the enemy is bringing onplanet, Major, and no intel on the composition of the new units. Until we do, we will fall back to the line of the Black River." The waterway had been the main point of contact between the two sides for years before the Earth forces broke through and began to advance 20 months before. The river was a perfect defensive position, very deep and 2 kilometers wide along most of its path. But pulling back that far surrendered almost two years' progress and threatened to let the battle for Oceania slip back into stalemate.

"Yes, sir." Sandrian saluted. "I will see to it at once." The aide turned abruptly and jogged toward the communications hut. He knew Halston was right or, at least, that caution was warranted. But terminating the assaults in progress and coordinating a fighting withdrawal over 60 kilometers was a complex operation. If they weren't careful, the retreat could turn into a confused rout.

Sandrian felt the stress in his chest and stomach. It was more than the complexity of the withdrawal. He was thinking about how hard it was going to hit the fan when UNGov heard about the retreat.

Chapter 22

From the Journal of Jake Taylor:

Am I stubborn? Tenacious? Dedicated? Pigheaded? How can words that are virtually synonymous mean such different things in practice? How can the same trait be both positive and negative? Is it degree? Context? Or is it something we assign later, after we see if the actions in question lead to success or failure? A tenacious general holds out, standing in the breach, saving the battle. A pigheaded commander gets his soldiers slaughtered because he refuses to retreat from that same position.

Tony Black is my best friend. Was my best friend, at least. For more than a decade we stood together on the burning sands of Gehenna, battling against an enemy we were both sure was evil. We ate together, marched together, shit together. We backed each other up in every way possible. He saved my life more than once, as I saved his.

He swore the same oath I did, to fight our way back to Earth and destroy UNGov, to free a world. How can two men, closer than brothers, see the same thing so differently? I feel the urgent, elemental need to destroy anything that stands in our way, to leave no force behind us, no survivors among those who challenge our Crusade and stand with our enemies. That doesn't mean I don't ache for the men lost, the victims of the Crusade. Later, when I have time, I will cry for them. But the Crusade is bigger than any of us, more important than any life, than any thousand lives, or ten thousand. If we succeed, we will free billions. Is there a cost too high to pay for that?

Now, there is yet another reason we must push forward. There is more at stake than just freedom. There is the survival of the human race, and the Tegeri as well. And other beings on planets far away. Tony doesn't know about the Darkness. I chose not to tell him, not to burden him with another weight. He doesn't understand the urgency as I do, the need to finish this fight as soon as possible, to press on to Earth and liberate mankind. To rally them to face a new danger. UNGov made the Tegeri into a false menace, a fraud to scare humanity into yielding to their rule. But now there is a real threat, one far graver even than we'd thought the Tegeri to be. We must have a world united, by free will rather than lies and totalitarian brutality, all mankind standing as one, fighting alongside the Tegeri against the greatest evil in the universe.

I want to tell my friend, to unload my burdens, even if only for a few minutes. I want to say to him I am not the monster he thinks I've become, that I feel the pain and death my soldiers face as acutely as I ever did. But I can't, I won't. It will do nothing but ease my own pain, and that is not a good enough reason. It is my place to endure, to be the pillar that supports this Crusade. I will not give my friend yet another load to carry. If the price of protecting him is his anger, even his hatred, so be it. I love Tony Black like a brother, and I will protect him any way I can. Whether he knows it or not.

"General, the enemy is advancing on all fronts." Black's voice was cold and efficient. Taylor had noticed the new formality in his exec's speech, "generals" and "sirs" replacing "Jakes" as he reported. "Major Samuels and Major Young are both falling back under heavy attack."

There had been communiques all morning, but now the data was becoming clear. There were thousands of enemy soldiers, apparently fresh formations, plunging into Taylor's exhausted and battered men.

What is this, Taylor thought, what the hell is going on? He'd hoped his troops' ceaseless attacks had broken the enemy's morale and shattered the combat effectiveness of their formations. For days his forces had pursued broken units, driving toward the Portal, the enemy's link to Earth and their source of supply and communications.

Perhaps this was their last reserve, he thought, a final desperate attempt to stave off defeat. If so, all his people had to do was hold on until the attack spent itself. But he had no idea what reinforcements were coming through the Portal, how many fresh units the enemy still had. He reminded himself his adversaries had all the resources of Earth behind them. If enough reserves were moving through the Portal, it wouldn't matter what his people did. They'd be overwhelmed eventually. That is why he'd been pushing so hard to crush the enemy lines and reach the Portal. As long as the enemy could bring in fresh troops and supplies, there was no hope of victory.

He looked at his oldest friend and second-in-command. He was hurt by Black's coolness, troubled by their quarrel. But he didn't have time for that, not now. The enemy counter-attack was unexpected, and it was a problem, maybe a big one. If there was enough force behind it, his army was in dire peril.

"We're going to have to burn the rest of our drones." Taylor's voice was somber, emotionless. "There's no choice. Launch a triple spread. That should just about clean out our stocks." He hated using the last of his recon drones, but there was no other option. He had to know how many troops the enemy was moving forward. He needed to know if it was just a diversion, or if they still had enough strength left to seriously threaten his battered army.

"Yes, sir." Black saluted crisply. "I will see to it now." He spun around on his heels and headed toward the communications tent.

Taylor almost called him back, but he stopped himself. There would be time enough to talk to Black, to mend fences, when the battle was over.

*   *   *   *   *

"All units, maintain position and keep firing." Young was shouting into the com. His hands were balled into fists, and his face was twisted in a determined grimace. He wasn't going to fall back any farther. Not a centimeter. Not if he had to nail his people to this ridge by will alone. "All platoons, detach a detail to strip the dead and wounded." Ammo was becoming a problem. It wasn't critical yet, but Young wasn't about to let it get there.

The enemy had counter-attacked three days before, and they'd been coming on nonstop ever since. He'd thought they were broken, but now they were getting new strength from somewhere. There were enhanced troops leading the attacks, but they were supported by thousands of regular soldiers, far more than he could account to UN Force Juno alone. Clearly, UNGov was pouring more troops through the Portal.

His people had almost made it; they'd almost broken through to make a move against the Portal. If they'd have gotten there, the enemy would have been cut off from all their supplies and reinforcements. It wasn't hard to defend a Portal entrance. One machine gun nest would do it, at least for a while. No more than two men abreast could come through at a time, and they'd be disoriented when they first stepped out.

But his men had fallen short of reaching the Portal. The enemy had managed to rush enough reserves through to seize the initiative and counter-attack, pushing Young's forces back along with the entire Army of Liberation.

His men were exhausted. They'd suffered massive casualties and, even with the reinforcements Taylor had pushed forward, he commanded barely half as many men as he had ten days before.

He'd launched the operation with a force that consisted entirely of enhanced Supersoldiers, but now half his men were unmodified planetary regulars thrown into the line as last-ditch reserves. They weren't anything close to a match for enhanced troopers, but the enemy forces were also mixed now. The brutal fighting had cost both sides many of their elite soldiers, and they were throwing anyone who could carry a rifle into the maelstrom.

Young watched as the enemy surged forward again. They'd charged three times already; this would be the fourth. They were mostly regulars coming now, the Supersoldiers deployed in small teams to stiffen the line. He stared for a few seconds as his enhanced eyes focused on the attackers, climbing over the bodies of their comrades to push forward. Enhanced or not, Young couldn't help but admire the courage of the men approaching his line. Such valor, he thought…has such courage ever been wasted for such a terrible cause before?

His men were raking the attackers' line, dozens falling, hundreds. He had his unmodified troopers in the front line trench, but his snipers and handpicked crack shots from his Supersoldier units were deployed among them. The rest of his enhanced soldiers, the survivors of the original two battalions he'd led forward, were organized as a reaction force, ready to counterattack anywhere the enemy broke through.

He stared out at the field. There were thousands of men coming at his line. His people were outnumbered at least 10-1. He didn't know where the enemy was getting so many troops, but he was beginning to realize there was no way his men could hold. Not against so many.

He heard a sound coming up from behind…gunships approaching. An instant later, his com crackled to life. "Major Young, this is Major MacArthur. I've got close air support inbound to your position. Prepare for FAE runs."

"Acknowledged, Major. And boy are you a sight for sore eyes." He flipped the com to the forcewide frequency. "Alright boys, grab some dirt. We've got friendly Dragonfires inbound!"

*   *   *   *   *

Macarthur's hand gripped the throttle as he veered his craft down toward the advancing enemy formations. The strike force was following him in, three ships total, the battered remnants of AOL's once powerful air command.

The fighting had been no less brutal in the air than on the ground, the opposing gunships tearing into each other, struggling with the last of their strength and ordnance to gain superiority in the sky.

Neither side had managed to achieve that, MacArthur thought grimly as he arced his craft downward in a sharp dive. They'd come close to mutual extermination instead. MacArthur's three birds were just about all the AOL had left, except for a few semi-wrecks the technicians were trying to get back in the air with a combination of recycled parts and good hopes.

He mourned all the men he'd lost, but there was pride there too, admiration for the way his outnumbered forces had grimly held their own. They'd knocked just about every enemy bird from the sky and, while he couldn't call his three remaining ships air superiority, he was proud of the near 2-1 kill ratio his people had achieved.

There hadn't been an airstrike from either side in three days, not until Taylor ordered MacArthur and his survivors take off and support Young's overwhelmed command. MacArthur knew the situation on the ground was desperate. He also realized this was going to be just about the last sortie for his forces. Even if his three birds made it through the AA fire and returned undamaged, they were loaded up with the last of the FAEs. They might manage one more mission with nothing but auto-cannon rounds, but then they'd completely out of ammo and grounded for the duration.

MacArthur had declared victory in the air war, at least in his own deepest thoughts. It was the only way he could reconcile with the losses. But he knew that success was only temporary. He had no more gunships and no way to get any. His birds were out of ammunition and spare parts. The Earth forces would get more of everything – ships, ammo, replacement parts - and probably soon. It would take a while to get new birds through the Portal and reassemble them, but he knew his last few ships would eventually be hunted down and destroyed. It might be a week, or two. Maybe even a month. But it would happen. And then the air would belong to the enemy. And Taylor's people on the ground would be in a worse holocaust than they were now.

MacArthur's eyes were fixed forward as his gunship streaked down toward the advancing enemy troops. He'd caught them cold, out in the open in a deep formation. Three ships was a small force, but he knew they would make their attack count. Maybe, just maybe, they could help the outnumbered guys on the ground win one more round.

He angled his ship, streaking toward the main enemy concentration. "Blue two, to the left. Blue three, to the right." He pushed the throttle forward, diving lower, positioning for his attack run. His two other ships pushed out to his flanks, the three Dragonfires forming in a perfect line as they made their final approach.

Three, two, one…MacArthur counted down in his head before he pulled the release. He could feel the slight bumps as his craft released the FAE canisters one after the other. He knew the other birds were keying off his release. His ersatz squadron was dropping a cloud of flaming death, 150 meters wide and over a kilometer long. For a few minutes, the ground below would become like a vision of hell. Men would be consumed by the fires, their bodies nearly vaporizing in the intense heat. Others would die from the low pressure at the center of the firestorms, their lungs torn apart as they gasped for breath.

It was a horrible death his ships brought the hapless infantry on the ground, the same nightmare the enemy aircraft had visited on the AOL's units. MacArthur felt a touch of regret, a small wave of guilt. He knew the men down there were not evil, at least not most of them. Not like he'd believed the Machines to be for so many years. They were conscripts, fighting because they had no choice. But war was war, and the sin of it all would be that much worse if Taylor's army lost. There was hope in the victory of the AOL, a chance all the suffering and death might lead to something positive. MacArthur and Taylor had never gotten along on Erastus, not until the very end. But the air commander had come to realize the heavy burden Taylor had taken on, and he was determined to support the cause…even if his last bird was grounded. Even if he had to pick up a rifle and jump into the line.

He looked at the screen, seeing the inferno on the ground below. The belly cameras on his ship gave him a tremendous view. His three ships had torn a 1,200 meter swath of utter destruction through the enemy ranks. Maybe, he thought, maybe that will be enough to save those guys on the ground.

"Alright, guys, let's get back home." He pulled back on the throttle, climbing hard, angling back toward base. An instant later the alarm sounded – incoming ground-to-air missiles. He jerked hard on the throttle, whipping the ship around in a wild evasive maneuver. MacArthur was the commander of AOL's air wing, a veteran pilot with more than a decade of combat experience. He wasn't about to let some random shot from a handheld launcher take him down. He was still thinking that when the rocket slammed into his ship, and it erupted into a roiling fireball, it's flaming remnants crashing hard to the ground.

*   *   *   *   *

Ralfieri pushed the headphone tightly against his ear. He'd listened to the recording twice already, but that didn't stop him from hitting play again. So that's what the dread Jake Taylor sounds like, he thought. But it wasn't Taylor's voice that made Ralfieri feel like he'd been gut-punched. It was what the man was saying.

The voice on the recording didn't sound like the psychopathic monster Ralfieri had been led to expect. Not even close. Taylor was almost pleading, a desperation obvious in his tone. It couldn't have been fear; Taylor's Supersoldiers could have easily crushed the unreinforced UN Force Juno they'd been facing when the transmission was made. No, it was a man beseeching his enemy not to fight, begging them not to make him kill them all.

Ralfieri had been troubled almost since the time he'd emerged through the Portal and taken command of the UN forces on Juno. It was little things, mostly…and a few big ones too. Nothing quite added up; nothing made sense. Now he was asking himself the core question at the heart of the matter. Was Taylor truly a villain, a madman rampaging across the Portal worlds massacring UN soldiers? Or was there more to it than that? Were Ralfieri and his men fighting on the wrong side?

"You say Taylor gave this speech before the fighting started?"

"Yes, sir. His people came through their Portal, but they didn't advance on us immediately." Captain Akawa spoke softly, his tones hushed despite the fact that he and Ralfieri were alone. "A lot of us believed him. His delay in attacking benefitted us, not them. We were talking about taking his offer when..."

"When?" Ralfieri had been looking out over the rocky ground, but now he turned to face Akawa. "When what?"

Akawa hesitated a few seconds. "Well, sir...it's..."

"Speak freely." Ralfieri could see the officer was uncomfortable. "Please, Captain."

"Well, sir, while we were discussing our options, we were called to an assembly. A number of men, mostly the ones who had been positioned on point and closer to Taylor's forces, tried to desert." He paused, swallowing hard. "Inquisitor Vanderberg's men captured many of them before they were able to make their escape. He..."

Ralfieri put his hand on Akawa's shoulder. "It's OK, Captain. Please go on."

"Sir, Inquisitor Vanderberg assembled the entire unit to watch while he..." Akawa paused again, taking a deep breath before he continued. "...while he had them shot, sir." Another pause. "He had them all shot, General, and the rest of the men in their units too, whether they had deserted or not."

Ralfieri felt the rage begin to boil over. He hated Vanderberg. He wanted to kill the miserable, arrogant butcher more than he'd ever wanted anything. He'd been close the day the Inquisitor had ordered the fleeing troops gunned down, but Anan Keita had gotten there in time to break up the conflict before it got too far. Ralfieri didn't think much of Keita either, but even his anger didn't blind him to the consequences of disobeying a member of the Secretariat. He'd backed down, reluctantly, angrily. Keita had managed to keep him away from

Vanderberg since.

"How did Taylor get his message through? I'm surprised the army commander didn't jam the transmission." Ralfieri was indulging his curiosity, trying to control his anger as he did.

"I don't know, sir. He was just able to transmit on our frequencies, somehow. As far as I know, every man in Force Juno heard the message."

Ralfieri looked down at the ground, thinking. There was more to the situation than what he'd been told. Much more.

He pulled out his com unit. "Major Evans, assemble a section immediately and report to me at the coordinates I transmit to you."

"Yes, sir." Evans' response was immediate. The officer was a reliable veteran and the man Ralfieri had come to trust the most.

"And this is a classified mission, Major, so you are to tell no one about it. Just pick your section and meet me at the coordinates."

"Yes, General." Ralfieri couldn't detect any confusion or concern over his cryptic orders in his subordinate's tone. "I will confirm when we are en route."

"Very well, Major. Ralfieri out." He turned toward Akawa. "Want to join us, Captain?"

"Where are you going, sir?"

Ralfieri paused for an instant. "I'm going to see General Taylor, Captain. I'm going to find out what the hell is really going on here."

Part Three
My Enemy, My Friend

Chapter 23

From the Journal of Jake Taylor:

There is a device in my head; they call it a Neural Intelligence System. It is somewhat misnamed, as it doesn't really have any intelligence of its own, artificial or otherwise. It is more of an amplification system for my brain, allowing me to retain and retrieve information far more quickly than I could on my own.

Most people would be amazed how disconcerting it is when you cannot forget anything. It's a strange, crowded feeling in my head, like there are too many thoughts and facts, far more than the human brain was intended to handle. It is extremely useful in many instances, yet I wonder sometimes if it will one day drive me mad, if nothing else does, that is. If I am not already mad.

While the device doesn't do any computation on its own, it does affect the way I think. I wouldn't say it makes me smarter, but my judgments, my reasoning are different because there is more information available to my brain. I don't waste effort trying to remember things, since it happens automatically. My thoughts and decisions have the benefit of far more data than most people's.

People and events rarely surprise me anymore. It does happen, but usually only when there is information of which I am unaware. The enemy's recent counter-offensive was a surprise because we didn't have enough drones to monitor their incoming reinforcements, and I had no information on the commanders involved and the forces they had available.

Every so often, a person will surprise me by showing initiative and character I didn't expect. General Antonio Ralfieri was one of those people. I felt the impact of his ability when my forces were pushed back, driven to their last stand along the battle scarred front. He surprised me again when the battle paused just before the final struggle. And without his courage and strength of will, my army would likely have died in the blood-soaked sands of Juno.

Bear Samuels slumped down and leaned against the slick mud wall of the shallow trench. The works had been hastily built, thrown up by groups of walking wounded and rallied routers. They weren't very deep, nor were they well planned or designed. A normal man could kneel or sit and stay in cover, but Samuels had to lean his massive frame forward to keep his head from poking over the top. The works were far from ideal, but even a poor quality trench was preferable to fighting in the open, and Samuels was glad to have them.

The battle had been fierce, the fighting nonstop. Samuels and his fellow officers had continually rallied the troops, kept them in the line far longer than they'd had a right to expect. Men, even cyborg Supersoldiers, had their limits, and Samuels' troops had been fighting for two weeks without a rest. They were nearing the breaking point, holding the line with the last of their strength. Samuels was enormously proud of his soldiers, but he also knew they couldn't hold out forever. If the enemy had enough fresh troops, they were going to win the battle. They had just launched a big assault that came close to success before it spent its impetus, and they fell back to regroup. Then, with no explanation, the enemy attacks just stopped. Completely. Even the harassing fire and mortar bombardment fell silent.

Samuels immediately ordered his forces to cease fire as well. He knew the battle was far from over, but his people were low on ammo, and they didn't have the resources to waste on long range fire at an enemy that wasn't advancing. Better to save what they had to repulse whatever attack was still to come.

He was grateful for the respite. His men were exhausted, and even a short break was welcome. He'd ordered half his units to stand down and pull back a klick, while the rest manned the defenses. Maybe they'd get enough time for a hot meal and some sleep. With a little luck, all his people would get a breather. Still, he had his recon teams on full alert. He was far from convinced the lull wasn't some kind of trick.

"Major Samuels…" It was Sergeant Welles on the com. Welles was the commander of the forward pickets.

"Yes, Sergeant. Report."

"Sir…we've got something…unexpected up here." Welles' voice was confused, uncertain.

"Go on, Sergeant. What is it?"

There was a short pause. "It's a group of the enemy approaching, sir. Perhaps 20-25." Another hesitation. "They appear to be unarmed…and…"

"And what, Sergeant?"

"They are carrying a flag, sir. A white flag."

Samuels paused. He knew what a white flag meant, though he'd never seen one employed on a battlefield. The Machines didn't surrender, and even when he'd been facing human enemies, any parley was easily arranged by com.

"Let them approach, Sergeant." Samuels was still confused, but he wasn't going to know anything unless he listened to what they had to say. "Keep an eye out for any kind of trick, any other enemy formations approaching."

"Yes, sir." A short pause. "No other enemy activity, Major. None at all."

"Very well, Sergeant. Bring them to me as soon as possible." Samuels' mind was racing. What was this all about?

*   *   *   *   *

"General Ralfieri, I'd like to welcome you to my headquarters." Taylor extended a hand to the commander of the army that had fought his people with such hellish intensity. "I must say, I am surprised at your presence." It was hard to speak calmly and courteously to an enemy, especially after the losses his men had suffered. But he knew Ralfieri and his soldiers had been lied to, just as he and his men had been for so many years. The very presence of the enemy commander here in Taylor's headquarters suggested he'd begun to doubt that propaganda.

"Thank you, General Taylor." Ralfieri reached out and grasped Taylor's hand. "I appreciate your seeing me." He paused. "It isn't easy for either of us, I am sure, after the ferocity of the battle and the losses we have suffered."

"No, it isn't." Taylor wanted to hate the enemy commander, but he couldn't. He saw a lot of himself in Antonio Ralfieri, and he couldn't question the courage it took for the general to come to Taylor's headquarters. "But that is no excuse for us to refuse communication. Even with an enemy."

"Perhaps we should not be enemies, General Taylor." Ralfieri stood silently for a few seconds, his eyes focused on his counterpart. He'd been told Jake Taylor was insane, a bloodthirsty villain determined to kill as many UN soldiers as possible. It never made sense to him. Even if Taylor had lost his mind, his soldiers would never have followed him with such devotion. Not if he was just a psychopathic monster. Now, seeing Taylor, hearing his voice, Ralfieri knew he'd been lied to…and he began to suspect the entire apocalyptic battle his men had been fighting was a tragic mistake.

"General, with all due respect, I need some answers." Ralfieri spoke softly, calmly. "I believe I have been lied to, that this terrible war we've been fighting is a tragic error."

Taylor took a deep breath. "It's not a mistake, General. At least not from the perspective of those who sent you here." Taylor couldn't keep the fatigue from his voice. "I am on a mission, General. All my men are. We are going back to Earth to destroy UNGov. To free humanity." Taylor hadn't intended to jump right to such a striking declaration, but he had a good feeling about Ralfieri, and something made him blurt it out.

"So it's all true then?" Ralfieri felt his stomach clench as he realized not just the war against Taylor's men, but the decades of conflict against the Machines had all been based on lies and propaganda. "UNGov started the war, not the Tegeri? The whole thing, 40 years of bloody slaughter, all to keep UNGov in power?"

Taylor nodded and exhaled slowly. "I'm afraid so, General Ralfieri." There was deep sadness in his tone. He'd know the truth for nearly two years, but he still felt the shock, the outrage, as keenly as he had that day in T'arza's underground complex.

Ralfieri looked back at Taylor. It was hard to gauge emotion from someone with cybernetic enhancements. Their metallic eyes tended to make their expressions mechanical-looking regardless of the underlying emotion. But he could feel Taylor's sadness, the heavy burden the AOL's commander carried with him. He wanted to know more – he needed to know – but in that instant he made up his mind. Everything Jake Taylor had said was true – he was suddenly sure of it.

He felt nauseous. His men had killed thousands of Taylor's people...and they'd lost even more of their own doing it. The battle had been a bloodbath, and it was all for nothing. Ralfieri felt the boiling rage inside, pressing against him, trying to find an escape. He wanted to track down everyone responsible and kill them with his bare hands.

Taylor knew what was going on in Ralfieri's head; he knew it all too well. "General...it's not your fault. I believed the same as you did for years. I was a good little soldier. I did what I was told. Until I found out the truth. As you have here today." Taylor paused, giving his guest a few seconds to absorb what he had just learned.

Ralfieri struggled to maintain his composure. "Forty years," he rasped. "All the dead. On both sides."

"I know what you're going through, General." Taylor reached out and put his hand on Ralfieri's shoulder. "No one knows better than I do. But you can't change what happened. None of us can." He paused. "But we are answerable for the future. You acted in ignorance before, but now you know the truth. If we let this go on, it is on us. Our responsibility."

Ralfieri exhaled. "Now that I know the truth," he said bitterly, "it will not go on. At least not here." He looked up at

Taylor. "This battle is over, I can tell you that much." He was tense, his hands clenched into fists. "I will never fight for them again. Never."

"We need to reach your people, General. We need to make them understand, all of them. Their place is with my soldiers, fighting for freedom, not as slaves for UNGov."

"You're right, General Taylor." Ralfieri let his eyes drop, a look of sadness dropping over his face. "So many dead. So many of your men, General, so many of mine." His voice was full of emotion...regret sadness, anger.

"I know, General." Taylor's voice was pure empathy. He understood what Ralfieri was thinking, the pain he was going through trying to adjust to what he'd learned. Taylor had been there; he was still there. But he'd learned to live with it after a fashion. At least, he'd managed to put duty first. There would be time for self-recrimination later, if he somehow lived through the Crusade. "The only question is, will those deaths mean something? Will you join me? Will you help me destroy UNGov and free the people of Earth from its tyranny?"

Ralfieri took a deep breath. The last day was a blur, and his mind was struggling to process everything he'd learned. But he didn't have any doubts, not anymore. "Yes, General." He spoke firmly, surely. "I am with you." He reached out his hand toward Taylor. "All the way."

Taylor grasped Ralfieri's hand and the two shook. "Thank you, General." Taylor forced a smile. "I am sure that together we will find a way to take down UNGov." He was actually far from sure, but he kept that to himself.

"I need to reach my men. I'm sure most of them will rally to us, but we need to contact them."

Taylor's hand moved toward the small amulet around his neck. "I believe I can help with that, General."

Ralfieri shook his head. "I know you have some method for long distance communication, General, but that's not the problem." His face twisted into an angry grimace. "There's a UN Inquisitor on Juno, General Taylor, and he has several hundred of his men with him. They executed every soldier who tried to come over to your side at the beginning of the campaign, even men who were just in the units of those attempting desertion." Ralfieri's voice was thick with anger. "I don't know what he could do if we issued a joint communique, but we can't take the risk."

Taylor nodded. "Then we have to take him out first." He opened his mouth to continue, but Ralfieri's com buzzed.

"General Ralfieri, we have a problem." It was Colonel Patel. Patel was the highest ranked modified officer left alive in Ralfieri's army, the tactical commander of the remnant of the Black Corps. His voice was strained, and Ralfieri could hear a commotion in the background.

"What is it, Colonel?"

"It's the Portal, sir. Something's wrong on Oceania." Patel paused, and Ralfieri could hear shouting in the background. "We were expecting new reinforcements and a fresh shipment of ordnance, but neither arrived. I dispatched three separate detachments through the Portal to check things out, and none have returned."

Ralfieri pressed the button on his com to mute the connection. "General Taylor, you don't have any forces on Oceania, do you?"

"No." Taylor had a thoughtful expression on his face. "Whatever is happening, my people have nothing to do with it."

Ralfieri snapped the com back on. "I'll be there as soon as I can. For now, I want that Portal heavily guarded."

"Sir…" Patel sounded nervous, uncomfortable. "Inquisitor Vanderberg is here, and he and his men have taken control of the area around the Portal."

"I'm on the way, Colonel. Do nothing until I arrive." He cut the connection and turned toward Taylor, a strange expression on his face. "Well, General, we know where Inquisitor Vanderberg and his men will be. How would you feel about dealing with this problem once and for all?"

Chapter 24

Private Communique
From Anton Samovich to Anan Keita

Your reports on the Black Corps' casualty rates have exceeded even my worst expectations. Despite our planning and efforts, we seem to have grossly underestimated the capabilities of Taylor and his men.

Your report suggests that despite our losses, the outcome of the battle rests on a knife's edge. We cannot take the risk that Taylor's forces may defeat the Black Corps and UN Force Juno. If the rebels are allowed to transit from Juno, our political position will be extremely precarious.

I am therefore authorizing the immediate transfer of veteran formations from all Portal Worlds within three transits of Juno. These forces should already be arriving through the Oceania-Juno Portal, and they will continue to do so until Taylor is defeated. I am diverting all new recruits from the training programs to Juno as well.

These transfers will endanger our positions on over a dozen Portal worlds. It is essential that you utilize this overwhelming force immediately to crush Taylor's forces. There can be no further delays. We must have an expeditious and conclusive victory, including the capture or death of Taylor himself, before any news of likely defeats on the weakened worlds reaches the Secretariat. I trust you fully understand what is at stake here, and I urge you to employ every possible measure to ensure our success.

"The enemy offensive on Oceania has captured the Portal to Juno, Secretary. Machine attacks have driven our defending units back several kilometers, and they now occupy the Portal area in considerable force." Under-Secretary Ramirez stood before Samovich's desk, a look of near-panic on his face. He'd dreaded bringing this news to his superior, but there was no way to avoid it. It wasn't the kind of thing he could delegate to a subordinate. "Colonel Halston is requesting immediate control over the reinforcements arriving onplanet to counter-attack and retake the Portal."

Samovich sighed. The bad news was coming nonstop. First, he had Drogov pounding away at him for permission to go after Li and Esteban. Li was up to something; there was no doubt about that. Drogov wanted to strike first. He knew his friend was tactically correct, at least in terms of executing the actual operations. There were few men as skilled at killing as Alexi Drogov. But Samovich knew very well that tactics and politics were two different things. He wasn't after blood for blood's sake. He wanted absolute power, and assassinations alone wouldn't attain that goal. Indeed, if he wasn't careful, they could easily backfire and cost him his chance at victory.

Samovich was also hesitant to unleash his friend. He had a surprise up his sleeve in Drogov, but it was one he could only use one time. Once he revealed that his top henchman was still alive, he had to make it count, and quickly. He'd lied to the entire Secretariat, telling them Drogov was dead. There would be considerable blowback from that. When he finally made his move with Drogov, there was going to be no room for any slip-ups. It had to be perfectly executed and lightning-fast.

Now he had this fresh hell to deal with. He'd taken a terrible chance stripping other Portal worlds of veteran formations – and doing it without even notifying the Secretariat. Now those troops weren't even getting through to Juno. If word got out that the supply line to the forces facing Taylor was cut, all hell would break loose. Even his allies on the Secretariat would be outraged. It was just the kind of thing Li needed to make a move against him.

"Authorize Colonel Halston to take command of all forces he requires from the units that have been diverted to Oceania for transit to Juno." Samovich's voice was hoarse and tired. It had been a long day. "He is to utilize anything he feels is necessary, but he is to retake the Portal within 48 hours, or he will answer directly to me." He glared at Ramirez. "Is that understood?"

"Yes, Secretary. Understood."

"He has 48 hours, Ramirez. Not a second longer. Make sure he understands that." Samovich's tone dripped of menace.

"Yes, sir." Ramirez moved sideways toward the door. "I will advise him at once, Secretary."

Samovich nodded and waved toward the entrance, dismissing his nervous subordinate. He watched Ramirez leave then he put his face in his hands. Why were the Tegeri suddenly so interested in Oceania, he wondered...why the big push after years of falling back? The timing couldn't have been worse...or better, he realized suddenly.

"Of course," he muttered to himself. "They're helping Taylor." He snapped bolt upright in his chair. "So that's what happened on Erastus." It all made sense now. The sudden rebellion among the forces on that world, the tremendous loyalty and fighting spirit of Taylor's men. It was the Tegeri. They contacted Taylor and told him the truth about the war. They were helping him.

His mind was racing. If he could connect Taylor to the Tegeri, it was a propaganda weapon against the rogue general, at least on Earth. Almost all of mankind still believed the aliens to be bloodthirsty monsters. But there was a dark side too. The Tegeri involvement also meant Taylor wasn't alone. If the Tegeri could launch an attack like they did on Oceania, what else might they do? Would they supply Taylor's forces? Equip them? He suddenly realized there was more uncertainty than he'd imagined...and even more need to put Taylor in a grave as soon as possible.

He sat at the desk as the minutes passed by, turning slowly into an hour. What should he do? He felt disconnected, uncertain. Should he wait, continue to bide his time hoping for victory on Juno? The situation there was spiraling out of control. He didn't even have a line of communications at the moment. Was there a realistic chance of getting the victory he needed in time? Or should he make a move against Li and Esteban now, roll the dice and risk everything in one bid for power?

He considered every possibility, imagined all the permutations that could result from each action. Finally, he made a decision. He grabbed the com unit and slowly dialed a familiar connect code. "Alexi, it's Anton. We're a go. Let's finish this now."

*   *   *   *   *

Alexi Drogov crept through the small patch of woods. The villa in the distance was probably the best-protected residence in the world. Raul Esteban had been a member of the Secretariat since UNGov seized power, and he'd been the Secretary-General and most powerful member of that body for the last 18 years. He was dying, everyone on the Secretariat knew that. But dying and dead were two different things, and if Samovich's coup was to succeed, nothing could be left to chance. A last minute condemnation from Esteban would be a huge problem. The dying leader had seemed to favor Samovich recently, at least mildly. But no one had seen the Secretary-General for weeks now, and Alexi Drogov intended to leave nothing to chance. He was going to tie up every loose end. Starting with Esteban.

"There's some kind of jamming, boss." Georgi Borgovich whispered as he trotted up next to Drogov. The team was on radio silence, but they were still listening, trying to catch any chatter between Esteban's security personnel.

Borgovich was one of Drogov's top men, another of Anton Samovich's childhood friends. Drogov had handpicked the assassination team. He preferred a small group that worked well together, one with men he could trust. And there weren't enough men Alexi Drogov trusted to fill out anything but a small group.

"That's got to be trouble." Drogov was compiling a mental list of reasons communications would be jammed. Right at the top of that list – Esteban's people knew his team was there. But if that was the case, why didn't they come at him? Without surprise, his few people didn't have a chance against the small army that guarded Esteban.

"It's heavy interference too." Drogov stared at his com unit as he listened to the static. "It's stronger away from the villa. The power source isn't in Esteban's compound, it's…"

The sounds of gunfire interrupted him. It was coming from the direction of the villa. For an instant he thought Esteban's security had discovered his positions and opened fire on his people, but then he realized there was a firefight going on closer to the villa. It took a few seconds for him to come to a conclusion, but then he realized. Someone else was attacking Esteban's compound. Li! It could only be Chang Li's people. They had made their move just moments before he had planned to launch his own operation.

"Chang Li's crew beat us to it." He spoke in a hushed tone as he turned to face Borgovich. "That's the only possibility."

Borgovich nodded. "So what do we do, boss?"

Drogov was silent. For better or worse, he'd never been an indecisive man. He assessed things quickly, and when he made a decision he went all in, without doubt, without hesitation. But this situation was so unexpected, he was unsure how to proceed. Should he try to take out both forces? No, he thought, that would be suicide. He considered trying to extricate his men undetected. That was a good plan…as long as Esteban's security foiled Li's attack. But Li must have other operations in place, moves intended to secure his position. If Li's people succeeded in killing Esteban, his coup might be too far advanced to stop.

They were probably going after Samovich too, he realized with a rush of concern. He had the urge to pull out and race back to protect his friend. But he knew that was pointless as well. Samovich was as secure as possible, and if Li had managed to arrange simultaneous assaults, Drogov would be too late to intervene anyway. The only way to be sure to thwart Li's efforts was to save Raul Esteban.

He turned toward Borgovich, his eyes staring intently into

his subordinate's. "OK, Borgo…change of plans." His voice was grim, deadly serious. He was gripping his rifle so tightly his fingers were white. "Pass the word down. We're going to hit whoever is attacking Esteban's people. We're going to save the Secretary-General." It was a 180 degree flip in the plan. They were going to save the man they had come to kill. "In one minute, Borgo. Sixty seconds."

Chapter 25

From the Journal of Jake Taylor:

I've made many command decisions in my life, but no matter how many times that responsibility falls on you, how many years you bear that burden, it never gets any easier.

Some of those decisions were made in haste, others after careful consideration. Some led to great success, others to disappointment and failure. Many were clearly important at the time, decisions I knew would have massive, long-lasting implications. Others seemed more routine, their true consequence not clear until much later.

Some of the most momentous decisions I have made did not reveal themselves as such at first. It was only later, after the results became clear, that I realized I had issued orders I would never forget.

When you think back later, after you know the terrible cost of your edicts, it is hard to imagine the routine, matter-of-fact way you made you snapped out those commands, issued orders with no idea how fateful they would become.

These are the hardest ones to live with afterward, those you didn't see as significant when you make them. It may have been impossible to foresee their true consequence, but you never feel that way later; you always wonder, questioning what you'd done, pondering if you'd heeded things more carefully if it would have made a difference. If a battle lost could have been won. If soldiers lost could have been saved. But there is no way to know. You are left only with doubt and regret. And the loss that resulted from your orders.

"Colonel Black will go with you, General. Until you are able to communicate effectively with your troops, and hopefully rally them to our cause, we will have to rely primarily on mine." Taylor's eyes shifted to the small cluster of men standing behind Ralfieri. "And your people here, of course." All of Ralfieri's companions had rallied to him, agreeing to follow their general in joining Taylor's Crusade.

"Thank you, General Taylor." He turned his head to face the officer standing next to Taylor. "And you, Colonel Black."

Black nodded. Ralfieri could tell there was something going on between Black and Taylor, some discomfort or disagreement at least. It wasn't what he'd expected between Taylor and his exec, but he didn't think too much of it. He realized he couldn't begin to appreciate the stress the men of the AOL had borne since they'd resolved to fight their way home to take on an entire world.

"Colonel Black, please organize a force of 300 men to accompany General Ralfieri. Your mission is to find Inquisitor Vanderberg and Secretary Keita." Ralfieri and Taylor had discussed everything that had to be done before they could safely address the troops still in the lines and seek to recruit them for the Crusade. They were both aware now of the terrible consequences of Vanderberg's interference with Taylor's original appeal to the soldiers of Juno, and they were determined to ensure that never happened again. "It is essential that Vanderberg and all of his men are hunted down and killed. Even his subordinates represent a considerable danger to our efforts."

Taylor didn't have any interest in capturing a UN Inquisitor or any of his henchmen. He couldn't even imagine the horrendous things Vanderberg had probably done, how many helpless civilians his people had tortured and massacred. How many men and women they'd dragged off in the night to disappear in some reeducation camp. There was no mercy in him for such creatures, no pity at all. There wasn't much point in ordering Black to capture the bastard just so Taylor could put a bullet in his head.

"If possible, you are to try to capture Secretary Keita and

bring him back alive." Keita was a different matter entirely. Taylor had no more empathy for a member of the Secretariat than he did for an Inquisitor, but Anan Keita was one of the most highly placed men on Earth. He was likely a treasure-trove of useful information, and Taylor wanted whatever intel could be squeezed out of the wretch.

"Yes, General." Black's tone was still chilly, though not as frigid as it had been. He stared at Taylor for a few seconds, his mouth slightly open, looking as if he wanted to say something. But he just saluted and turned to walk away.

Taylor turned back toward Ralfieri. "Good luck, General."

"Thank you, General Taylor." Ralfieri saluted Taylor, the first time he had done that. Then he spun around on his heels, following Black and motioning for his small group of men to follow.

Taylor watched them walk away. He knew the mission was difficult and dangerous, but there was no other way. The stakes were enormous. There were at least 12,000 of Ralfieri's men still in the line. They were remnants of both the Black Corps and UN Force Juno. If the mission succeeded, if Vanderberg and Keita were neutralized, there was a good chance most of those soldiers would join the AOL, swelling its depleted ranks. Taylor and Ralfieri would address them together and, without the Inquisitor's brutal repression, he was optimistic they could reach most of them.

If the mission failed, the blood would continue to flow. Taylor's battered survivors would carry on their apocalyptic fight, a wasteful struggle against men who should be their allies, not their enemies. Even if they won in the end, there would be so few of them left they'd have no chance of success on Earth.

Taylor watched the party walk slowly away, wondering if just over 300 men were about to undertake the decisive operation of the war.

$$*\qquad*\qquad*\qquad*\qquad*$$

The sergeant at the checkpoint held up his hands, signaling

the lead transport to stop. The trucks were from the AOL, but they bore no markings or insignia. They were the same kind the Juno forces and Black Corps used, but with no identification they aroused suspicion from the sentries.

Evans jumped out of the front cab and walked slowly toward the cluster of troops standing in the convoy's path. He wanted to keep the guards away from the transports, hoping they wouldn't decide to do a search. He held his hands out in front of him, making it clear he had no weapon at the ready. "I am Major Thomas Evans, Sergeant. My detachment is transporting captured trucks and supplies to the rear."

Evans continued walking forward. His stomach was tight. The trucks were filled with Taylor's veterans, their weapons at the ready. If the sergeant insisted on checking out the vehicles, there was going to be one hell of a firefight more than ten kilometers away from the Portal. There was no doubt Black's men could take out the sentries, but the alarm would be raised, and they wouldn't stand a chance of making it to their destination.

"Excuse me, sir. Inquisitor Vanderberg ordered tightened security around the Portal zone." The Sergeant sounded a little nervous. A veteran major was a terrifying beast, and the noncom was trying hard to sound respectful. "I just need to do a positive ID before I wave you through." He reached down and pulled a small palm scanner from a box at his feet.

"Very well, Sergeant." Evans took another few steps and held out his arm. "But then we must be going. We're on a tight schedule."

The sergeant held the scanner out, and Evans placed his palm on top. The device lit up briefly then beeped softly. "You can remove your hand, sir." The sergeant looked down at the scanner. "Very well, Major Evans. You may proceed."

Evans turned and walked back to the lead transport. He wanted to run, to get through the checkpoint as quickly as possible, but that would only raise suspicion. He moved smartly, but not too quickly, and he made sure not to look back as he did.

Evans climbed into the cab of the transport and signaled for the driver to move. He was relieved to see the sergeant and his men moving the barricade out of the convoy's way. He allowed himself a small sigh as the trucks moved forward, carrying Colonel Black and his 300 men plus General Ralfieri and a section of Black Corps troopers.

Evans was a veteran with years of combat experience, but he could feel the sweat soaking his shirt, and his heart was beating like a drum in his chest. He'd never been in a situation like this, sneaking to the rear of his own army. It wasn't just the fight he expected with Vanderberg's men. It was what came next. Could Ralfieri and Taylor get through to the forces deployed along the line? Would they manage to convince them all of the terrible truth? Or would the Black Corps and UN Force Juno fracture, begin fighting each other? In the coming battle, his fate would be in his own hands, at least to a considerable extent. But once they secured the Portal and dealt with Vanderberg's men, he would have nothing to do but sit back and see what happened. And Thomas Evans hated feeling helpless.

They were through the first hurdle, at least. Now they just had to take on an Inquisitor and all of his men – and any other troops stationed around the Portal if Ralfieri couldn't get them to stand down.

*   *   *   *   *

"Let's go, boys. Move!" Tony Black stood behind one of the transports, waving his arms as he urged his men forward. "Kill any of the Inquisitor's men on sight. Everyone else is off-limits unless you're in a life or death defensive situation."

Ralfieri was on the com already, ordering the Black Corps and UN Force Juno soldiers to stand down, not to fire on the forces attacking Vanderberg and his men. He was their commander, and they had no love for the brutal Inquisitor who'd ordered hundreds of their comrades executed. But they had all grown up in the UNGov era, conditioned their whole lives to fear Inquisitors. Black liked Ralfieri, and he could see his former enemy was a capable and charismatic leader. Hopefully his men would obey his commands and ignore the inevitable counter-orders from Vanderberg. The forces on Erastus had all rallied to Taylor, but it had been a close thing there too, and they'd almost come to a fight. Could they get lucky again?

Black watched the last man hop out of the cargo hold, and he spun on his heels and followed his men. He had his assault rifle in his hands, and he set it for single shots. The Juno forces were going to be scattered all around with Vanderberg's men. It wasn't a situation where Black's people could go in blazing away on full auto. Not without killing a lot of potential new allies.

"All UN soldiers, this is Colonel Black of the Army of Liberation. We are here with the authorization of General Antonio Ralfieri, and our sole targets are the Inquisitor and his men. You will not be attacked if you do not fire upon us." Black knew Ralfieri had already issued orders to stand down, but he figured it might be useful for the men on the line to hear it from the leader of the armed force bearing down on them.

He switched back to the forcewide com and addressed his own men. "Take fucking care who you shoot, all of you. You know what the targets look like. The first one of you who hits anyone but a deputy is going to have to deal with me. And that's before General Taylor gets to you." Vanderberg's men wore black uniforms, and the UN regulars wore light brown, so there was no likely confusion there. Despite the name, the Black Corps wore charcoal gray fatigues. The color was close enough to black to get confused with the Inquisitor's men unless his people were careful. Black knew that one targeting mistake, one idle Black Corps soldier shot by one of his troopers, could start a huge firefight between forces who should be allies. "So be fucking careful, all of you."

There was a commotion all around the Portal as they approached. Vanderberg's deputies were taking positions behind crates, trucks, whatever cover they could find. Ralfieri's transmission had tipped them off, but there had been no other choice. Ralfieri's address was the only chance to get the Juno forces to stand down and stay out of the fight.

Black heard gunfire up ahead. A rattle of singe shots from his men, followed by automatic fire from the defenders. He crouched down and advanced cautiously, stopping at a pile of crates covered with a tarp. It was good cover, and the position offered him a strong vantage point.

The Inquisitor's troops were in good positions, behind cover and firing indiscriminately, unconcerned with any collateral damage they inflicted. His own men were pinned down behind whatever cover they could find, returning the enemy fire slowly, cautiously. It was hard to pick out and positively ID the enemy targets in cover, and they could see there were plenty of Juno regulars in their fields of fire too.

Black sighed. This was a must-do mission. There was no easy way in, no method to distinguish the targets at this range. His people were going to have to rush the position and finish the fight at close range. He didn't want to think about how many of his men were going to be slaughtered racing across that open ground, but he couldn't think of any option. His people were never going to pick off the Inquisitor's people at this range, not without hosing down the whole position. And that would kill hundreds of the regulars too.

He took a deep breath, willing himself to order his people to attack. His bent his legs, muscles tense, ready to spring forward. If he was ordering men to charge through that fire, he was god-damned going with them. He was just about to give the command when all hell broke loose in the enemy position.

It was fire, but it wasn't the machine guns of Vanderberg's people. The sound of assault rifles, hundreds of them, ripped through the air, firing irregularly. The automatic fire dropped off and nearly stopped, and he could hear shouts and the sounds of battle from the enemy position.

Ralfieri's men! That was the only answer, Black thought, his stomach clenched with excitement. It all made sense. They hated the Inquisitor and his thugs who had slaughtered their comrades. Ralfieri's message gave them the courage to rise up, Black thought, and by God, that's just what they are doing.

"The Juno forces are fighting the Inquisitor's troops, boys. Let's get in there and help them." Black popped his half-spent cartridge and reloaded. "Remember, we don't want to hit any

friendlies, so make sure what you're aiming at before you fire."
There will be close fighting before this is over, Black thought.
Knife work.

"Charge!"

Chapter 26

From the Writings of T'arza, Elder of House Setai:

I have become more certain than ever that the Ancients foresaw the Tegeri and the humans fighting side by side against the Darkness, that it was their design from the beginning. I have come to realize that the humans are essential to our chances of victory, for they excel at war and strife in a way we Tegeri are simply not equipped to match.

Tegeri will fight when threatened or when their freedoms are attacked, but it is a necessity to us, a last resort when all else fails. Humans will fight over anything – land, currency, power, women, pride, vengeance. They will fight at the command of unworthy leaders, embrace causes they don't understand, sacrifice their sense of self to feel they are part of something larger.

They profess to want peace, but this is a fiction they create, a salve to protect them from the realization of what they truly are. They want to believe themselves peaceful beings who value freedom, but their actions and their history speak against this self-assessment. Humans retain a primitive, feral side, something that was bred out of the Tegeri race eons ago.

I have led more forces to the planet the Earth people call Oceania, and we have attacked the human armies and taken possession of the Portal leading to Juno. We have stopped the flow of reinforcements and supplies to the forces fighting Taylor, though I do not know how long we can hold. Perhaps this will be the respite he needs to win his fight and continue on to Earth, to overthrow the despotic regime that rules his people

and bring freedom to mankind...then to lead them against the
Darkness, to take their rightful places as our brothers and allies
and not our enemies.

I am reminded how terrible is war, what a scourge it is to
those forced to fight. The New Ones I led here have suffered
terrible losses, and I shall carry the burden of their deaths as
long as I live. The battlefield is a horrific sight, covered with the
dead and dying. I dread the thought of the coming war against
the Darkness. If the carnage I witness now is the result of a
misguided war with the humans, what nightmare will the fight
against the Darkness unleash on the galaxy?

T'arza stood outside the headquarters structure, watching
the columns of newly arrived troops move toward the front
line. The New Ones were manufactured beings, produced in
sophisticated crèches the Tegeri constructed expressly for that
purpose. Their genetics were carefully designed by their creators, and they suffered from no diseases, no defects. They were
physically similar to both Tegeri and humans, but they lacked the
weaknesses that plagued naturally-evolved beings.

The Tegeri created this new race as their protégés, to follow
in their footsteps. Tegeri were long-lived beings, but their race
was slowly dying. Reproduction rates had been declining for
centuries, and no effort of Tegeri science had been able to determine a cause or cure. Slowly, inexorably, the Tegeri were dying
off. At the current rate of decline, it would be millennia before
the last of them was gone, but far sooner there would be too
few to maintain the infrastructure and industry of Homeworld.

The New Ones were created to fill that void, to take over the
roles that became vacant and to continue the legacy of Tegeri
civilization when the last of the ancient race had departed this
plane of existence.

The Tegeri had poured all their knowledge and centuries
of effort into the creation of the New Ones, but they had not
yet fully achieved their goal. The New Ones were intelligent
and capable, physically superior to their creators in many ways,

but they were incomplete. They could not reproduce on their own; they had to be quickened artificially. They required bio-mechanical implants to function properly. The Tegeri had tried for centuries to make them self-sustaining, but all their efforts had failed. The New Ones were capable of thought but not true free will.

The Tegeri had not created them as slaves – indeed, such would be anathema to their culture. Yet the New Ones acted almost as slaves, seeking the guidance and approval of the Tegeri in all things, despite the wishes of their creators that they embrace their own independence. The Council had debated many times whether the New Ones had yet attained true sentience, but they had never reached a conclusion.

T'arza realized how similar the New Ones were to the humans in some ways, yet different in others. The New Ones lacked the baser instincts of humanity, greed, dishonesty, thirst for power. Yet in other aspects, there were eerie correlations. Their subordination of will to the Tegeri did not have the same terrible effects as the human tendency to follow leaders unquestioningly, but T'arza recognized the similarity of the traits. Perhaps the difference between the two is merely providence, T'arza thought. The New Ones subordinated themselves to the Tegeri, who were their creators, but the Tegeri did not fight wars of aggression or seek to impose their will on others. The humans bended their knees to the worst of their own kind, men who sought to dominate others for their own gain and accumulation of power. Would the New Ones behave the same way when the Tegeri were gone?

Perhaps there was less difference between New Ones and humans than he had thought. Had the Tegeri been different, more violent or conquest-minded, T'arza didn't doubt the New Ones would obey as readily when they were ordered to fight.

Did we err long ago, T'arza wondered…did we leave the humans on their own when they needed us to help them understand freedom and self-determination? There was no way to know if his people could have altered human history, helped their sibling race avoid its worst mistakes. Intervening would have required dominating the humans, and that was against all the Tegeri's moral and ethical principles. Should they have ignored their own beliefs, become mankind's masters to save them from their own folly? The question was irrelevant. That time had passed, and the humans, for better or worse, had been left to develop on their own.

All T'arza could do now was hope Taylor was victorious and that he managed to sway his race, to lead them from slavery and bring them, as a free and united people, to their place alongside the Tegeri as guardians of the entire galaxy.

"Honorable T'arza." A voice called, pulling him from his introspection.

"Yes, Commander Jemorah. Speak your mind."

The New One soldier stood before T'arza, clad in battle armor and fully armed. Jemorah was a High Commander, one of the highest ranked of his kind. The Tegeri were generally uncomfortable with hierarchy and authority. The members of the Council served out of duty and obligation, and beneath this top level, Tegeri society had very little stratification. They had been compelled to create a more complex rank structure for military units, but they had never become comfortable with the concept, and their armies had far fewer layers than those of their human counterparts.

Humans thrived on dividing themselves into ranks to such a great extent the Tegeri had tremendous difficulty comprehending their motivations. The human economy, government, and army – even families and informal social groups - were divided and sub-divided into an almost unimaginable series of levels, each claiming its own perquisites and authority. Humans relentlessly sought control over others and exalted status, and they considered themselves superior to any of their own race who had achieved a lesser position.

It was a trait that had led humanity to most of its worst disasters, but it was one uniquely suited to war. On the battlefield, there was rarely time for debate and discussion. The way humans naturally subdivided themselves into ranks made them excellent soldiers. Tegeri leaders had to force themselves to issue orders to their New One subordinates, but human commanders didn't hesitate to exercise their authority – or to submit to those ranked higher. Blind obedience, so destructive to a society as a whole, was tailor made for the battlefield, where discipline often meant the difference between victory and defeat.

"Honorable T'arza, the human forces have launched a massive counter-attack against our positions near the Portal." Jemorah bowed as he spoke. His people knew the Tegeri had created them, and they considered their patrons to be superiors, masters. "They have deployed massive numbers of fresh troops, newly arrived. Our lines are beginning to crumble, Honored T'arza."

T'arza paused, his face impassive. He hadn't expected to hold the Portal indefinitely, but he had hoped to maintain the interdiction of the human supply line until Taylor's people defeated their enemies on Juno. He didn't know what was happening on that world, but he doubted there had been enough time for the battle to be over. If the humans pushed through to the Portal now, they would get reinforcements to their forces, possibly enough to turn the tide and defeat Taylor's army.

"Commander, you are to deploy all reserves to hold the Portal as long as possible, without regard to the longer term effect on the war." T'arza knew he was sending thousands of New Ones to their deaths in a hopeless struggle, but days counted, even hours.

"Yes, Honorable T'arza." The commander bowed his head and turned away to execute the orders. He expressed no doubt about T'arza's command, no animosity that the Tegeri had just condemned vast numbers of his people to death in a futile battle.

T'arza watched Jemorah leave. He felt sickened, ashamed at the orders he had issued, but he kept that inside. There was no time for weakness, none even for morality. Such is war, he thought, wondering how the humans could excel so at something so terrible.

*   *   *   *   *

"All units, advance!" Halston stood at the forward command post, his brand new general's stars gleaming on his otherwise soiled and worn fatigues. The battle to reclaim the Portal had been raging non-stop for three days. His forces had taken enormous losses, but the message from Earth had been clear. Retake the Portal immediately – at all costs.

"The 17th and 23rd Battalions are to advance and attack at once." He'd been feeding in fresh troops to replace shattered units as quickly as he could get them forward. There were over 100,000 men on Oceania now, most of them originally bound for Juno. But they weren't going to get to the fight on that world unless they broke through and retook the Portal. And Halston intended to get them there. The message from Earth had also promised him promotions and wealth and privilege if he succeeded. It didn't say anything about what would happen if he failed, but he was well aware UNGov handled the stick with greater skill and readiness than the carrot.

Halston stared down at a small tablet, reviewing the OBs for the various units crowded behind the lines. He didn't know how UNGov had gotten so many troops to Oceania, but now he had control of all of them, the largest army fielded since UNGov had taken control of Earth's governments.

He'd never seen the Machines so aggressive. This was the first time he'd seen the Tegeri increase force levels on the planet too. Previously, they had simply replaced losses. They'd have crushed UN Force Oceania utterly by now if it hadn't been for the new reserves. There were at least 20,000 casualties on each side, but the fighting was still going on. The Machines were determined to hang on to the Portal, and his people were going to keep coming until they took it back.

He watched the new reserves marching by, heading up to the front. He could hear the battle from where he stood, the explosions almost constant as his forces shelled the enemy line continuously.

He'd cut off the enemy's reinforcements, positioning a blocking force to interdict their lines of supply and communication. The Machine reserves were attacking the blocking units just as ferociously as his own men were pushing toward the Portal. But he had more reserves, and whoever had the last soldier to commit to the fight was going to win.

The Machines had been pushed back, almost to the Portal itself by his constant attacks. He knew his people would break through soon. All he had to do was keep feeding new units into the fight. He could feel the tension, the excitement in his gut. The adrenalin in his system was temporarily keeping the crushing fatigue at bay. He knew how important the next 12 hours would be.

Yes, he thought, it is just a matter of time. And dead men.

Chapter 27

From the Journal of Jake Taylor:

Everyone experiences conflicts in life, interactions with people they dislike, even hate. This is natural. There are many people who do bad things, hurt people, engender justifiable enmity from others. Man is a fallible creature, and many lose their way, become something dark and hurtful.

Then there is true evil. It is something we think about, write about, a concept we fear but often can't describe clearly. It is pure malevolence, pitiless, soulless. It is something impossible to truly understand...until you go to a dark enough place and see it staring back at you.

I already had a list of reasons I despised UNGov, why I would give my all to destroy it, to track down and kill its leaders. But what they did to the men of the Black Corps, their own soldiers, was pure evil.

Black was in the thick of the fight, pistol in one hand, blood-stained knife in the other. The Inquisitor's men were tough, but they were bullies at heart, without the stomachs to fight men like Black's Supersoldiers.

He still hadn't found Vanderberg, but there weren't too many places the Inquisitor had left to hide. Most of his men were dead, and the rest were trying to flee...or begging futilely for mercy. Black had no pity for men who had killed and tortured so many civilians back on Earth. He'd seen Inquisitor teams at work before, during the food riots back in Philly. They were merciless, savage. They crushed the uprisings without pity, killing even the children as they tried to flee.

You're all very brave when you're facing starving, unarmed civilians, Black thought as he watched the terrified remnants of Vanderberg's forces fleeing in a disordered rout. They wouldn't get far. There were at least a thousand men from UN Force Juno waiting. Black didn't know if those men would join the Crusade, but he was damned sure they were out to avenge their slain comrades. He knew Vanderberg's men would get no pity from them either.

Black swung around to face another of the Inquisitor's thugs. He thrust his arm forward, hitting his foe in the face hard with his pistol. The deputy was stunned, and he hesitated for an instant. That was all Black needed. He shoved his combat knife hard, jamming it into his enemy's armpit with all the force his enhanced muscles could manage.

The deputy's blood poured down Black's arm as the man slid off his knife and fell to the floor dead. Black's combat reflexes didn't allow him a respite. He leapt forward, moving toward another of the deputies when a message came over the com.

"Attention Black Corps soldiers. This is Inquisitor Vanderberg." The message was broadcast over the Black Corps' frequency. The voice was deep, angry. "You are hereby commanded to attack and destroy all forces from the opposing army as well as all Juno regulars currently assisting them. This is a Priority Yellow-9 order."

There weren't many of the Black Corps men in the area, but the few that were there began firing immediately. Black was about to turn when he felt a pain in his shoulder. He was pushed forward by the round, and he spun himself around as he fell. It was one of Ralfieri's people, from the detachment that had come to Taylor's headquarters. Black hadn't known what to expect from the troops positioned at the Portal, but he was shocked that the men who'd accompanied Ralfieri were attacking his people.

His veteran reflexes took over, and he raised his pistol even as he fell, putting at least 5 or 6 rounds in his attacker. He dropped to the ground and clicked on the com as he lay there. "It's a trap, men. Take out Ralfieri's escorts. Now!"

He took a deep breath. The shot to his shoulder was nothing, at least not enough to keep Tony Black out of a fight. He took a deep breath and got up, spinning his head around, looking for any of the Black Corps troopers who'd come with him. There was vengeance in his eyes. Black could stay cool in the maelstrom of combat, but he had no place for backstabbing traitors.

*   *   *   *   *

"Stand down!" Ralfieri's voice was raw, but he kept screaming into the com. "All Black Corps personnel, cease fire immediately and stand down. I repeat, cease fire at once."

He didn't know what was happening. His people were firing on Black's troops, even the detachment he'd taken with him to Taylor's camp, men who'd listened to the truth and sworn to join the Crusade. They were attacking the Juno troops too, trying to aid the remnants of Vanderberg's force. He didn't know why they were following the Inquisitor's orders now and ignoring his.

Black's people had been taken by surprise, and they'd lost 20 men before they realized their new allies were attacking them. But then they fell on their attackers with unimaginable fury. Black's men were Supersoldiers too, and they were hardened veterans of Gehenna. No warriors ever made could stand against them.

The men of Ralfieri's detachment fell, one by one cut down by Black's enraged soldiers. Black's people assumed the entire mission was a trap, and all of the UN soldiers present were part of it. They fired away indiscriminately, unconcerned with collateral damage. A few of the Juno troops were caught in the crossfire, but most of them were off in pursuit of the last of Vanderberg's men, cutting them down, tearing apart the ones they were able to catch and shooting down the others as they fled.

It took a few minutes, but Black realized it was just the Black Corps soldiers fighting his people. The Juno forces were finishing off Vanderberg's troops, but none of them were attacking his men.

"Do not attack the Juno regulars!" Black shouted into the com. "Only the Black Corps troopers are attacking us." Black saw another Black Corps man running across his field of view, about 50 meters away. His combat reflexes took over, whipping around his rifle and firing half a dozen shots. One of his hits tore half the target's head off, and the body spun and fell to the ground.

Most of the Black Corps troopers in the immediate area were dead, only a few still standing. Black still didn't understand what had happened, why Raflieri's men had suddenly switched sides. He'd spoken with them all, and he'd been sure they were sincere. Could he have read them that incorrectly? It didn't make sense.

"I want prisoners," he abruptly yelled into the com. "Take the last few captive if possible." He wanted to get to the bottom of this, and he needed prisoners to question.

"And find Inquisitor Vanderberg. I want him dead. Now!"

*   *   *   *   *

Taylor stood before the disarmed, shackled prisoners. Black's people had managed to take three alive and send them back. They also found Vanderberg, or what was left of him, at least. The Juno regulars had run the Inquisitor down a few klicks from the Portal. By the time they stopped shooting, there was almost nothing left of Vanderberg's mangled body, nothing solid at least.

The prisoners were all wounded, but they were still ambulatory. The nanotech in their bloodstreams was already at work, healing their injuries and pumping them full of antibiotics and stimulants. They stared back at Taylor with strange, blank looks on their faces, as if they were in some kind of shock.

"Why, Major Evans?" Taylor's voice was calm, though he

was enraged that the Black Corps soldiers had attacked his people. "Why did you disobey General Ralfieri and ambush my men?"

"General Taylor…" Evans looked up at Taylor, his watery eyes struggling to meet the general's. There was a strip of cloth wrapped around a wound on his leg. The bandage was covered with dried blood and caked in mud and filth. "I don't know, sir." He forced himself to look Taylor in the eyes. "I just don't know."

Taylor glared down at Evans. "You're going to have to do better than that, Major."

Evans swallowed hard. "I really don't know, sir. I…I just couldn't…not do it, General." His voice was cracked and emotional. "I…really don't know, sir. My memory of the whole thing is very spotty."

Taylor took a step toward Evans. "Major, do you understand how crazy that sounds? Almost 30 of my soldiers are dead, shot in the back by your men." He paused and took a deep breath. "Do you know how hard it is for me not to put a bullet in your head right now?" Taylor glared at the prisoner. "You'd better start making sense. Now."

Evans stared at Taylor piteously. "Yes, sir, I understand sir. I know it sounds insane." His voice was a miserable rasp, and tears were streaming down his face. "But it is the truth, General. I couldn't stop myself. I just couldn't."

Taylor was about to speak when he heard a fast hovercraft approaching. The light transport pulled up about 20 meters away, and General Antonio Ralfieri jumped out and strode purposefully toward Taylor and the prisoners. His left hand held a pistol and his right was clenched into a fist.

"Why Evans?" His voice was unfiltered rage. "Why did you do it?" He stopped right in front of the sobbing major. "You have one chance to explain yourself. One." He held out the pistol, aiming it right at Evans' head.

"Antonio…wait." Taylor walked up slowly behind the enraged general. He put his hand gently on Ralfieri's arm, pushing it slowly to the side. Taylor couldn't explain it, but something told him Evans was telling the truth. It didn't make sense, but he wanted to get to the bottom of just what had happened at the Portal.

"General Taylor, this treacherous vermin killed your men." Ralfieri was enraged, and he struggled to control his tone when speaking to Taylor. "He should die for his crimes."

"Antonio, just relax." Taylor's tone was calm, soothing. "If he is guilty I assure you he will pay with his life. But he says he couldn't stop himself. That sounds like some kind of conditioning to me."

Ralfieri looked skeptical. "General, I don't want to believe what happened any more than you, but I don't believe a word from this man's mouth."

"I'm not saying I do either." Taylor glanced at the prostrate Evans then back to Ralfieri. "But what he is describing sounds a lot like conditioning of some kind. And I wouldn't put it past UNGov to condition your men without your knowledge." Taylor's voice became darker, angrier when he mentioned UNGov.

"I swear to you both, it was like someone else was controlling my arms and legs." Evans spoke softly, his voice deep with sadness. The men kneeling next to him nodded as he spoke.

"Yes, sirs," one of them said. "The Major is telling the truth."

Ralfieri still looked skeptical, but Taylor turned to face him again. "It doesn't make any sense, Antonio. They could have killed us both right here before you left if they'd wanted to. Why wait until they are in action, outnumbered 15-1 by my men? Unless they had no choice. Unless it was the Inquisitor's order that activated their conditioning."

Ralfieri just stared back at Taylor wordlessly. His mind was racing, wondering if Evans and his men had indeed been subjected to some kind of mental conditioning...if all of the Black Corps had.

Taylor flipped on his com. "Dr. Harris," he said softly. "I need you here now. There are some men I want you to examine."

*   *   *   *   *

"It would take me months to figure out exactly what was done to these guys, General, but I feel pretty comfortable saying they didn't attack our people of their own free will." Doctor Harris was the AOL's chief surgeon and the commander of its medical services.

"You mean some kind of conditioning?" Taylor sounded uncertain. He wasn't sure he believed that any kind of psycho-babble could have caused the Black Corps men to behave as they had.

"Yes…conditioning certainly, but something more than that too." Harris' tone changed, became darker, angrier. "General, these guys have all had some sort of invasive brain surgery."

"Surgery? You mean they were modified somehow to control their behavior?" Fresh anger crept into Taylor's voice.

"That's exactly what I mean." Harris was angry too. The thought of UNGov cutting into the soldiers' brains so they could control them more effectively was anathema to him. He wondered what kind of doctor would perform such a heinous procedure. "I seriously doubt they are capable of resisting the orders of a command figure."

"But they ignored General Ralfieri's orders to cease fire."

"If I had to guess, General, I'd say there are certain command phrases as well as pre-programmed preferences for a designated hierarchy, one that may be very different from the military organizational chart." He paused for a few seconds. "A UN Inquisitor is a high-level authority figure. It would not be at all surprising if the programming gives higher priority to orders from such an individual. Indeed, from UNGov's perspective, that makes perfect sense. If a general were to go rogue, a government enforcer could take control of his men. I suspect the whole thing was instigated by our rebellion, General."

Taylor stood silently for a minute, looking down at the ground and thinking about what Harris had just told him. Finally, his eyes shot back up to the doctor. "So how do we reverse the conditioning, Bill? Can you do it without surgery, or do you have to open them all up?" He began to think of the monumental task of performing brain surgery on thousands of

Black Corps soldiers in the field."

"There's nothing I can do, General." Harris' voice was sad but firm.

"You mean nothing you can do here? What kind of facility do you need?"

"No, Jake." The doctor spoke slowly, grimly. "There is nothing anyone can do. The procedure is irreversible."

The words hit Taylor like a sledgehammer. "Are you sure?"

"I'm positive, General." Harris spoke softly. "It's intentional. Whoever did it designed the procedure to be permanent. At least to current medical technology. Any attempt to modify the affected area of the brain would be immediately fatal."

The implications of Harris' words were sinking in to Taylor's mind. "So these men will always follow the orders of whomever they are programmed to obey....forever? No matter what the men themselves want? No matter what we do?

"I'm afraid so, General." Harris took a deep breath. "Whoever did this knows his business."

Taylor didn't reply. He just stood there looking to the side, his mind racing with implications. He hadn't thought it was possible to hate UNGov more than he already did, but the rage inside him was stronger than ever. What kind of monsters, he thought, would do this to thousands of their own soldiers? But he didn't need an answer. He already knew.

Chapter 28

To All Member of the Supreme Secretariat:

An emergency meeting of the Secretariat is called for 1pm, this afternoon, Geneva time. All members are required to attend. – The Office of the Secretary-General

"I am here today on a matter of the gravest import." Raul Esteban sat in his place at the head of the table. He was leaning back, half sitting, half lying in a motorized chair. The plush leather seat he normally occupied had been pulled aside. He was weak, his voice a barely audible whisper, amplified by a small microphone attached to a headset. There were loosely bandaged sores all around his neck and the lower part of his face. His eyes were filmy, and only a few strands of his once-thick hair still hung from his bald head.

Four large guards, fully-armed and wearing body armor, stood silently behind Esteban. It was a violation of Secretariat rules for armed personnel to enter the chamber, but no one questioned the Secretary-General.

For only the second time in its history, the Secretariat had been called to an emergency meeting, its exalted members roused from whatever else they were doing and summoned to UNGov HQ. They were now gathered, save two. Anan Keita was on Juno, his chair next to Samovich empty. The seat on Esteban's left was also vacant. Chang Li was conspicuously absent. He hadn't responded to the emergency call, and no one knew where he was. His allies looked around nervously, not sure what to expect.

"Last night there was an attempt on my life." Esteban's amplified voice was weak and tinny, but his anger was obvious. "It was a well-planned and executed operation, one that likely would have succeeded without the timely intervention of Secretary Samovich's internal security forces."

There was a ripple of surprise around the table. Everybody knew Esteban didn't have long to live, but they were shocked and outraged that anyone would make an attempt on the life of a member of the Secretariat. They considered themselves untouchable, and most of them viewed any attack on one of them as a dangerous precedent.

"I want to thank Secretary Samovich for his efforts. I will now yield the floor to him so that he may enlighten us further on this criminal act."

Samovich rose and looked out at the faces around the table. "Thank you, Secretary-General. I would like to begin by expressing my own outrage at this appalling crime." He glanced back toward Esteban for an instant before continuing. "In cooperation with the Secretary-General's security team, my operatives were able to capture several of the perpetrators alive." He looked around the table again, watching for any reactions from Li's allies. He suspected none of them had been in on the scheme, but he hadn't been sure, not until he saw the shock in their eyes.

"The prisoners were brought to Internal Security headquarters and questioned through the night." He struggled to keep the excitement from his voice. "We discovered the truth, and I'm afraid it is extremely unpleasant. All of the prisoners have confessed, and their stories support each other. They were sent to kill Secretary-General Esteban by none other than Secretary Chang Li." His tone was one of sadness, shock. Anton Samovich was a good actor.

The room was silent, stunned looks on the faces of most of those present. This was a development none could have foreseen, an astonishing turn of events. Li's allies looked skeptical, as if they suspected some sort of trick by Samovich.

"Bring in the prisoner." Samovich turned to face the sentry at the door as he spoke.

A few seconds later, two guards brought in Zhao Min. They were half dragging, half carrying the barely conscious man into the chamber. They stopped behind Samovich, holding the slumping form of Chang Li's top henchman.

"This is Zhao Min, my esteemed colleagues, one of Chang Li's personal operatives." He turned toward the prisoner. "Tell this body what you told me last night. Who sent you to attack the Secretary-General?"

The captive turned his head slowly. Samovich had ordered Zhao cleaned up for his appearance, but he still looked haggard and exhausted. It was clear he'd been through a very harsh interrogation. He stood, shaking, shrinking away from Samovich.

"Come now, we have your confession on video, along with those of your co-conspirators. There is nothing to be served by a refusal to cooperate now."

Zhao swallowed hard. "Yes," he croaked. "Chang Li sent us to assassinate the Secretary-General."

"There," Samovich declared, slamming his fist on the table. "An admission from one of the lead perpetrators." He motioned for the guards to remove the prisoner, and he looked over at Li's empty chair. "And where is Secretary Li?" He turned toward Li's closest allies. "Why is Chang Li not here? Why did he not respond to the summons?" He turned and faced Esteban. "Because he is guilty, that is why. Because he is hiding from the justice he knows he will find here."

Esteban's labored breathing was loud through the amplifier. Samovich had briefed him before the meeting, but he was still enraged about Li's attempt, and hearing the operative acknowledge Li's involvement made his blood boil. He knew he didn't have more than a week or two left anyway, but his ego couldn't accept that anyone would have the audacity to challenge him.

He cleared his raw throat. "In consideration of the information Secretary Samovich has presented, I would like to propose several actions." Esteban paused, catching his breath before he continued. "First, I propose that this body strip Chang Li of his Seat, effective immediately and, further, that a Warrant of Execution be issued at once, directing all state security forces to terminate him on sight."

Samovich rose again, restraining his excitement and doing his best imitation of regret. "It is with great sadness that I must second the Secretary-General's proposal. An attack on one of us is an attack on all of us and cannot be condoned." He stared over at Li's allies. "All in favor?"

His own people raised their hands immediately, as did those of the neutral block. Li's allies paused, the shock heavy on their faces. He knew they were realizing it would be suicidal to continue to support Li. They glanced back and forth at each other before slowly, reluctantly raising their hands. Samovich watched, struggling to keep the grim expression on his face, to fight back the broad smile that wanted to escape. After years of planning and waiting, he was about to win the ultimate victory.

"It is unanimous. Chang Li is hereby expelled from this body and declared an enemy of the state. He will be arrested and executed as soon as he can be found." Taylor managed a solemn tone of voice, as if he regretted the entire situation.

"Now for my second piece of business." Esteban turned his head slowly to look over at Samovich. "You all know I am dying. It is now time for us to consider the future of this body, the leadership that will bring our noble experiment in world government into the future. Therefore, I propose that I step down from the Secretary-Generalship, effective immediately, and assume an advisory role as Secretary-General emeritus."

Surprised murmurs rippled around the table. No one had expected Raul Esteban to resign his position and power, not while he was still breathing.

"This government, and this august body, are very dear to me. I am the last of the Founders, the final member of the first Secretariat, and nothing is more important to me than to ensure that UNGov moves into the future boldly, and with continued success."

Esteban struggled to raise his head, angling to stare directly at Samovich. "It is for that reason that I propose that Secretary Anton Samovich, who has served this body long and faithfully, be appointed the new Secretary-General of the United Nations World Government, and that he be sworn in and invested with the powers of the office immediately."

Samovich sat quietly, trying to keep the grin off his face. All the planning, all the second guessing, years of calculating and debating…and Drogov's people blunder into Li's attack on Esteban's compound. Luck could make or break the most carefully conceived plans, and this time providence had cast its vote for Anton Samovich.

"I second the motion." It was Pierre Aguillard, one of Samovich's creatures.

"All agreed?" Esteban looked out across the table. One by one, hands were raised.

Samovich was watching Li's closest allies, trying to imagine what was going through their heads. Li was gone suddenly, expelled from the Secretariat with a death sentence on his head. Now his avowed enemy was about to step into the Secretary-General's chair. They were realizing, he knew, that they had to supplicate themselves to him, to ease themselves away from the disgraced Li and into his good graces. Samovich smiled as he watched each in turn raise their hands.

"It is unanimous." Esteban's weak voice silenced the room. "Anton Samovich, you are now the Secretary-General of the United Nations World Government." He waved to the guards standing behind him, and one of them pull his chair back slowly. "Rise and take your place at the head of this table."

Samovich walked toward the Secretary-General's seat as one of the guards slid the chair back into place. He stood for a few seconds looking out over the rest of the Secretariat. "I want to thank you all, and especially Secretary-General Emeritus Esteban, both for his confidence and for his years of exemplary leadership, from which I have learned more than I can easily list."

A round of applause followed, loud and enthusiastic. Finally, he thought, as he lowered himself slowly into the chair…after all these years. Anton Samovich was Secretary-General, the most powerful man in the world.

Chapter 29

From the Journal of Jake Taylor:

I feel a strange kinship to General Ralfieri. I see in him myself two years ago, struggling to deal with the terrible truths he has learned too quickly. I pity him also, for I know where the road ahead of him leads. I understand the pressure, the self-loathing, the dark path he must tread. I know, because that has been my road, and still it goes on, into the darkness with no end in sight.

Ralfieri was silent, staring at Taylor with a look of horror on his face. Part of him couldn't believe what the AOL's commander had just told him, but in his heart he knew it was true.

"I'm sorry, Antonio." Taylor was sympathetic. He couldn't imagine what his new ally was feeling. He put his hand on Ralfieri's shoulder. "I know it is hard to accept."

"There is no way to reverse the procedure? No way to prevent UNGov from controlling those men?"

"I'm sorry, Antonio." Taylor had felt the same outrage and despair when he'd first learned what had been done to the men of the Black Corps. "Dr. Harris knows his business. When he says he is sure, I've never seen him be wrong. And he had no doubt, no doubt at all." Taylor paused, giving Ralfieri a chance to absorb what he'd said. "The irreversibility is deliberate."

"I don't know what to do. Colonel Black's people have captured Secretary Keita, so that buys us some time, at least." The word had just come through. They'd found Keita hiding in a large crate in a supply dump. He was on his way to headquarters under heavy guard. "With any luck there isn't anyone else currently on Juno who can override your orders. And Colonel Black's rearguard is on the Portal, so we'll know if anyone else arrives."

Ralfieri took a deep breath. He'd addressed all the soldiers on Juno, and virtually every one of them, Black Corps and UN Force Juno alike, had rallied to Taylor's cause. He'd been surprised at the response, at how quickly the men of his army were ready to join their former enemies. Some, he was sure, were more enthusiastic than others. Many were probably going along with comrades. But he realized they all knew what UNGov truly was. They'd all been taken away from friends and family and shipped to a foreign world. They had fought well, but not for UNGov. They'd given their all for their comrades, the men standing next to them in the line.

He'd been relieved by the reaction. He'd been dreading how he would handle a splintered force, with thousands of men under arms remaining loyal to UNGov, and he was thrilled not to have to go down that road. Things were under control for the moment, but he realized as soon as UNGov got someone else of a top command level to the planet, the Black Corps men would be turned against him again. They would struggle to control their wills, to stand with their new allies, but they would fail. And they would attack Taylor's army and the men of UN Force Juno. It would be a bloodbath, and a tragedy Ralfieri didn't want to imagine.

"We need to get the Black Corps off Juno, Jake. As quickly as possible. Before another Inquisitor gets here and turns them on us."

"My thoughts exactly." Taylor nodded as he spoke. "And then we need to get the rest of the army offworld while we have this respite, before the enemy starts sending men through the Portal. If we stay on Juno, UNGov will simply send more and more troops through until we are destroyed."

Taylor turned toward Major Samuels. "Bear, go with General Ralfieri and help him coordinate getting his people through the Portal. Commandeer any available transport you can find."

Samuels nodded. "Yes, sir."

"Thank you, Jake." Ralfieri extended his hand toward Taylor and the two shook warmly before Ralfieri and Samuels turned and walked away.

Taylor pulled out his com, punching in the code for Major Young. "Karl, I need you to begin coordinating our people and getting them to the Lorus Portal. We're leaving Juno."

"I'm on it, Jake."

Taylor could hear the relief in Young's voice. He knew his people would fight if he ordered them to, but the war on Juno had been an apocalypse, and his people were all near the breaking point. It only served the enemy if they stayed to fight wave after wave of UN forces. It was time to go.

"I've assigned most of our transport to ferry the Black Corps and Force Juno troops to the Portal, so do the best you can with what you've got." Taylor paused then added, "Keep them moving, Karl. I want us off this planet as soon as possible." He thought of Black and his men at the Portal, alone and exposed.

"We'll manage, Jake. I'll get them there."

"Thanks, Karl." Taylor cut the line. No one would force march the men harder than Frantic Young…except maybe Hank Daniels. And Taylor had another job for Daniels.

"Hank, you feel up to some serious duty?" Daniels was standing a few meters away. He'd just been released from the field hospital, and that only because he'd driven every doctor in the place crazy until they let him go. He looked ready for action, but Taylor knew he wasn't 100% yet. But he needed every senior officer he had, and Daniels was one of his best. And he was perfect for what Taylor had in mind.

"I'm good to go, Jake. I'll take care of anything you need." Daniels was still in moderate pain, but he masked it perfectly. "What can I do?"

"I want you to put together a force of 1,000 men, all Super-soldiers, and position them here." Taylor held up a small pad, pointing to a spot on the map it displayed. The position was a strategic one, along a defensible ridge and positioned to cover the army's retreat to the Lorus Portal. It was a good spot to intercept any forces moving from the Oceania Portal.

Daniels smiled. "You got it, Jake. I'll start with the survivors from my battalions and add what I need from other units."

"That's fine, Hank." Taylor knew he was going to have to do a lot of adding. There weren't many of his own men still in the field. Exactly 202, Taylor's NIS forced into his memory. "Take anybody you need, but choose them well. You're going to be the last people to leave Juno." Taylor reached out his hand. "Except for Blackie's rearguard and me, of course."

Daniels grasped Taylor's hand and shook it briskly. "Thank you, Jake." Daniels was a true warrior, and the idea of sitting idle at a time like this was unthinkable. He was grateful to have an important job and to see that he hadn't lost Taylor's trust. The disaster that had befallen his troops when the Black Corps first appeared wasn't his fault, but he blamed himself anyway.

Taylor knew exactly what Daniels was thinking. "You're welcome, Hank." He paused then added, "Take it easy. No heroics. You're people are just there in case. With any luck, Blackie's people will fall back on your line, and we'll all transit together."

*   *   *   *   *

"General Taylor, Colonel Black is reporting enemy forces moving through the Portal!" The aide was rushing toward Taylor, shouting the report as he approached. "He has placed his forces in a defensive position around the Portal, and he reports that all enemy efforts to push through so far have been repulsed."

Taylor felt like he'd been slapped in the face. The cessation of enemy traffic through the Oceania Portal had never been explained, but he'd hoped it would continue until he and Ralfieri managed to move the rest of the army through the Lorus Portal. About a third of the forces had passed through already, mostly Taylor's unmodified units and the wounded who could be easily moved. The Black Corps had been spread out across 200 square kilometers, and the shortage of transport was slowing their move to the transit site. The Lorus Portal was hundreds of klicks from the battlefield, across a long stretch of difficult and rocky terrain. Even force-marching Supersoldiers needed time to travel that far.

Now there was nothing but Tony Black and 272 of the AOL's best men standing between the withdrawing army and whatever enemy reinforcements were trying to push through. Taylor knew Black and his people would fight like lions. He was sure they could hold the Portal, at least for a while. But eventually the enemy was going to push through. He had to get his people moving.

"General Black is to jam all communications around the Portal immediately." He knew that was going to cut Black's people off from HQ, but he didn't have a choice. All it would take was one man with the proper rank and codes getting through the Portal, and the Black Corps would be fighting his people again.

"Yes, General Taylor." The aide turned and ran back to the communications structure to relay Taylor's command.

Jake stood silently for a minute, imagining the situation at the Oceania Portal. Blackie would have his men deployed all around the transit point, back far enough to avoid any enemy efforts to lob bombs and grenades through. He would have every vantage point covered, multiple fields of fire converging on the narrow exit of the Portal. His people would kill hundreds of the soldiers who tried to force their way through, maybe even thousands. But they would become fatigued, run low on ammunition. If UNGov was pushing enough people through, sooner or later they would overwhelm Black and his men.

The evac had to be completed before that happened. He had to get everybody off Juno and send the transports back to get Black and the rearguard, and he had to do it before they were wiped out. He almost commed Ralfieri and Young to check on their status, but he stopped himself. They're good men, he thought, the best. And they understood what was at stake. They would get the job done as quickly as humanly possible without him harassing them.

Taylor turned and looked off in the general direction of the

Oceania Portal. Tony Black and a handful of men were standing in the breach, as they had so many times, buying the army
time to escape. Taylor wanted more than anything to be with
them, to be the last man to fall back from that crucial defensive
position. But the burdens of command were there, as always.
He was responsible for thousands of soldiers, not just the 300
fighting to hold the Portal. But one of those 300 was his best
friend, a man closer to him than any brother. He stared off into
the distance, his mind replaying the last angry words Black had
said to him. And thanks to the NIS, he remembered every syl-
lable, as he would until the day he died.

*   *   *   *   *

"Keep it moving, Frantic. I want the rest of those men
through in an hour." Taylor was riding everyone's last nerve,
pushing the contingents to move through the Portal as quickly
as possible.

"I'm on it, Jake." Young sounded exhausted. Even with
surgically-enhanced muscles and adrenalin-producing nanobots,
there was a limit to what men could do with no rest. Taylor
had been pushing his people to that limit, and none had worked
harder than Karl Young. "I'll get them through."

Taylor nodded and turned as he saw Samuels moving toward
him. "Bear, what's the status on the Black Corps?"

"Assembled one klick from the Portal, Jake. Ready to go any
time."

Taylor nodded. "Are you sure they're all there?"

"Yes, sir. General Ralfieri and I triple-checked."

"Very well, order Captain Larken to set up a jamming perimeter around them and cut the interference around the Oceania
Portal." Taylor's people had been jamming all communications
across the field, trying to ensure that no orders could reach the
Black Corps soldiers and activate their programming, even if
someone managed to slip past Black and his men. It was effective, but blanketing a wide area took enormous power, and it
was burning through the army's dwindling supply of fuel. The

wide-area jamming was also interfering with communications with Black's rearguard. And Taylor wanted to know what was going on at the Portal.

"Yes, Jake. I'll take care of it now." Samuels turned and trotted off toward the com station.

Taylor walked up and down the ranks of troops moving toward the narrow Portal entrance. His army was leaving a lot of its equipment and supplies behind. He knew that would come back to haunt them later, but there was no choice. Disassembling power units and heavy transports and manhandling the parts through the Portal would take days, even weeks. Time he knew his people didn't have. Not with the enemy trying to smash through the Portal with fresh troops.

"Jake!" Samuels' shouted from the front of the com station as he ran back toward Taylor. His voice face was stricken, his voice distraught. "We just reached Colonel Black, sir. He is mortally wounded, and most of his command is destroyed. Enemy troops are pouring through the Portal."

Chapter 30

From the Journal of Jake Taylor:

How much pain and loss can a man bear and still push forward? I would welcome death in battle, the quick release from all my burdens. Perhaps, I think, I will stay on Juno, meet the enemy alone, die in arms, responsible for no one's death but my own. But then I remember the cause, the Crusade. My death would hand UNGov the victory, and all those who have died in our efforts would have paid that great price in vain. My destiny is not in my control; my life is not mine to give. It belongs to the dead from our battles, men who stood in the line and gave all they had to give...because I asked them to, because I promised never to yield until Earth was free of its cancerous government. I must find a way to go on, to muster the strength and will they deserve. Anything less would be unforgivable.

"Blackie!" Taylor's voice blasted through the com, his tone almost frantic. "Blackie, can you hear me?"

Black tried to pull his body up against the small rock behind him, slowly raising his head as he propped himself up. He sat for a few seconds, trying to catch his breath, but he was too lightheaded, and he allowed himself to slide back down. He lay on his side and took a shallow, painful breath. His throat was parched. He reached for his canteen, but it had been holed, and all the water had drained away.

"Jake..." He coughed, feeling the blood slowly filling his lungs. He could feel the nanobots working too, but he suspected this time the extraordinary technology was going to meet its match. His body was riddled with enemy projectiles, and he was covered in burns. He was kilometers from the nearest hospital, and nobody could get to him, not in time. Not without jeopardizing the whole plan. His men had dragged him back from the front lines, but now most of them were dead, and he could hear the sounds of the enemy troops getting closer.

"What's the status of the rearguard, Blackie?" Taylor's voice was choked with emotion. He could tell his friend was wounded, but he struggled to stay focused.

"Dead, Jake." Black's voice was strained, throaty. "Most of them are dead, and the rest are pinned down. They won't last long now."

Taylor felt his stomach clench. Black had taken 300 men with him, the toughest and longest-serving veterans in the army. Now they were all dead, their lives the price of the army's chance at escape.

"Sit tight, Blackie. I've got Hank Daniels and his crew on standby. I'll have help to you as soon as possible."

"No. Not this time." The words sliced through the com like daggers piercing Taylor's chest. "I'm done, Jake." There was sadness in Black's voice, and concern for his friend, his brother.

Black gritted his teeth against the pain. He could face his own death, but he couldn't let Jake endanger the remnants of the army in some futile effort to save him. Knowing his death was buying the army its escape was a comfort, and he wasn't going to let Taylor get everyone else killed out of some sense of duty to him. "I'm not getting out of this one, buddy."

"To hell you're not." Taylor roared through the com, his voice determination itself. "I'm not leaving you. I'm coming there myself. You just stay low, and wait."

Black could hear the tension and grief in Taylor's voice. He didn't know how much more his friend could take. He regretted his crisis of faith, his earlier anger at Taylor. It was the crushing stress they'd all been under since they'd begun the Crusade. The pressure was maddening. It was almost impossible to bear, and Taylor had it worst of everyone.

"You sit tight, Blackie. We're on the way."

"No." There was a firmness to Black's voice. "Don't make me die here knowing you and half the army are going to get killed in a useless effort to save me." There was pleading in his tone too. "I'm shot to pieces, and whatever survivors are still hanging on will be dead in a few minutes. You'll get here too late, and the relieving force will be trapped and overwhelmed." He paused, coughing up blood as he rasped for air. "Let our deaths mean something, Jake. Let us know we saved the army before we die."

Taylor didn't answer for a few seconds. He couldn't force the words. Finally, he said, "Blackie, I'm so sorry."

"Forget that, Jake. It's just war. Death's waiting out there for all of us. Today is my day." Black hesitated for a few seconds. "I'm sorry we fought, my friend." Black's voice was getting weaker, and Taylor could tell how much effort it took for him to speak.

"Don't worry about that, Bla…"

"Just let me finish, Jake." He paused, gasping for air. "Please." Black sucked in another shallow breath, gritting his teeth against the pain. "I was wrong before. I wish I could take back what I said, Jake." Another pause. "I don't want to die with this between us. I regret it all. You're the closest friend I've ever had…and the best man I've ever known. None of this is your fault, any more than it's any of ours. And if there's a chance to end it all, to get back to Earth and destroy the monstrosity that rules all mankind, there couldn't be a better man in charge."

Taylor's felt a tightness in his chest as Black's words tore at him. "No, Blackie." He spoke softly, struggling to hold back his tears. "You were right. We should have gotten out of here sooner. It was my pride, my arrogance. I couldn't leave the field to the enemy."

"No. There is no one else who could lead this army, no one but you. We look to you, expect you to be perfect, to know what to do in every situation. It's an impossible burden we put on you, Jake, but it's the only way we can push ourselves through this nightmare." He paused again, gasping for breath. "We lost a lot of good men here, Jake." Black's voice was fading to a whisper, but he forced himself to continue. "I'm just one more, my friend. When you get to Earth and crush those miserable bastards at UNGov, raise your glass one time to me, to old friends who didn't make it back."

Taylor tried to speak, but he couldn't push the words from his throat. There were tears streaming down his cheeks, and his hands were clenched into tight fists. The rage and despair threatened to consume him. He was ready to order every man that remained to march to Black's position, to toss the plan and fight one last battle to the death. But he knew he couldn't. Duty. It had become the bane of his existence, an irresistible force that tormented him constantly. But he was its slave, and he knew he could never escape its bitter embrace. He had to get what remained of the army through the Portal...and back to Earth. That was more important than anyone's life. Even Tony Black's.

"Now go, Jake." Black's voice was softer, weaker. "Go now while you still can. Get everyone through the Portal...and kill those bastards on Earth."

Black took one last rasping breath, and then he fell silent. Taylor knew his friend was gone.

*   *   *   *   *

Evans stood facing Taylor. The columns were moving quickly through the Portal. There were UN Force Juno troops marching through now, survivors of the initial planetary army. The original force had lost well over half its strength, but virtually all of those who were left had rallied to Taylor's cause.

Taylor was trying to focus on getting everyone through the Portal before the enemy could get enough forces through from Oceania to mount an attack. If they hit his people all strung out at the Portal, with half their force already transited, it would be a disaster.

He was grateful for the distraction, for anything that kept his mind busy. He'd staggered behind one of the small shelters and fallen to his knees right after he spoke to Black. His stomach emptied, and tears poured down his face. He was grateful Black had forgiven him, that they hadn't parted on bad terms, but that didn't change the fact that his closest friend was dead. He'd died performing the mission Taylor had given him, alone and in pain. He'd died so the army could survive, so it could move on with the Crusade. The time Black and his people had bought with their lives would save thousands, allow them to transit to Lorus before the new UN forces could attack and overwhelm them. Taylor had taken a few minutes to mourn his friend, but then he'd pulled himself back together and gone back to work.

"You know we can't go with you, General Taylor." There was sadness in Evans' voice, and grave resignation. "As soon as they can get a signal through to me – to all of us – we'll attack you again. You know it, and so do I." He took a deep breath. "They did this to us, General, and there's no undoing it. As long as they can communicate with us, we're their slaves. We can't fight them, can't raise a hand against them…and we'll do whatever they command, even though our conscious minds are screaming no."

Taylor opened his mouth, but he didn't know what to say. Evans' words hit him hard, but he realized they were true. He knew what had to be done, but he didn't want to allow himself to believe it, and he certainly didn't have the strength to do it. These were good men, veterans who had fought in good faith against the Tegeri before they were drafted into the Black Corps and turned into cyborgs. They'd been lied to just as he had been. Worse, UNGov had cut into their brains, stolen their free will. Taylor couldn't command these men to stay behind, much less order his soldiers to attack them. He knew the Black Corps would remain a deadly threat to his army, but he simply couldn't face the reality of doing something about it.

"Don't worry, General." There was a strange tone to Evans' voice, an eerie calm. "We will take care of things here. You just get your people and the unmodified survivors from the Juno army through the Portal before the new UN forces can deploy and attack."

Taylor felt like nauseous. He had an idea what Evans was planning. "No, Tom…" He put his hand on Evans' soldier. "We'll find a way. We'll…"

"There is no way, Jake." Evans forced a smile. "You know that as well as I do. My people have a choice. Wait until UNGov gets new commanders here to make us slaves again. Or…" Evans took a breath. "…or take matters into our own hands."

"Tom…"

"Please, Jake. Go now. Get everybody through the Portal. Don't waste the time Colonel Black and his people paid so dearly for. Finish the Crusade. That's what you can do for us. Make sure those bastards can never do this to anyone again. Ever."

Taylor knew Evans was right. There were probably thousands of troops pouring through the Portal from Oceania. They were men like just those of UN Force Juno, but they had no idea of the truth. They all believed Taylor's men were the worst traitors imaginable, killers who had slaughtered their counterparts on Juno and a string of other worlds. Taylor had considered trying to address them, to convince them to come over to his side along with the remnants of UN Force Juno. But he knew there wasn't time. There would be UN security among the arriving soldiers, maybe even another Inquisitor. No, there was no choice. If his people were going to have any hope of reaching Earth they had to leave Juno. Immediately.

Taylor looked at Evans, his respect for the man growing by the second. He didn't know what to say. He struggled for words, but they eluded him. Finally, he snapped a perfect salute to Evans. "Major, it has been my honor to serve with you." He extended his hand.

Evans reached out and grabbed Taylor's hand. "And my honor to have served with you, however briefly. Please accept my renewed apologies for the losses you suffered when our programming was activated."

Taylor winced. He'd been ready to kill Evans with his bare

hands when he'd thought the Black Corps officer had betrayed his men. But now he saw the true quality of the man.

"Fortune go with you and those you lead, General Taylor. The spirit of the Black Corps will be with you. Always."

Taylor nodded and turned back toward the column. Evans stood and watched the men marching. He stood there silently, for a good long time…until the last man stepped through the Portal. He finally nodded and allowed himself one brief smile. The Army of Liberation was on its way. Then he straightened his uniform and walked back to where his men had gathered.

Chapter 30

From the Journal of Jake Taylor:

Earth. Home. Or is it home anymore? Do we even have a home, we men of Gehenna? What will we find when we return? A hostile world, one that thinks us traitors and murderers? A grim battle to destroy an entrenched government?

Will the people listen to us? Will they follow us, rise up and free themselves from the shackles of UNGov? Or has their spirit been destroyed by years of repression? Does mankind have the spirit to stand for itself, to demand freedom, to fight however long it takes to break their chains?

I don't know. I see men like those from the Black Corps and UN Force Juno, and I want to believe...I want to believe man's spirit is indestructible, that no amount of oppression can extinguish it. But I remember Earth too, how the people cringed in fear and did as they were told. I remember men like my father, those who still felt the spark of independence, ridiculed and hushed by their panicked families.

I was no better then. I didn't listen to what my father told me, what he tried to teach me. I believed what they told me at school, what the media said. It took a manifestation of hell as brutal as Erastus to change that.

Will our friends and relatives still be alive? What will they think of us after so many years? We are grim creatures, all of us, dark and violent. We know little now but war and the brutality of the battlefield. Those of us with the modifications are cyborgs, monstrous to the eyes of those who have never

seen such creatures. Will we terrify those who once loved us? Are we fit to live among parents, siblings, old friends? Will they open their arms and welcome us home? Or will they fear us, shun us?

"Men of the Black Corps, by now you are all aware that we have been surgically altered, rendered incapable of refusing orders issued by designated authorities from UNGov." Evans looked out over the men assembled in front of him. All the survivors of the Black Corps were there, just over 4,000 out of 20,000 who had marched through the Portal. "What has been done to us cannot be undone. There is no cure, no way back. UNGov has made slaves of us, puppets waiting to dance for their masters."

Evans looked out over the soldiers before him, standing silently. "We cannot follow General Taylor and his army. There is too great a danger our conditioning will be used against them, and we cannot allow that. Taylor and his forces are the only chance to destroy UNGov, to free all the generations that follow from tyranny, to ensure that they can never do to others what they did to us. We will not be the cause of that effort's failure." His voice was grim, determined.

"We have two choices, brothers, and each of us must decide for ourselves what road we will tread. Even as I speak, new soldiers are marching through the Portal. These forces will undoubtedly be accompanied by UNGov personnel, probably another Inquisitor team. If we do nothing, if we remain here, they will give us orders...commands we will be unable to disobey. They will tear from us our free will, makes us slaves to their purposes. They will compel us to follow General Taylor and his forces, to continue to fight a dishonest and evil war. To kill men who are the only hope to end this nightmare and lead Earth to a better future."

Evans took a deep breath. He was scared and sad, but anger was his strongest emotion, fueled by a deep and growing hatred for UNGov. He thought about Taylor's men reaching Earth, rallying the people of the world, destroying those who had done this to him, to his soldiers. He didn't know if they could do it, a few thousand men taking on a world, but he liked to believe they would prevail.

"I will give you no orders. Each of you must make your own choice…and choose well, for whatever you decide, it may be the last decision you make for yourself."

Evans reached down to his side, pulling his pistol slowly from its holster. "Here then, is my decision. I shall never live as a slave again, never surrender my free will, never be made to serve such an evil master again."

He looked out over the soldiers assembled before him. A murmur rippled through their ranks when he pulled out the pistol, but now they stood frozen, silent, watching their commander in terrified awe.

"Goodbye, my brothers. I have been honored to serve with you and, briefly, to command your ranks. You deserve far better than that which fate has given you." He paused for an instant, his eyes panning across the assembled ranks one last time. "Fortune go with you wherever you go, my friends."

He took one last breath and raised the pistol to his head. A second passed, possibly two, seeming impossibly long to the men watching their leader. Then a single shot rang out, and Major Thomas Evans fell to the ground.

The men of the Black Corps stood in stunned silence for a moment, staring at the body of their leader. Then a single shot rang out, as if in answer. And another, and another. Throughout the massed ranks, men began to fall, singly at first then in clumps, following the example of their commander, choosing death over slavery.

When it was over the air was still, and in the silent, fading twilight, 4,000 men lay dead by their own hands, a last rebellion against those who had taken their humanity and made them into slaves.

*   *   *   *   *

Keita stood before Taylor, trying to maintain his composure despite the panic building inside him. He was exhausted and more than a little disoriented. He couldn't reconcile with how he'd gone from discussing Taylor's army in the safety of UN Headquarters months before to being their prisoner. He was scared, wondering what the rebels would do with him. Years of arrogance as one of Earth's masters wouldn't let him believe they might seriously harm him. It didn't occur to him that Taylor might ask himself what treatment he would get at the hands of UNGov if he had been captured. If it had, Keita's meager control would have broken down completely.

Taylor walked toward Keita, his stride grim and purposeful. When Keita saw the expression on Taylor's face, his heart sank, and he began to shake with fear. This was a man like none he'd ever seen before. It wasn't the fiery heat of rage the captive saw on Taylor's face. It was something far worse, an icy stare as cold as death itself. There was no humanity in the man approaching, no pity, no mercy. Only grim purpose. And a hatred Keita couldn't begin to understand.

Taylor stopped about a meter from Keita and looked over his shoulder, toward a small cluster of officers. "The army will prepare to march toward the Yanvar Portal. We're moving on as soon as possible. No more delays." The new forces arriving on Juno would eventually pursue his people, and he wanted to be off Lorus before that happened. The Yanvar Portal was in a remote area. It would take any pursuers a long time to find it. By the time they did, Taylor and his men would be on Earth.

Taylor didn't know if his battered group of survivors from Juno qualified as an army anymore, but he didn't know what else to call it. The remnants of Force Juno had brought his numbers up, but the ranks of his Supersoldiers were sorely depleted. No more than a third of the Ten Thousand had survived the holocaust of Juno, but those men were as grim and deadly as any who had ever taken up arms.

"We have a job to do on Earth, and it's past time we got there."

"Yes, sir." The senior officer of the group replied crisply.

"With your permission, sir." He snapped off a salute and, at Taylor's nod, he turned and trotted off to carry out the order.

Taylor turned toward one of the guards standing next to Keita. "Escort Mr. Keita to storage hut 7. It has been prepared for him." There was a menace in Taylor's voice so terrifying, Keita's legs gave out and he slumped to the ground. "He and I have much to talk about."

Taylor watched the guards drag Keita's limp and cowering form toward the hut, but he wasn't really seeing it. Taylor couldn't see anything but Tony Black, one instant the cheerful, smiling image of his friend, the next his imagining of the dead and bloodied face of his second in command, lying unretrieved and unburied on the battlefield. Whatever was left of Taylor's humanity, of his ability to grant an enemy mercy, had died in that bloodsoaked mud with his friend.

He turned and walked grimly toward the storage hut. He had a lot to discuss with Keita.

*   *   *   *   *

Taylor walked slowly away from the hut, wiping his hands on a small cloth, once bright white, now almost completely covered in red. It was blood mostly, but other fluids too. Keita's interrogation had not been an easy one, but Taylor was sure he'd gotten everything the prisoner knew. It was all there now, stored in the eidetic memory UNGov's scientists had implanted in his brain. Names, locations, vital government installations, force strengths…everything. It really had been foolish, Taylor thought, for UNGov to allow a member of the Secretariat to fall into his grasp. He couldn't even begin to assign a value to the information he'd gotten from Keita.

The UN Secretary had talked, almost from the start, but Taylor had been forced to press harder to get the truly classified data. There were others Keita was afraid of too, and Taylor had to work his way through that before the dam burst, and the prisoner hemorrhaged truly sensitive information. By the time Taylor put a bullet in Keita's head, it was nothing but a mercy, a thank-you for the tremendous intelligence Taylor would now use in the quest to bring down UNGov.

He gave a passing thought to the brutality he'd just employed, the soulless expediency with which he'd tormented his prisoner. He tried to imagine his younger self, what he would have thought. But he quickly put it aside. That boy had been a fool, a child with no idea how dark the universe truly is. Still, Taylor had interrogated Keita alone. He would allow himself to become a monster to see the Crusade achieve victory, but he wouldn't ask any of his men to tread down that path with him. Those nightmares would be his and his alone.

He'd done what he had to do, and there was no use whimpering about it. He had work ahead, so much work. They'd won the battle on Juno…or at least they'd escaped from it. He had no idea what Evans and the remnants of the Black Corps had done. He had some suspicions, but they were too dark, too terrible to think about. He hated himself for hoping they made the choice he thought they had. It was horrifying, but it also meant there was no chance he would have to face them again, that more of his men would die. The holocaust on Juno had been enough.

He didn't have time for such musings. There was still a long way to go. And whenever he felt his resolve weakening or pity creeping into his soul, there was the image of Tony Black, his friend, his brother, alone, lying dead on the cold ground.

The battle for Earth would be next, and it would be like nothing Taylor's people could imagine. His army had left almost 70% of its strength dead in the sands of Juno, thousands of loyal soldiers, dedicated fighters…friends. He didn't begin to know how he could destroy UNGov with what was left. But he knew he would try, his men would try…and if they didn't succeed, none of them would survive. They owed nothing less to the thousands who had died on Juno, giving their lives so the fight could continue.

He knew victory on Earth would only be the start, that the Darkness was coming, and man had to be ready to face it. He still bore that burden alone, the only human being who knew what was coming. There was a limit to what men could endure, and his soldiers had enough to carry.

He stopped and turned to look back toward the Juno Portal. "Well, my friend, we are on our way back to Earth, as we planned when this all began back on Gehenna.

He had a picture in his mind, Tony Black the day he'd reported for duty fresh out of the Portal. He'd been a cocky little shit, plucked straight from the streets of the Philly Metrozone. Taylor had been a newly promoted sergeant, eager to prove he had what it took to whip new recruits into shape. They'd clashed at first, but it wasn't long before they'd become fast friends. For more than ten years, they'd marched together, fought together, ate together, pulled each other through the hell of Erastus. Taylor knew he would never have survived so long in Gehenna without Tony Black.

"Goodbye, my friend." Taylor's voice was soft, mournful. "I will drink that toast to you standing in the wreckage of UNGov HQ.